Malcolm McKay has been a writer/director in television, radio and theatre for many years. His theatre work includes productions in the UK and internationally. His television writing includes the award winning *A Wanted Man* trilogy, and the adaptation of Mervyn Peake's *Gormenghast* He has made three films for the BBC, *Redemption*, *Maria's Child* and *Cruel Train*. His novels include *I Am The Gong Man*, *The Lack brothers*, *The Path*, *Breaking Up* and *Thistown* for young people.

# The Many Lives of Francis Riley

MALCOLM MCKAY

Tangent Arts



A CIP catalogue record for this title is available from the British Library.

ISBN: 978-0-6451995-4-3

# DEDICATION

This novel is dedicated to all the actors I have worked with over the years. Many have been good friends. They have entertained me, charmed me, sometimes infuriated me and taught me many things with their undaunted courage, insatiable curiosity and absolute determination to live as open, generous, imaginative and creative human beings.

# 1

'He is so gorgeous!' Miriam squirmed in her seat with a wild gleam in her eye and whooped as an American beside herself with joy. 'He is so charming and so funny!' She clapped like a demented seal and I thought she could do some serious damage to her hands.

'Alright Miriam, I've got the point,' I said through grinding teeth.

She didn't hear me or even notice. The object of her awe - and believe me that's no exaggeration - was standing with his one hand flopping over the lectern; the other held as modestly high as he could without appearing too triumphant. He bowed low with a self-satisfied smirk on his face. An actor? He couldn't have been anything else. Star of stage and screen, and now an honorary PHD from Barr-Lyon University, Doctor (Hon), Sir Alexander Hudson, should he care to use his full monicker, stood above us like some all-conquering hero.

Ok, he'd been amusing, I'll give him that. And alright, attractive too, with his long grey hair, craggy face, sweet little boyish grin and slender body in a black suit with trousers that would have been too tight on a teenager. They encased slightly bandy strutting legs and a groin which he thrust towards us like a rakish old stallion. Was I jealous of him? Probably. But despite that, and despite Miriam's over the top reaction which irritated me, I had to admit I did admire him, and actually found myself as the clapping died fantasising about having him as a mate, my best pal.

I know all about thespians; my sister, Annie, is one and so is her husband, Paul. In fact I remember vaguely some occasion when Paul had spoken of the great Alexander like he was his closest mucker. I hadn't taken much notice at the time. Actors were always telling you they were best pals of the famous when the truth was they'd had half a line in the same scene, or stood by them at the catering truck munching a sausage sandwich and sharing the mustard. But getting any closer than that to Sir Alexander Hudson, Hon. Doc? Come off it, I don't think so.

I'd seen the man's work though. I'd watched him on TV, and once on stage about ten years ago when I'd taken a group of kids to see his famous Mad Hamlet. He'd been dressed in his pyjamas, even appearing in the court scenes like some lunatic somnambulist. The reviews were raves and the kids thought he'd been hilarious. 'There's more things in heaven and earth, Mr Riley!' they'd laughed me off the bus back at the school. How could I argue with that? And I had to admit it took some balls or agnorance or genius to deconstruct the greatest play in the English Language into a festering dream of revenge with a pair of underpants on your head. And all that mischief and charisma had been right up there on the stage in front of us. A star's a star, no doubt about it. There must be some reason for it. Although I wouldn't have admitted it I actually imagined for one second, being him, being Alexander. Straight up, I tell you, being Alexander.

We left the university theatre and walked the fifty yards along the old concrete path through pretty manicured lawns, past the yellow lit-up windows of the student blocks, to the refectory, an architect's wet dream of high-arched wooden beams and hanging glass. There was a long white cloth-covered table of drinks laid out along one wall. Students bribed by an evening's pay, free food and the chance to be in the same room as Alexander Hudson, squeezed through the crowd offering large trays of canapés. These were miniature meals in themselves; tiny hotdogs, tiny sandwiches and even tinier eclairs. The students silently objected if you actually helped yourself to anything. They wanted to stuff it all into their own great hungry gobs in between slugging back as much booze as they could on the quiet. I didn't blame them, student grants being what they were. There was one in particular, a tall boy with an amazing frizz of blond hair who I recognised as having been in a class of mine a few years before. He clinked up a couple of bottles of red and managed to take a giant swig out of both at the same time as he disappeared into the kitchen. Obviously my teaching hadn't been entirely unsuccessful. By the end several of them were so inebriated and their trays sloped at such perilous angles that anyone reaching for a miniature bite was in serious danger of getting a hot puppy (small hotdog, keep up) down the front of his pants. No-one seemed to care too much. It was all loud and cheerful and sated. The women especially (and I include Miriam), were jigging with excitement and arousal - and that's no exaggeration either. Old Alexander had done his job; his audience were intoxicated and exhilarated and they heaved towards him at the far end of the room like worshippers clamouring for their high priest. Miriam's height was against her but her sheer bloodymindedness made up for her lack of inches as she ducked low and sharp-elbowed herself into the throng.

I stood by the back wall, with a couple of glasses of red silently glugging and observed the crowd with my cynical eye. I wondered why I had no appetite to join them. Am I aloof, am I superior, do I aspire to greater things? No, no, and maybe - though what those other things are I have yet to discover. Anyway I wanted to get out of there and Miriam had dissolved herself into the mass so I had to wait.

There were a couple of other honorary doctorships. The first was a world renowned geneticist who'd been involved in the discovery of the human genome. Bearing this in mind I'd have thought he'd have been aware enough of our qualities to have known what boredom was. I'd actually nodded off during his twenty minute ramble. He should have stayed in his lab counting his Nobel prize. He stood a few yards away talking to an earnest young female academic in thick black-framed brainy glasses and thick black-cloth brainy dress and shoes. I assumed their conversation was beyond me. I moved a couple of yards further away hoping to avoid contamination by my own ignorance, and almost collided with the third honorary PHD. She was a rather homely looking Indian multi-millionaire who'd donated millions to the university in order to plaster her name all over it. She smiled at me with her mouth only.

'Maybe we should go with the crowd,' I said politely and nodded towards Hudson at the other end of the room.

'I could buy the lot of them,' she answered. Her eyes flickered some amusement then went dead.

Not so homely after all.

'Star attraction, isn't he?'

'Huh,' she muttered. 'Look like me and make one point eight three million a year out of baby food and car parts, that's star attraction.' Then she did smile with her whole face, eyes included.

I said, 'One point eight three? That's very exact if you don't mind me saying so.'

'Not at all.'

'Is such attention to detail the secret of your success?'

'Point eight four next year!' Her smile broadened, 'I'm kidding you, my dear. And that's the secret if you want to know. Kidding people.' She was homely again. 'I'd better go and find the rector and tell him they can name the medical school after me. The Monica Mahdpuri Wing. Get two of them and I can fly.'

She winked and wandered away down the side of the room looking like she was just popping into Marks and Spencers for a sandwich. She was kidding me? It's not that difficult; confusion is my natural state. And she was clearly an extraordinary woman of the type I needed to know. Unfortunately I didn't have the wit to realise it until it was too late, which is my usual disposition; the last to the party.

I watched her yellow sari disappear through the crowd

wondering who she was going to befuddle next. After thirty seconds with her you'd be so upside down you'd give her the moon in a bucket.

I looked around for another drink. The students had fulfilled their function and the booze had run dry. Miriam came towards me with a broad grin on her face. She was clutching a programme which she thrust in front of my eyes. Scrawled across the front was, Love and best wishes to my friend, Miriam Diamandis, Alexander Hudson.

'My friend? He doesn't know you from the pimples on my arse.'

'Oh for God's sake.' she stuffed the programme angrily into her bag and marched off towards the door.

I followed her as I always had in the eight years that I'd known her. She was from Athens, at least her parents were. 'You're all Greek to me,' I'd said it more than once, which she hadn't appreciated. She'd come into my life after what she'd called my wild times which actually existed only in her imagination. I'd made the mistake of telling her about my passion for Dolores Morales another Mediterranienne who years before had caused me heartbreak and downfall. I'll admit there'd been other skirmishes along the way but none as bloody as Dolores with her long fingernails. Miriam had regarded all that with a kind of superior amusement in the three years we'd been an actual couple.

Our relationship had faded into an understanding; a kind of stand-off with both of us wishing we could maybe get out of it, or assumed we actually were out of it and weren't entirely, or were content with it as it was. It wasn't even as if I'd been in love with her, or even just plain loved her. Or had I? That was a question I'd failed to answer so many times I'd stopped asking. Seeing each other had become a habit which neither of us could break. At odd times we stopped meeting for a few weeks, once even for six months, but then found ourselves again in a bar or cafe on the High Street, swapping the bits of our lives that we'd hidden from other people. We knew each other so well that there were virtually no secrets between us, except those we didn't admit to ourselves. We were two lonely singles heading for forty and hanging on to what intimacy we could clutch at as the days passed and the world disappeared into the inevitable.

It wasn't that I didn't find her attractive. She was slim and solid with good square shoulders, a strong stride and a nose always pointed in the right direction. Her face was round and cheerful under cropped black hair which stuck out here and there and made me laugh. She also had a far greater energy than me, and a frightening will, also fiercer then mine. And to top it all she was more popular than I was. But, and here's the but. She was also a controller of all events and discourse, which drove me crazy. I said to her, 'You're sucking the life out of me!'

'I'm injecting it into you. You're a stuck-up English person...'

'Irish person...'

'English. And you need life. You have no soul, or passion, and too many words.'

This didn't happen too often but it was always there, waiting for its moment like a small dog waiting to nip your pants. But the other problem, maybe it was the big problem; she was a lecturer in psychology at Barr-Lyon, higher up the academic scale than me. She never mentioned it, but I always felt patronised because I spent my working hours trying to interest unimpressed fourteen year olds in Jane Austen, while she was engaged in the far superior challenge of analysing the analysis of Melanie Klein which gave me a headache. Either way it left me thinking that I was, in some imperceptible way, inferior - although, let's face it, Miriam wasn't the only cause of that.

## 2

We left the refectory, walked round the rotunda and across the sweet campus grass which had been cut that day. It was a sultry dusk at the end of June, the air smelled bright, the black green branches of the trees above us were silhouetted against the electric blue of the sky and I was beginning to feel almost Dylan Thomas. The streetlights came on as we reached the top of the town's High Street and a yellow haze descended on the winding row of shops and small businesses we passed: my barber's, her hairdresser's; the metro-market where I bought my food, the delicatessen where she purchased her's; the pub I never went to, the Flying Duck coffee bar where we met and talked; Guiseppe's, the Taj Mahal, the China Palace, the Polish deli, the Welsh dentist, all of Merrie England grinning at itself from one side of the road to the other; my territory - where we both lived.

I was pleased to be out of the university, the bright air in there suffocated me. Miriam strode ahead, her long shadow stretched back like a rope flicking round my feet and dragging me along. Somehow at the end of events like that I always ended up with her. I'd have felt guilty if I hadn't and would have been wondering for the rest of the night if she was unhappy. I knew she almost certainly wouldn't have been, but that's what I'd have been thinking.

I stopped and lit a cigarette.

'When are you going to give that up?' she said without turning her head.

'When I'm ready.'

Over the years that conversation had been abbreviated to the minimum, no further subtractions or additions possible. I wanted to sit on a bench and enjoy my smoke but Miriam once on track never veered; her short heels clicked on the pavement a yard in front as my trainers padded soft behind. We said nothing else and went into The Forlorn Calf, a pub in a back street. Why it was called The Forlorn Calf beats me. I've never heard of any other pub in the country called the Forlorn Calf. Sad young cow? What's that all about? English humour? Some kind of comment about the life ahead? Get pissed while you can? Anyway that night it suited me as my mood shifted, settling downwards. There'd been something about Alexander Hudson that had depressed me. And so had Monica Mahdpuri, the millionaire Indian. Sure, they'd both had an ease and confidence in their different ways but it was more than that; they possessed a sense of purpose, an intensity of being I couldn't quite catch, as if their footstep, hard or soft, was always certain.

'I enjoyed that,' said Miriam as we sat down. I pulled a sad face and went to the bar to get the drinks. The pub which I knew well, only too well, was low-lit and filling up. The walls were dark wood panels and on one was a small print of Francis Drake, another man of his moment - maybe he'd like to meet Francis Riley a man not of his? Most of the crowd had come direct from the investiture. Investiture? Is that what I was calling it? Was Alexander Hudson a monarch? And if he was, where did that leave me? A serf?

'I'm not miserable.' I put our drinks on the table, a pint for me and a vodka and tonic for her. 'That's before you accuse me of it.'

'I wasn't accusing you of anything.'

'What you don't get is that I have an interior life.' I waved my hand vaguely round my head. 'It goes on in here all the time. I'm running marathons in my brain while you're taking a walk in the park.'

'Nice of you to say, darling.' She took a sip of her vodka.

'It's all just breath and heartbeat in the end.'

'Saint Francis, the stoic.' A glimmer of a smile.

'You want to hear amusing stories all night, do you?'

'Would be a change'.

'I'm sure Alexander's still over there. You could walk back.'

'Is that what this is all about?'

'So what's so great about being an actor?'

'As you said, they tell amusing stories.' She pursed her lips and looked round the pub as if she might get lucky and find someone more interesting to talk to. I knew she wasn't going to listen to me. The moment I started thinking about anything she lost interest; either because she thought my thoughts were boring, or too convoluted, or too confused, or she'd heard it all before. Her eyes were glazing. But I wasn't to be deflected, there was something niggling me.

'Seriously, what's so great about being an actor? Listen to me, Mitzy. You pick up a magazine and there's an actor on the cover, you open it and there are five interviews with actors inside. What's the fascination? Why does everybody want to be an actor?'

'No particular reason, Frankie, fame, money, sexual charisma, can't imagine why.' She pretended to yawn, tapping her mouth with her hand.

'That's just him, Alexander Hudson, not everybody's going to be in the papers, rich as Croesus, and have a bed full of sex are they?'

'Not going to stop people wanting it, is it?' she said. 'Or not going to stop them wanting to read about it either. Or being attracted to charm and wit.'

I ignored the obvious inference. 'Why doesn't everybody want to be scientists, or writers or politicians?'

'See above,' she said.

'Anyway what does an actor do? He pretends to be other people. What kind of life is that? What kind of person is that?'

'Why don't you try it, Frankie? And pretend to be someone who's witty and charming?'

'Excuse me, I know a lot of actors.'

'Oh yes, your sister.'

'There's no need to take that sarcastic tone. She's a perfectly nice and reasonable woman and she likes you.' I wasn't too sure how true that was, but pretty certain that Miriam wasn't too keen on Annie, although she pretended to be her greatest pal, hanging on her every word and laughing out loud at her stories. In my opinion, if anyone was an actor it was Miriam.

'Alright, Francis. I'll get another drink. You?'

'Jamesons. A large one. If you don't mind.'

She went to the bar.

I admit she was probably right about actors. Through my sister and her husband I'd met a lot of them over the years. They were charming, charismatic, intelligent, and not believing I had too many of those qualities, I'd often found myself in Annie's kitchen laughing so much at their stories, that I wished I did. Maybe that was the answer to my question. They were everything I wasn't.

Miriam came back with the drinks.

She said, 'sorry, I was a bit over the top there in the refectory with Hon. Doc Hudson. Did I look stupid?'

'No, no, you were fine. Why not get excited? You like getting excited.'

'He made me feel like a little girl.'

'I could see that.'

She shrugged. 'There was something joyous about him, made me remember it in me. The joy, I mean. It must be there somewhere.' She raised both eyebrows sorrowfully nonplussed. There were little moments when Miriam could be so revealingly honest that it made me want to hug her. In that brief instant she'd shown the vulnerability of age, the fact that she wasn't married, or in a relationship, and didn't feel like a kid anymore; and she regretted all of it.

'I know what you mean. Sorry, I've been a bit grumpy myself, so peace, Ok?'

She smiled and raised her glass.

'But listen.' I leant forward onto the table. "Why do you think everybody wants to be an actor? Seriously? I mean, are we all so unhappy that we want to be someone else? Is that it? Look, I know about the fame and money and all that, but I can tell you from my experience that the truth is most actors can hardly afford breakfast and spend their entire lives waiting to get cast in some commercial for laxatives. I mean getting a cheque for having a crap.'

'Please, Francis.'

'Or it's one line in a TV serial, or if they're lucky a part in a play that pays them for a couple of months even less than I get which is saying something. That's the truth of it, Miriam. What are they, mad? Come on, you call yourself a psychologist.'

'I don't call myself a psychologist, I am one.'

'Alright, sorry. So tell me what's so good about it?'

'Perhaps they like to be free.'

'Free to work as gardeners, or in a pub, or cycle messengers?'

'Free to be themselves, Frankie.'

'What?'

That was the first thing that night that had sounded interesting to me and I wanted to talk about it, but we were interrupted by the drinkers on the table next to us getting up and being immediately replaced by a new group who'd just come in from the university.

'Hi Miriam. How are you, darling?'

It was Theo Skinner, Miriam's head of department. He sat on the chair closest to her. If Miriam was occasionally superior towards me, Skinner acted as if I actually didn't exist. He was a younger version of Alexander Hudson with the same grey hair, lean figure, thin weasily face, but no black suit. If he'd showed up with a leather manbag over his shoulders I wouldn't have been surprised.

'Hullo Frankie, how are you?'

Only close friends and acquaintances were allowed to call me Frankie, and Skinner wasn't one of them.

'We were just having an interesting conversation,' I said.

He ignored me and introduced the others who sat down

around him.

'John you know, Louise you know.'

I didn't know either of them.

'And this is Professor Abebi Musa.'

Skinner gave a toe-curling grin as a gorgeous woman sat down at the other end of the table. I gulped. And I did, literally, I gulped. She was a show stopper, the opening number and the curtain call all rolled into one. Why was I thinking in these theatrical metaphors? She was tall and slim although I suspected she had a voluptuous figure subtly hidden beneath her pale green dress which showed off her shoulders and the top of her chest. She sat, pert and sexy, dark hair softly curling round an oval face and large black eyes. She was heartbreakingly lovely, her pale brown flesh gleamed gold in the last rays of the sun coming in through the windows. Now you know why I gulped. She was it. I was taken. Her smile would have lit up the pub in deepest winter and lit me up for the rest of my life. She nodded to Miriam and then to me.

'Hi.' It was a croak, all I could manage.

'Abebi,' said Skinner, 'is a visiting professor from Moretown University in Baltimore.' He obviously fancied her as much as I did. But then he flirted with everyone including Miriam who returned the favour enthusiastically. Did I care? I don't think so, but there might have been another deeper level of ancient festering jealousy which could force its toxic fingers up the back of my throat if I let it. Anyway, who cared? There was this gorgeous woman at the end of the table. The arrow had landed and I was quivering.

'Abebi's over for the conference,' Skinner said, flashing piranha teeth.

Abebi was still smiling, 'Hi,' she said, 'it's so great to be back in a real British pub.' She looked around, her mouth slightly open as if she was breathing it all in. 'I'm so happy to be here.' Her accent was rich and husky American.

Skinner leaned over and put his hand on Miriam's arm. 'And I hope you've decided to join us. Have you?' He squeezed her wrist.

He was talking about the small conference the psychology department held every summer. He'd offered Miriam a non-participant pass which allowed her to attend but not give a paper, which meant essentially she'd be his dogsbody. And it also meant that the July trip to France that we'd thought about, wouldn't happen - even if I'd wanted it to.

I caught Skinner looking at Miriam and thought it incredible how he could smile with his mouth, or his eyes, or both together, and whatever combination he decided on you knew none of it meant a thing except he was demonstrating that he was smiling at you. He could have sent you a text.

'Yes, I'd love to Theo,' Miriam said.

'You will?'

'Yes!' She seemed delighted with herself. 'I've decided.'

And without a word to me. Goodbye Dordogne.

'Ah that's a great relief,' said Skinner with another grin from the depths of the ocean.

Abebi didn't give me another glance. They talked about the conference, university gossip and briefly, which surprised me, led by John, who wanted to show off his working class credentials, to football. Being the one subject I knew something about I said proudly, 'Hey, look, I'm a Spurs fan!'

Professor Abebi stunned me by replying, 'Wow, so am I!'

This was my chance. 'You should see the new stadium! It's something else.' And for that moment we were together on a cold floodlit night wrapped in Spurs scarves and hugging each other as...

'Anyway,' said Skinner. 'Abebi, you're probably still tired from the flight. I think it's time I walked you back.'

Fuck you Theo.

As they left Abebi gave me a brief smile and widened her eyes. I grinned back but didn't think she noticed. Soon after, Miriam got up to leave but then sat down again on the edge of her seat with her mouth turned down and her face full of olive-toned concern. I thought she was going to apologise about France.

'Maybe all this about acting,' she said, 'is because you don't know who you are, Francis. Perhaps none of us do. As far as I know there isn't a list of existential questions, but if there was, that one would be close to the top.'

'You mean, who you are?'

'Exactly.' And she got up again before I could mention the Dordogne. 'See you soon.'

I watched through the window as she walked away down the empty street past a line of parked cars. Her head was low and her shoulders thoughtfully hunched. She stopped, raised her head for a second and walked on. I thought she must be talking to herself. Probably to Skinner and certainly not to me. Had she been as affected by the beauty of Abebi as I had? Perhaps she was recoiling from an attractiveness she'd never thought she'd had herself? Mitzy was a bright and sharp woman but there were some things she couldn't hide and one of them was her sadness.

I didn't feel like going home. I finished my Jamesons and went to the bar. It had been quite some day. The end of the summer term had finally arrived and the kids, having done their exams, were restless and joyous and itching to hang about on dusty estates or laze around on the streets causing indolent mayhem. As they filed out after my last class Molly Chang had shuffled her feet by my desk wanting to talk. I knew she didn't have much to look forward to. Her father had died and she'd told me that the trip to Hong Kong with her mother and sister had been called off. I wanted to get out of there, but should have been more sympathetic. After all I knew about absent fathers. My own was deeply retired to Cork. He'd gone back there eight years ago after Ma had passed. 'Now's the time for me to go home, Francis.' he'd said, 'Gilly's there and the grand-kids, and you'll be alright here, won't you? You've got Annie.'

'Don't worry about a thing, Pa.'

I hadn't meant it. I'd liked my old man being just up the road. It somehow helped me place myself. I'd been over to Cork a couple of times and had enjoyed the craic in the local pub with him and his mates. We'd even been fishing once, but hadn't talked much, just looked out over the river through wet Irish rain which in its own unfathomable way didn't seem to dampen my spirits. I was alright, knowing Pa was happy enough. Another thing not to feel guilty about anyway.

I ordered another Jamesons, and sunk into new thoughts about a summer in Ireland seeing that Miriam had curtailed our non-existent holiday plans. I'd had no particular regrets about that but saw no reason why the possibility should have been so rudely interrupted. Do you not think I have a heart and soul, Miriam Diamandis? Well I do. Well actually I didn't. I'd told Molly Chang to forget Hong Kong for the next hundred years or at least until Chinese Imperialism had run its course. I should have at least seen in my own father that being ripped from the old root was only ever just temporary.

I ordered another Jamesons. Alexander Hudson had really got to me as some paragon of everything I wasn't. Did I really want to be him? My heroes as a kid had been William Shakespeare, David Bowie and David Ginola - not that he was a great player but because of his haircut. There were no peacemakers or saints on that list I noticed. Did that mean I was insensitive to the woes of the world? Probably. I had enough of my own. I hadn't been exactly thoughtful towards Molly had I? But Alexander Hudson? I refused to accommodate him in my empty cupboard of heroes. Except that Miriam's statement, actors are free, was wriggling around in there somewhere, waiting to be shown the light of day.

I ordered another Jamesons, they were going down so quick now I'd stopped feeling the heat or the rasp. But what was really on my mind was Professor Abebi. She'd bit deep.

How did you get to be a professor and that beautiful? Maybe that's exactly how you got to be a professor? I refused to believe it of her. I tried to tell myself she was just another little fancy to light up my sad little world. Forget it Francis. Forget it? How could I? Are you kidding? Forget her? And anyway what about that tiny smile and eye-widening as she'd left? She'd hardly spoken to me, but what a conversation we could have had about the football. She secretly fancied me and asked Skinner for my number. Skinner had put her onto Miriam who'd told her I was probably still in the pub, the phone rang and the landlord shouted out, anyone here called Francis Riley? And ten minutes later she walks in with those shoulders and that pale green dress and....

I ordered another Jamesons. As it was poured over the pub's last ice cube I caught himself in the mirror behind the optics. I wasn't Brad Pitt, but not too bad considering. Considering what? Considering that his face was rounder, his nose stubbier, his eyes smaller, and he didn't look like me at all, though his hair was roughly the same colour. 'Hey pal, hey, you Francis? You wanna be me? Actors are free, you know?' Christ, things were writhing away down there in Brad's pit and I had no idea what they were. I decided I'd better stop before I started comparing our careers which admittedly wouldn't take long. To hell with it, I raised my glass. To both of us!

I downed the shot and wandered away up the High Street for the short walk up to my flat. The night was curiously light although the dawn was hours away. Is there a Francis Riley in the bar? There's a professor wanting to speak... I stopped suddenly outside the Welsh Dentist's and stared at a blow-up of great white smiley teeth as I realised that if Miriam would be attending the psycho conference. That meant I had an excuse to go too! And who else would be there?

# 3

The term was over and done. I'd never seen the school empty so fast. The only one who didn't seem too happy about it was Molly Chang. She walked sadly down the drive with her bony shoulders round her neck, no doubt not looking forward to the next six hot weeks in the small steamy flat she lived in on the fourth floor of a council block with its endless tiny balconies hung with clothes and littered with abandoned nursery toys. At least her home would be tidier than mine and she'd get a decent chilli prawn and rice every now and again.

I wandered through empty corridors past deserted classrooms and didn't miss at all the joyous clamour, the pounding of the feet, the unedited laugher, and all the second by second improvisation of teenage life. My head felt lighter, my headache fading. No more literature for the illiterate, no more drumming Dickens into the dim, no more trying to channel their anarchy into a literature that tried to show them what they knew already. I wasn't even convinced myself. How could an artistic construct be greater than the free spirit of their natural lives? Larking boys and flirty girls; why constrain them at all? "Leave it out, sir! Let us go! What we've got is better than what you say!" And the writers we studied knew it too; they knew that there were no words that could encapsulate this wild liberty. All they could do was despair, point at it, and sigh at the impossibility of their art. Ah, but I loved the books - a bookish man, me - and I loved the kids, and tried to instil the artifice because that was my job; how it had to be, I guess. This was the way we constructed ourselves, the way we constructed our children to be ourselves. What a thing hey, to make them like us? What was I to do about that? Nothing. But it didn't stop me yearning to be as unfettered as them.

There was no-one in the staffroom. I emptied my locker

of the stink of twelve weeks of unwashed clothes, sticky bags, crumbled biscuits and forgotten papers. I was having a quiet sit down to reflect on my coming indolence when my mate Tony Braithwaite came in. He was the head of maths, a long tall and brilliant Yorkshireman from somewhere in the wastelands north of Sheffield. God's own country, mate. Tony was his name and maths was his game. He saw everyone, including me, mainly me, as a problem to be solved numerically. As far as he was concerned I was just a set of genetic codes with a mal-functioning laptop between my ears. 'Reason, son, reason;' his catchphrase repeated endlessly whenever he heard a loose or emotional thought or especially a poetic angle - something he never took seriously.

He sat his great bulk opposite me. I sometimes thought his strength was terrifying; he pulsed with it, like a deep power, molten down there and ready to burst through his grin from beneath his low forehead, his widow's peak and his heavy black specs. Tony always knew pretty well everything, and I knew he knew, though I did my best to contradict him - usually no contest, his rationality strode into all the corners of my mind and tied me up in a weird and impenetrable psychic tangle.

His face contorted into a knowing grimace. 'How is it, Frankie?'

'I think I'm in love.' The silken image of Abebi had grown stronger and stronger as the days passed which was certainly a sign as to how desperate I was for some object on which to spill out this deep well of something or other that had been building up in me for far too long. Maybe I should have bought a cat.

'Love? What's that?' said Tony. 'And who with? And do you have a chance?'

'Beats me. A gorgeous professor. No.'

'Forget it, mate.'

'Ok.'

'That's that then.'

Tony had spoken. I sighed and looked round the room. My delight at the forthcoming holiday had evaporated at this dose of Braithwaite reality. The staffroom didn't help. I seemed to have been staring forever at the same old scraped beige paintwork and the same old red and green chairs worn bare by the same old arses and farts of a thousand teachers wondering why, oh why, and what was in it for them? It all seemed to sum up the deadly creeping apathy that was slowly swamping the inner contortions of my life. The room reeked of years gone by. And years to come? The question begged itself like they do.

Tony put his big hands behind his huge head, scuffed his hair and yawned. 'Ah, forty-three days of empty-headed bliss. That's one thousand and thirty hours, which if you're interested is sixty-one thousand, nine hundred and twenty minutes.'

'And how many seconds?'

'A lot.'

'Come on Tone, you know you love it.' And he did. It was his party trick.

He closed his eyes for a couple of seconds and said, 'that'll be, three million, seven hundred and fifteen thousand, two hundred, less the three it took me to say that. Always know time, it's all we've got. That's another two seconds just gone. You should introduce maths into literature.'

'I'm doing Oscar Wilde next term.

He laughed and looked at the ceiling, then said, 'Ah? What was the percentage of homosexuals in London in the late nineteenth century? If it was low then the intolerance was high. Keep taking the numbers every few years and you could do a graph. One function homosexuality, increasing, the other intolerance, decreasing, and sooner or later, I reckon, the lines would cross and you'd probably discover we're all gay.'

'Sure Tone, things change, thanks very much.'

'You can predict it, son, you'd be surprised.'

I gave up, 'Want to come to a party tomorrow? My sister's throwing a bash for a garden full of actors. She's been ill, so it's a kind of comeback tour. Miriam can't come, she's preparing for this conference. They'll love you. You can work out the percentage of their earnings compared to the rest of us.

'Many there?' he asked.

'I don't know.'

'Any good looking women?'

'Figure it out for yourself,' I was pleased with my pun though Tony, genius that he was, didn't get it. If there was anything that would distract him from numbers it was his undying quest for the female. Forget graphs, or notches on the bedpost, his success rate was beyond computation. He once told me he could find a fuck in a haystack.

'Alright, I'll come,' he said it as if he was doing Annie a favour.

I gave him her address and heaved the rucksack of books and papers I'd need for the prep of my next years curriculum onto my back and walked out of the school gates. I strolled through the baked, dry and empty terraces the half mile to my flat letting my depression fade in the absence of a specific grouse to hang it on. What could be better? Seven weeks of nothing. It was a glorious day, the sun was stark and bright and hot on my head, birds flipped and spun in the plane trees and the pigeons shat. My spirits rose even further as I imagined seeing Professor Abebi again at the conference. This was a long-shot I had to admit. The food of dreams can fill the empty belly of life. Who said that? We're married and live in Los Angeles, Beverley Hills maybe, on the Strip? I decide on Mulholland Drive in a small but tasteful chateau up on the white hill. I'm a visiting professor of English literature at - the name of the university escapes me - and I've published my first novel, which is a low level but much admired literary sensation. 'It's a start honey, buy yourself a new dress, I'm getting a prize.' I've found myself and become the man I always knew I truly was. I unlocked the front door of the basement flat I'd lived in for ten years and dumped my sack onto the heap of clothes I'd once recognised as a sofa; there was a faint ancient smell coming out of the bathroom or maybe the bedroom. I didn't look in the kitchen. Maybe it was my feet. I didn't care, I could live with it. Without a seconds delay I whipped my phone out of my pocket and called Miriam.

'Can't talk, I'm busy,' she said.

It was her usual first response.

'Ah the conference. You're working hard?'

'Theo wants me to organise the opening gala. I really wish he hadn't asked, but he was so persuasive as usual.' She went on to describe how difficult it all was; the guest list, the invitations, the paperwork, the schedules, how she's being used and abused and at the same time delighted to be asked. 'It just shows how much Theo trusts me,' she said. All this took at least ten minutes from someone too busy to talk.

'Gala? Very impressive. Will everyone be there?'

'Yes, Francis, I have to go.'

'Everyone?'

'Francis, I have to go.' She sighed as if she was being pestered by a kid tugging at her skirt with sticky hands.

'Can I come?'

'What?'

'To the Gala?'

'Since when have you been interested in psychology?'

'I want to see you Miriam. It looks like it's my only chance. Maybe we could get a bite after?'

'I'll be tied up with Theo.'

As far as I was concerned she could spend as much time as she liked with Skinner; in fact Skinner could be my salvation, tying up Miriam and the rest while me and Abebi slunk to the Calf. Dreams can come true, you know? 'Don't worry about a thing, I'll put the crisps in the bowls.'

'We have caterers for that.' Her voice was getting more

faint as if she was holding the phone away from her ear.

'When is it?'

'Next Thursday.'

'Perfect, I'll be there. What time?'

'Francis, I haven't invited you.'

'When else am I going to see you, Miriam?'

She couldn't turn me down. It was unspoken between us that no matter how badly we got on at any particular time we would see each other again. To have denied that would have been to take our relationship into the area of sulks and retaliation which we both knew would indicate some other need which neither of us were prepared to admit.

'I'll pretend I'm Sven Murphy from Trinity College and giving a paper introducing maths as the determining, underlying factors of psychological development.'

'What are you talking about?'

'I could wear my suit. Do you know I haven't worn it for...'

'It's 6.30 in the refectory. But I'm going to have to be...'

'Schmoozing. I know. Don't worry about a thing. I'll look after myself. I'd like to know more about your world, I really would.'

'I'm going, Francis.'

'Bye, Mitzy.'

Cracked it.

## 4

Annie wanted to express her thanks to all her friends who'd helped her through her illness with flowers, chocolates and interminable anecdotes, so she'd arranged just a small gathering in the large garden of her and Paul's nicely detached house on the other side of the town from me.

Paul, capable of being ironic about his profession, winked and said, 'They've all been. One visit from each of them. No more, no less. Job done.'

I was happy to go along with him because I knew it would irritate Annie. 'Part played, when's my next audition?

My sister, a tall woman with a long face, longer fair hair and dreamy Celtic eyes which could shaft you if you didn't watch it, was laying the snacks on the counter top. 'They can't come all the time! They have to go for a call, or a reading, or a tech! They're busy people!'

I smirked at Paul and having come early to help out, took the crates of booze out into the garden and lined the bottles up on a couple of trestle tables. I usually volunteered to be a kind of unofficial waiter at these parties, it gave me something to do and released me from standing around weaponising stories about the last job or audition I hadn't had.

The party was at Annie's whim but Paul had entered into the spirit of things with his usual generosity. It was to do with keeping up the appearances of his success of a few years back when he'd played a leading lawyer in a long running TV cop show which had gone to his head. He'd graciously received recognition on the street and had even been happy to dispense legal advice to fans who thought he was an actual lawman - until some real time thug threatened him when he'd declined to represent him in court. Now that he was accepted as a known if slightly faded face who maybe you could remember or maybe you couldn't, he still felt obliged to throw money around even when he didn't have any. I envied his brief moment of fame anyway.

As I lined up the bottles I thought I may as well open one as it was a hot afternoon and there was a long evening ahead. This could have been a mistake. Guests started arriving at four and I did my duty going round topping up glasses, which was also a handy way of weighing up the women. Most of them were gorgeous with a lot of chat and sparkling flirty eyes that told you that they knew exactly what you were looking at. The actor men strode about the lawn with straight backs, heads held high, laughing loudly, and flicking glances at the women and the occasional cigarette butt into Annie's bedraggled flower beds which she'd had rapidly tended by a couple of kids from down the road for a tenner each.

Tony arrived at five forty-eight. I knew this because when I glanced at my watch, he said five forty eight without looking at his. Tony Braithwaite, time machine. He took a bottle of beer from me and said, 'No real ale then?'

'No mate, they're actors, reality doesn't exist.'

He glanced round the garden and settled his gaze on an attractive artiste called Miranda Vee, a friend of Annie's who I'd noticed at a previous party. Her hair, pride and joy, was very long, very straight and very golden, her body long and slim, her face long and getting on a bit which didn't stop her eyes fluttering as she appraised every man in the garden.

'She looks interesting,' said Tony, and then walked straight over to her. I should have known, and for a jealous second was sorry I'd invited him. I took a couple of bottles over to Annie and Bernadine, her fourteen stone pal from back in the Kilburn days who was bulging out of her party dress and kept shifting her arms as cover for the worst of it. They were sitting on a bench under an apple tree.

'Where's Miriam?' said Annie.

'Otherwise engaged.'

'And what about you?' said Bernadine flicking her thin black hair behind her ears. 'Know what it means? To be married, you know?'

What is it with sisters, mothers and female friends of the family that all they want to know about is the marital status of all brothers, nephews, uncles etc? Did I ever pry into their relationships? No I did not.

'Too engaged with himself.' said Annie.

I kept my mouth shut.

'I like Miriam,' said Bernadine. 'Isn't she Greek?'

'Red or white?' I held out both bottles.

'He's forty...what is he?' Bernadine wasn't letting it drop.

'Soon enough.' said Annie.

'Never ask a lady his age,' I said.

'He probably doesn't know,' said Annie. 'Was going to be a footballer once, that was a laugh, though wait a minute. he did get a trial for someone once. Who was it?'

'Kilburn ladies?' said Bernadine.

'Red or white?' This was getting boring.

'My little brother,' said Annie. She blew me a kiss with a loving big sister smile.

'He's got a nice face though' said Bernadine. 'And not a bad body either. Could do with a haircut.' She let out a great gulp of laughter. 'Look at it!'

They were at the Francis as livestock phase.

'Oh outwardly he's passable,' said Annie. 'Our mother always said...'

There was no hope when my sister started bringing up the historical reinforcements. 'You can get your own drinks.' I walked away, but had only gone five yards when I bumped into Paul.

How is it? he asked. 'Your mate's doing well by the look of it.' He grinned over at Tony who was standing noticeably closer to Miranda Vee. I observed not for the first time Tony's broad shoulders and remembered once he'd said he'd played rugby for Sheffield Youth.

'He's probably counting on her,' I said, bitterly smirking at my own little joke. I found a chair, sat on it and watched as the noise level rose and the anecdotes opened up like machine gun fire all over the lawn. I have to say they were an attractive bunch. They'd broken into small circles, all pretending to listen, laughing a lot, and each waiting patiently for their turn to stand and deliver. There was a deathly fascination about this as each went on with their story, unable to stop until they could think of a punchline. Sometimes they found one and everybody roared. Other times they didn't and it all ground to an embarrassing halt. But that didn't matter. They just said something like, 'Oh it's the script, darling, I need a better writer!' And everyone fell about. No actor audience ever lets you fail; they'd be too terrified that you'd do the same to them if they did. Best of all were the anecdotes about how they'd just missed getting a lead opposite Al Pacino, or in a Ken Branagh film. These could last half an hour; the casting director was bitten by a dog, the video link failed, or Pacino's third cousin got the gig. I had to admit to a sense of sad admiration at their refusal to admit defeat, always turning the rejection into glorious failure at the same time as humbly downplaying success. 'Oh I got the lead, I was so lucky,' or 'I'm terrified I'll forget my lines, there's so many of them,' or 'I'll probably never work again, well, you don't do you after such a huge....'?

I got up and wandered from group to group topping up glasses. They were funny and innocent and honest and all shared the same dreams and were in the same gang which I wanted to join, which made me love them, and hate them too because I wasn't one of them. I left bottles on tables and chairs for them to help themselves.

Finally I settled myself behind the booze table with my own bottle. It was going down well and I was feeling pleasantly dreamily half pissed although Annie's comments had bitten deeper than probably she'd intended. She'd been the eldest child when we'd moved over to England and, aside from Pa, had retained not only the strongest accent, but the most intense old family loyalties. Having become a substitute mother to me after our own had died she knew only too well my sense of failure, and felt obliged to point it out by the simple device of lavishing me with praise and encouragement. This was a deadly double act I could do without but couldn't deny its truth. I'd failed twice to get promotion to run the English Department; the last time being a bare six months ago, when Mr Pontini, the school head, had said, 'We all love you Francis and you're a wonderful teacher, but...' But? I knew well enough what that meant; I didn't have the leadership qualities or the gumption to lead where others would follow. How could I argue with that? I wouldn't follow myself except into a maze of speculation that exited only where it had started. Annie and Paul had been sympathetic (and so had Miriam which made it worse), but I couldn't escape the feeling that they were all patting me on the head for trying hard and coming in just outside the medals.

I looked around for Tony but he'd disappeared, and so had Miranda Vee. It didn't take long to work that one out. I decided I needed a piss and was about to stand up when Fat Dick crumped down onto the chair beside me. Richard Guest was an older actor who made a living playing large and evil in horror films; eighteen stone of blubber and a trilby puffing up the stairs with a hacksaw in his hand.

'Can't stand up for longer than ten minutes,' he said. 'Feel the greatest sympathy for my knees. How much longer can they bear the burden? Anyway, heard all the stories, know all the faces, cut the cackle and get on with it, hey?'

'Get on with what?'

'The last sad rites.' he laughed. 'Don't mean to depress you, dear boy. Haven't got much longer, you see?' He put his hand on my leg. 'I like you, my friend, there's a fresh-faced honesty about you that's somehow reassuring. Gives me faith in humanity.'

'What do you mean, not much longer?'

'Anyway.' Richard beamed 'How are you getting on?'

'Badly, I keep getting introduced to people and I ask them how they are and they take about forty-five minutes to tell me and then look over my shoulder and ask something like, and what are you doing these days, which most of them know anyway, and I say, Oh I'm still just teaching, and they wander off to talk to someone else.'

Richard looked around the noisy gathering. 'Actors never

interested in others. It's in the nature of the calling.'

'But you know what gets to me? It's me using that word, just. Just teaching. What's wrong with teaching? Why's it just teaching?'

I was getting tetchy.

'Sorry, Annie upset me.'

'Oh she's a bitch. Always has been.'

'Excuse me. She's my sister.'

'Oh but I love her, dear boy, and Paul, delightful man. We're all bitches and beautiful. Look at me!' He laughed again. 'And we're all *just* something or other.'

'Did you just say you haven't got much longer?'

'Another six months so my doctor tells me...' He turned and looked at me from beneath the bushiest eyebrows you've ever seen. His eyes were round and large but not a trace of self pity. 'We come, we go, darling, and to be honest carrying this weight is becoming daily more tiresome.'

'Six months?'

'It's enough, dear.' He turned away and for the first time I saw a sadness in him.

'I'm going to miss you.' I meant it. Fat Dick was a real person. Not that everybody else wasn't, but Fat Dick wasn't afraid to show it.

That's what I like about you, dear boy. You don't make a tragic face and weep, you move right along to the nub of it. My absence. I wonder myself what that would be like.'

'Sorry, I didn't mean...'

'I know you didn't. Come and have lunch with me soon? I've time for that anyway. Would you do that?'

'I'd like to.'

'And we can talk about the romantic poets. I think I'll take them with me to my grave.' He perked up. 'Perhaps I shall meet them! Good morning Mr Wordsworth, how's Johnny Keats? Lord Byron passed through? Such heavy boots don't you think?' His eyes sparkled as he looked up. 'Ah, Geraldine!' An older, grey-haired woman had appeared in front of us wearing a long, flowing summer coat. 'I won't get up if you don't mind.'

'Of course not, darling,' she smiled sweetly.

She looked as much in need of a seat as Richard so I stood up and let her sit. I left them to their hugs and kisses and wandered into the house and up the stairs to the bathroom. On the landing I stopped for a moment and held onto the bannister.

Fuck me, Fat Dick is going to cop it.

What did I think about that? Well I'd better stop calling him Fat Dick for a start. My friend Richard Guest was going to die. He was going to be absent. I'd never see him again. He'd be an absent friend. How many friends can be absent before there's only you left? Over the years I'd often imagined myself on my own deathbed. What would I say to my loving big-eyed kids gathered round me in some Dickensian pageant waiting for the last wise words from Francis the ancient sage? Live your life to the full, son! Don't waste time, dear daughter! Life is for living now! And then I'd pass quietly away leaving them with the cliches of the ages echoing forever in their dim little minds. I'm determined that my lunch with Richard won't be a lachrymose last supper. Oh no. it's going to be a celebration, a fucking riot of suckling pig and port with white table cloths and a hundred sommeliers all speaking Parisienne dear boy. I'll give the old fellah the send-off he deserves, even if it would be in his club and he'd pay for it.

I moved on up the stairs. As I passed a bedroom door I heard a series of grunts. I knew exactly what that was and couldn't resist. I opened the door and there in front of me was Miranda Vee back flat on the bed, her skirt rucked around her thighs and her bare legs wrapped round Tony Braithwaite. She was squeezing his naked arse with beautifully manicured green fingernails. As the coverlet was blue and his bum pink, it looked like a giant peach bobbing up and down in a swimming pool. Tony turned as I went into the room.

'Six minutes,' he said, thrusting and panting.

'In seconds.'

'Three sixty,'

'Do you mind?' said Miranda as she poked her head up over Tony's shoulder.

'Sorry, just looking for the bathroom.' I grinned myself out of the room and closed the door. Tony had been fucking for six minutes and Fat Dick would be dead in six months. Maths in everything. Sex and death. Maybe I should write a novel. I did the necessary; zipped up and went back down the stairs. As I reached the bottom I sensed something was different; it was quieter, the party babble had subsided. I went on through the kitchen and the conservatory and could see that the circles of happily gambolling gossiping actors in the garden had broken up into one large ring and there in the middle of the lawn stood himself, Honorary Doctor Sir Alexander Hudson, like a star with the rest in orbit. He was smiling graciously at his old pal Paul, who clearly had been telling the truth about their being friends. They were chatting uneasily to each other as the rest of the party looked on pretending not to. I immediately noticed that Paul hadn't done his hostly duty and I picked up a couple of bottles and a glass from one of the trestles.

'Drink, Mr Hudson, sir?' I said with my best obsequious smile.

'Ah thank you.'

'This is Francis, Annie's brother,' said Paul.

'Someone who knows the necessary.' Hudson smiled at me.

'Years of practice,' I said with a carefully raised eyebrow,

'Get yourself a glass,' said Alexander, 'and join us.'

I heard someone laugh as I stood, back arched and head bent forward, paying the greatest attention as whatever was said by the great man flowed by barely comprehended in my anxiousness to show how engaged I was.

I said, 'I'm just a teacher.'

Well never mind,' said Alexander.

At least he was honest. And that's all I remembered. My creepy homage had broken the ice and everybody returned to their circles of joy as if nothing had happened. Paul took him over to the food table and I, seeing my presence was no longer required, went back and sat under the tree where Richard had been talking to Geraldine. They'd both gone to talk to Hudson and stood with him like an ageing citadel in the castle of the free and easy. The rest of the evening went by in a bit of a blur. I remember a tall woman with a large bust in a grey dress sitting by me. She told me something about working on a biblical story. For some reason I was fascinated by this and asked her endless questions about her research.

'Where's it set?'

'Oh? Palestine, I suppose.'

'Big production?'

'Oh I wouldn't say that.'

'Is it for film or theatre?'

'Sorry?'

'Film or theatre? Or TV?'

'I'm the local vicar,' she said.

'Ah. Well.' But only momentarily stumped, I said, 'Bet you get a load of jokes.'

'What jokes?'

'Vicar jokes. There's hundreds of them.'

'Oh I love jokes, especially vicar jokes. Tell me one.'

'Can't think of any.' My head lolled backwards and I felt the prick on my scalp from the stub of a twig on the trunk of the tree behind. My head shot forward again. 'I know a poem. "There was a priest, a dirty beast, his name was Harry Moses. He had a prick nine inches thick and balls as red as roses."'

'Ah,' said the vicar. 'I think I can see someone I know.' She wandered away giving me a strange look back as she went.

I thought I saw Tony again, and Miranda Vee, but wasn't sure. Then I fell asleep. When I woke up the garden was empty and I was lying in a lounger staring up at the night sky. I thought I was counting the stars then realised there was one standing in front of me.

'Paul says you live in the town,' said Alexander Hudson, 'I have a taxi outside. I'll drop you off.'

## 5

I was so shocked by the sudden appearance of the great actor that I sobered enough to walk in a reasonably straight line out of Annie's front door, across the pavement of a sultry night and into the back seat of a waiting black cab, its engine humming with anticipation. My last memories of the party were of Alexander hugging Paul like a long lost brother and of Annie falling slowly backwards into the house as we pulled away. Alexander was silent on the seat next to me. My brain refused to register what was happening.

Finally he said, 'enjoy yourself?'

I felt like crying. 'Oh yes.'

'Fancy a night cap?'

'Ah....?' my mouth fell open.

'I know a place.' He said something to the driver and a couple of minutes later we pulled up at the end of an alley in the town. I remember a flight of steep stairs heading down into a dark well with the faint echo of music coming from below. I held onto the rail and slowly eased myself into the depths. We entered a low-ceilinged smoke filled red-lit basement room with a small bar along one wall and a piano at the far end. There were half a dozen shadowy figures at small tables and a couple by the bar. They were all men. I sat with Alexander on a beat-up red banquette that curved round one of the corners of the room. The only girl in the place came up to us and Alexander ordered two whiskies as I tried to remember whether I'd asked for one or not.

'Where am I?'

'Don't worry, you're safe, said Alexander. 'Little place I know. Haven't been here for years.' He nodded hello to a man by the bar who smiled back. 'Always perfectly peaceful. To be honest I find parties these days something of a trial. You can get too much attention, can't you?

'Absolutely.'

'How would you know?' he laughed.

'Thanks very much.' For a second the thought crossed my mind that this must be a pick-up. Alexander had even touched my leg, but just like Fat Dick it was in the friendliest possible way. Gay men seemed to like me. Maybe it was because they knew I was too soft for any kind of judgement, or in this case so far off my head that I couldn't possibly make one anyway. I felt like my feet were rooted to the ground and my head was floating. I certainly wasn't going to brighten anyone's night with sparkling repartee. The girl brought the drinks and put them on the table in front of us. She was wearing an indecently short skirt above legs that went up to her armpits. For a second I saw myself as an ant on a celestial ladder. 'What a pair,' I said.

'Extraordinary, aren't they?'

'Excuse me, but why am I here?

'Company,' said Alexander. 'I didn't want to go home. Do you mind?'

'No, no. Absolutely no. It's fine by me.'

He looked over at the bar and for a second a sad shadow passed over his face. I decided with the too obvious clarity of booze that there lounging on the beat up old sofa next to me was Alexander Hudson, world famous celebrity and actor, who was as lonely as fuck. So lonely in fact that he was happy to pass the time of night with me; that's how lonely he was. I wanted to give him a big hug. Or at least say something that sounded like intelligent conversation. I said, 'What's it like, being an actor?'

He laughed out loud and said, 'oh dear.'

'Sorry, really extremely boring question, I know, I know. I'm drunk, you see?' I very carefully placed my scotch back on the table. 'Sorry.'

'Oh don't apologise,' he said with a wave of his hand. 'Sometimes the simplest... actually I adore being an actor. There are of course times when I hate it but I couldn't be anything else. It's what I am my dear, probably the most irredeemable narcissist is the truth of it. We're all narcissists aren't we?' His mouth turned down as he seemed to think about his own question. 'Unfortunately like the man himself the image slowly fades.' He fluttered his fingers into the air as if he was watching the thought disappear into the dark corners of the room. 'As we look into the stream desperate to see the beauty in ourselves, we slowly ripple away. Don't let me get too maudlin.' He breathed in deeply as if trying to keep himself in check. 'But I keep it up, you see? I go to the parties, the old friends smile as they pay their compliments, but I can see it in their eyes, it's a kind of farewell.' There was a hint of an actorish tear. 'Well done, Alex, you did what we all strive for, you've been a beacon, showed us all it was worth while, but we know as you do that it can't last. That's why he killed himself.'

'Who?'

'Narcissus, dear. Keep up.'

'Sorry. I've had enough of death for one night' Fat..., I mean Richard...'

'You know Dick Guest?'

'He told me he's got six months.'

'So terribly sad. He's one of the most generous men I've ever met. I shall miss him terribly.'

'He's always been nice to me.' Now there really was a tear in my eye. 'You're not thinking of topping yourself, are you?'

'Who me?'

'Sorry. Another totally stupid question.'

'Ha! Not likely, darling.' Alexander sat back on the banquette. 'I'll squeeze every ounce out of it, don't you worry about that. But you can't help thinking, can you? I mean going back over it, wondering who you are, what you've been?' He looked away, his voice was getting soft and dreamy, then abruptly more harsh and judgemental. 'My mother died a couple of years ago. I loved her, absolutely adored her, but do you know the awful truth? There they were in the church, all spread before me as I delivered the eulogy. I knew I was watching myself, checking the cadence, keeping the emotions just so, the delivery, waiting for a laugh or a smile, shedding a tear or two, not too much, not too little. No doubt about it, I was performing. Even at the funeral of my mother who I loved more than anybody in this world, I was giving them a show.' He was suddenly angry. His feelings seemed to come and go at will. 'I was disgusted with myself afterwards but what could I do, other than admit finally that I was a fucking actor, and everything I did was a fucking act?' He looked down at his drink. 'I'm sitting here with a glass of scotch. The booze is real but I'm not, I'm acting.' He stared at me. 'Life's an act, isn't it?'

'Is it?'

'Oh yes, we all do it. You do it. You prepare a small performance for every second of your day The truth is you civilians do it better than we professionals. Of course you're better at it than us because we can't see you doing it and no-one assumes you are. A performance, darling, perhaps that's all life is. Like another?' He turned his eyes toward the bar, raised one finger to get attention, then two to indicate what he wanted, then pointed down at the table. He turned back to me, 'Did you think I was going to try to seduce you?'

'Ah? The thought had crossed my mind.'

'In another time you would have been right. You're a very attractive man.'

'I'd say I was pretty ignorant.'

'No you're not, you're a teacher.'

'Teacher's are pretty ignorant.'

'Always remember that the student knows what he or she needs better than anyone else. All you have to do is help them see it. That's what actors do, you see?'

'Do they?"

'Oh yes, we give you permission to act and here's your stage.' He gestured, looking around the club as if it were the world.

The legs brought a couple more whiskies over. 'I don't know if I can drink much more.'

'Last one,' said Alexander.

'It's been a great pleasure to meet you, Mr Hudson.'

'And you.'

I stared at the new scotch on the table in front of me. 'You see, Mr Hudson...'

'Alex, darling.'

'Sir Alex...'

'I don't think that's necessary.'

'You see, I don't know who I am.'

He laughed out loud. 'Who does?'

'That's what I was told anyway.'

'Well I certainly don't know who I am,' Alexander arched his eyebrows which gave him the look of a surprised clown. 'I'm an actor, I play this or that and then move on. We like to think that we admit the truth about ourselves every now and then but I don't think I ever really have. I don't know what it is. One perhaps uses a character as a kind of shield or conduit but that's a kind of cowardice isn't it? You can always say afterwards, oh it's the part, it wasn't me at all. They always believe you. Was it the truth or wasn't it? Don't ask me, dear.'

I took a good slug of the whisky. It was all getting a bit beyond me.

'I'm not answering you, am I?' he said. He looked at me.

His eyes were dark, his gaze direct and thoughtful. 'We think,' he said, 'that somewhere down there beyond all the pretence that there's the real me, the absolute, unchangeable, eternal me. I've wondered about this myself, said all sorts of things that I've thought were truthful and honest, that were the real me, usually when I've had too much of this.' He raised his glass. 'And the next day I've realised that everything I've said was just drunk, self-pitying nonsense and I've been ashamed of it. There is no true self, Francis. That is what I've come to believe anyway. There's only the me that I choose to be and sometimes that choice is successful and sometimes it isn't. People will swallow anything, and if you're sure about who you are then so will they be. Decide, then be it, that's my advice to you. Your good health.' He raised his glass to lips, then inclined his head towards me and stage whispered, 'Choose wisely, act fiercely.'

'Ah well, I'm grateful for that. Thank you.'

'Are you Irish?'

'Can you hear the accent?'

'No. You don't have an accent. It's the rhythm. I can hear the rhythm of your native land. That's my job, you see, to hear people, see them, imitate them I suppose.' He gave me a long piercing look and pursed his lips as if considering the problem. 'Is the Irish the real thing, do you think?'

'I don't know.'

'Something Celtic, depressed, dreamy, that's Irish, isn't it? None of my business of course but I suspect you're a bit of a romantic.'

'Saint Francis the stoic.'

'Oh God, no. A concrete post is stoical, standing there in all weathers. Ask it what it wants and it would probably say, "can you get me out of this fucking rain."' He laughed and finished his drink. 'If you ever need anything get in touch. Paul knows where to find me.'

We staggered back up the stairs. The cool night air hit me like an ice wall and I stumbled after Alexander as we walked back up the alley. He took my arm. 'I'll find another cab.'

'It's alright.' I could see my barber's and realised we were only a couple of hundred yards from where I lived. 'I can make it from here.'

I watched as Sir Alex strode briskly away down the street, seeming to be hardly touched by the booze, or anything else.

## 6

I woke up next morning at eleven and stared up at the crack in the ceiling above my bed and wondered as usual where it led. My gaze travelled down to the white chipboard full length cupboard built-in to the alcove ahead of me. One door was open and I stared for a while at the jumble of half-sorted, dull-coloured forlornly-hung and tangled charity shop rejects that you might call my wardrobe, all my various selves hanging there waiting for the actuality of me to inflate them. As my eye travelled further down I spotted my own legs stretched out away from me on the bed. My duvet had slipped to one side and I could see my left limb with trouser on and the shoe and sock off revealing my toes. So far so good. The right side was the problem. The trouser leg was off but the shoe was still on and tightly laced. I wondered how this could be. Receiving no answer my survey continued down to the jumble on the floor by my bed which I briefly studied; there was my ipad, an earplug, several books, three used tissues, a triangle of pizza on a dirty plate, a wine glass, two empty bottles, several T-shirts and the sock and left shoe that I'd obviously removed the night before without continuing on to the trouser leg. This was the depressing detritus of my life. What could this be other than an indication of mental disorder? But on the other hand it could be a sign not only of creativity but of the huge love within me just waiting to be disentangled and come bursting forth. There before you is the whole of me laid bare over my bedroom floor. I am open for all to see. How vulnerable and honest I am!

Then I was grinning. What a night I'd had. An hour alone with Alexander Hudson. I'd an overwhelming desire to call, write, or email him and inform him of the wonder of his good self as a human being and could I be his best pal for the rest of my life? You Alexander are a true star lighting heaven's way for the rest of us. I could almost have cried such was the extent of my love and adoration. How can I be like you? I thought I should call Miriam and boast about my deeply intimate heart to heart with the greatest actor in the country and make her jealous. The idea made me smile through the throb in my temple, but then I remembered Alexander's wise words. 'Life's an act isn't it?' I couldn't make up my mind whether I should perform the humble acolyte and keep a respectful shtum, or boast about it to Miriam. To boast or not to boast? I called Miriam. She wasn't available. Probably hanging around Theo Skinner somewhere up in psycho land. Such was my relentless delight in myself I sent her a text. Had long conversation with Alexander Hudson at Annie's party and interesting little club later. Sorry you missed it. Cu Thursday. Frankie x.

Actually I wasn't sorry that Miriam had missed the party. If she'd been there I wouldn't have got near Alexander. She always had the words and I didn't. I sometimes felt that I actually disappeared as the air around me was sucked into her orbit. Still, to hell with that. I thought of Thursday, the conference and Professor Abebi, then realised I'd forgotten her surname. Maybe I'd never known it. But all that would be rectified as soon as I read the plastic ID dangling deliciously over the deep and mysterious chasm of her cleavage. Such was my delight in all this and the amount of alcohol still in my veins that I reached my hand down to my conveniently naked thigh. Strangely Alexander's face kept appearing in the midst of my fantasies of Abebi. I didn't know whether he would approve of what I was doing or not.

I wondered what to do with the rest of my empty day. I could spend it reading the end of term essays handed in by Year Twelve, but remembering Alexander again - choose wisely and act fiercely! - I called Tony and arranged to meet him for a drink in the Calf.

We settled in our usual corner by the window with a couple of pints in front of us. Tony was looking spry and brimming with health, his muscles bulging out of a red short-sleeved shirt and his great thighs stretching the legs of his khaki shorts. Despite three cups of tea and a piece of toast as a bed for the booze I still felt wretched and took a long gulp of bitter hoping it would perk me up. 'How'd you do that with Amanda?'

'Miranda,' he said. 'Miranda Vee. She was in that TV show, Random, you see it? She were a middle-aged sex goddess from Rotherham. 'Bout time you caught up with popular culture.'

'How d'you do it?'

'Watch TV.'

'With Miranda?'

'Comes natural.'

'Come on, I need to know.'

'You have to understand basic principle.'

'What basic principle?'

'Sex. Always there. Like picking apples off the tree.'

'Cheers, Adam. I'm going to be seeing Abebi, so maybe a bit more information?'

He leant forward, his big shoulders and arms crowding his pint. He stretched his lips up the sides of his face and exhaled as if considering the most basic aspects of his art. 'Tell them they've got beautiful breasts.'

'You what?'

'Tell them they've got...'

'You must be fucking joking.'

'Fucking not, son.' Tony took his own first slug of the beer, then tapped his nose. 'Sex is always there, right?'

'So you just come out with it, just like that?'

'Fucking right.'

'It's offensive.'

'Calm down, son. I'll tell yer.' He leant back and breathed in deeply., propping his glasses back up his nose with a meaty finger. 'Suppose you're at some party or summat. You see this nice looking woman. You have a quick glance, she has a quick glance, mebbe a smile or mebbe not. You edge closer, you smile, you talk and soon as you can, you say summat like, you got nice breasts.'

'What age are you living in? You actually say that?'

'Why not?'

'Go and ask any woman.'

'You think women don't want sex?'

'You ever heard of subtlety?'

'Just listen to me, alright? You say it, Ok? And you're right, she's mebbe immediately offended. She gives you a filthy look like you're an unreconstructed male or whatever, and walks off in a huff, celebrating her assault on primitive man and thinking how she's going to tell her mates about it and write a letter to the papers. I know all this, Frankie.'

'So why do you do it?'

'Because I like sex. And so does she.'

'But you didn't get any. She's walked off.'

'Haven't finished, have I? She's ten yards away, angry as some clucking hen, and firing dirty looks at you across the room and you leave it there for about ten minutes or a quarter of an hour, mebbe twenty; judgement son, that's what it's all about. Anyhow you know something and so does she. The matter has been raised, see?'

'Raised? Right.'

'She may or may not want sex with you, but it's there on the table.' He grinned and nodded as if agreeing with himself. 'Then after a while, you glance at her again, cross room. She turns away still pissed of at you, but the thought is... raised as you say. After a while you glance again and if she's interested you see the slightest little smile on her face, just a little tweak, you know? Because she's actually liked the compliment, see? I mean she might not have done but least she knows what's available. Tha's the point, isn't it? You get closer again and mebbe you say, sorry did I offend you? Which of course you have in the front part of her mind, but underneath there's...'

'...the big fucking snake.'

'Which she's as aware of as you. She's no fool, Frankie. She knows game. And so you get talking, you both know exactly what you're talking about. If she continues to strop, buy her a drink and forget it, you can't win 'em all. But if she's warming up you can sooner or later get round to discussing dimensions and so on.'

'Dimensions? You mean you tell her how big your dick is?'

'Could do.'

'Fuck off.'

'What's the matter with you? Sex is an animal act. It's exciting to talk about it. Women aren't just mini-mouses, you know? They're up there, fucking sex goddesses. They're wild and they're free and they want you to recognise that. And once you get past all the bullshit, you're both in the field. You and her. And she loves being there as much as you do.'

'So you tell her the size of your dick?'

'I don't think you're understanding the deeper philosophy of the approach, Frankie. I'm talking about what's really happening. Some of them don't want it. Fair enough. They tell you to fuck off. We're all grown ups, alright? Anyhow you don't have to talk about actual dimensions, just mention summat like it because sometimes it's the way. And sometimes she really likes it. And by the way you don't want to exaggerate or you'll look stupid later.'

'Like six inches when it's five...?'

'Speak for yourself. Anyhow you don't have to do it. You can finesse it. You know, create metaphors. Metaphors can be fun. You should know, you're an English teacher.'

'So I go up to Abebi, who's the most gorgeous woman in the world, who's a professor in cognitive consciousness and start talking about bananas?'

'Doesn't matter if she's a professor or a bar sweeper, she's just like the rest of us.' He gave me a look over his glasses like he's talking to his apprentice. 'We all know about sex. Me and Miranda, we both got what we wanted, didn't we?'

'What did she say about us doing arithmetic as she had your metaphor between her legs?'

'She thought it were funny. She was enjoying herself, see? But I'll take your point for a moment. A professor?' He thought about it as he finished his pint. 'Mebbe you need a more intellectual approach, but I'll tell you something, intellect can get in the way of sex, too much thinking, too much worrying, stops you getting what you want. Not enough soul, see? Not enough admitting. Shall I tell you what they really want?'

'Sex?'

'Sure, that's part of it, but what they absolutely want is respect, respect for them as proper human beings, body and soul. They want a man standing in front of them who's big and bold enough to lay it out, all his desires, and everything he wants, and then he says, how about you, you interested?' He was prodding the table with his finger now. 'Because you, lady, you're as big and powerful as I am, and you've got a right and so have I. So there it is. Two grown-ups being honest with each other and respecting each other and either wanting the same thing, or not. Another pint?'

I gave him my glass and watched as he went to the bar. I wondered how many women I knew would have listened to all that and reacted in the way Tony said they would. I could just hear Sophie Rayner, a geography teacher at our school, laying into him. How would Tony have taken it? Sophie was a handsome woman with slanting eyes, a dark fringe, and a great figure. I'd fancied her for years but she could see misogyny in the way you held your pen. Everything I said would be taken as some kind of assault. She scared me so much that I instinctively retreated to the farthest corner of the staffroom whenever she entered. But I knew Tony was as attracted to her as much as I was. In fact, now I came to think of it, I'd actually seen them sitting together one lunch time, and talking closely at a social, and didn't she and Tony once accompany a group of kids on some field trip? Why hadn't I ever asked him about it? Had I been too jealous? Probably. He came back to the table with the drinks.

'What happened with you and Sophie Rayner?'

'Who?'

'Sophie Rayner, geography.'

Tony sat down. 'Oh we had a little... you know?'

'You fucked her?'

'For about three months, off and on.'

'You fucked Sophie Rayner?'

'Just told yer, Frankie.'

'Did you tell her she had great breasts?'

'Ah?' Tony searched his memory. 'Not immediately, no. Sophie's a particular kind of woman as you know. You've got to respect people for what they believe, see? But you've got to take them on too, or they don't respect you. Matter of fact I prefer strong women, you know where you are with them. And Sophie's a very intelligent person.'

'You amaze me, Tony.'

'Amaze meself sometimes. It's just the road, son. Take it as it is. They love it more than we do. Never stop talking about it, do they?'

'You have any feelings, Tone?'

'Feelings for what?'

'You know, feelings, like feelings.'

'Course I do. They come and go. Don't build your house

on shifting sands, mate.'

'You ever been in love?'

Tony sat back on his seat, brought his beer to his mouth, then put it back on the table. 'Now you're going deep, Frankie.'

'Tell me.'

'Alright.' He took a good half of the pint in one gulp. 'You know something the beer's shit in here. Don't know why we keep coming.'

'You ever been in love?'

'You're like a dog with a bone, son. I was in love once, matter of fact, learned me lesson. Her name was Debbie, beautiful girl, left me, broke my heart.'

'How long ago?'

'Bout ten years, before I came down here. I cried for a week. Pal of mine said you're grieving son, go see someone, help you out. Think he meant some kind of counsellor. No thanks. Well truth is I thought about it. I do have feelings, see Frankie? Know what I did? I wrote a book on arithmetic for ten year olds. Really simple stuff, basic numbers, nothing you could argue with. Understood, see, how things add up. Facts, mate.'

'That's it? Facts?'

'Things you can rely on.' He looked at me straight in the eye. There was something frightening about the glance, as if that was the truth, and what was I going to do about it?

'Fucking hell, Tone.'

'I get what I want, so do they, that's all there is to it.'

'You had your heart broken and so you wrote a book on arithmetic?'

'Made a couple of thousand quid. Been meaning to write another.' He finished the pint.

'It's my round.' I began to get up.

'No I'll get them.' Tony looked over at the bar and I could see why. The landlord had been replaced by a nice looking girl with a low cut blouse. 'I'd like to have a word.' He went and stood under the horse brasses as she pumped the handle smiling at him and pulling as the beer gushed. Immediate metaphor. The girl leant forward as she put the pint on the bar, giving Tony a good shot of her cleavage. He grinned. I wondered when he'd be moving on to dimensions. How about the fourth one, Tone, the emotional universe? Maybe the girl would enlighten him. I don't know why but suddenly I felt very protective of my friend, wanting to put my arms round him and say don't worry about Debbie. Tony would have told me to fuck off, but I loved him anyway. Good old Tone. Mutt or marvel? Either, neither, or both. Whichever it was he was a huge presence in me. He made me think of the wildness in the kids I taught. He'd had it once too. I could imagine him on a rugby field on the Moors charging through the northern wind; a mutt, wild and marvellous. He'd taught me many things, mainly how to gather my vagueness into common sense, and I loved his booming laugh and northern wisecracks, even his 'reason, son, reason...' And in this sudden wave of sentiment, just for a second I loved myself too, good old Frankie, lovely little Francis.

It was getting ridiculous, my hangover was descending into full-on self-pity which I knew would soon descend to that mysterious ailment, the unnameable, the nervous ball inside, all unformed and swirling, sending up the fumes of pain and joy, of wonder and confusion; everything I needed and didn't, and couldn't work out anyway, except by maths according to my Yorkshire therapist. Maybe this was the come down from the alcohol, or maybe it's what's always there, only visible or felt in times like these.

Just five days ago Abebi had sat there in this very pub, at this actual table. Twenty minutes of paradise. And then Skinner and Paradise Lost. Not him. Please God, in your absence, don't let it be him. How could I stop him? I looked down at the ancient wood floor hoping antiquity might provide the answer, then up at the window as the sunlight poured in.

My phone rang. It was Paul.

'What are you doing, tomorrow?' he said. He told me, his son, Arnold, who was in his final year at film school was making his end of course film and one of his actors had let him down. 'He wants me to step in,' said Paul, 'but I can't, I'm doing a commercial, so I suggested you. It's a student film, you don't have to do anything.'

'I'm not an actor.' My heart was suddenly beating with the panic of my own wildness.

'It's two lines. You're always so scathing about acting. Here's your chance to prove yourself wrong. Annie thinks it's a great idea. I'll tell Arnold you'll do it.'

'No Paul.'

Paul rang off. Two minutes later Arnold himself called and said he'd get someone to push the script through my letterbox that afternoon.

'Wait a minute....'

'You've got to do it, I'm desperate, Uncle Francis.' said Arnold, He'd never called me that before. In fact he'd hardly ever spoken to me.'

'I can't.'

'This is my finals project. If I don't get it in, I'll fail the course!'

What could I say? I imagined my sister's face. 'You've let down a member of the family, even if he is a stepson!' Two minutes later she called in person, 'Well you'll have to find your character now!' She rang off with a cackle.

Tony came back with the drinks. I'm seeing her tonight, my place,' he said. And winked at the girl behind the bar.

# 7

Arnold's film was called And So They Thought They Knew. The script was hardly more than twenty pages long and came with a short note saying, You're playing Scarborough, 10 am Lewisham High Street outside the MacDonald's. Cu there, Arnold. I lay on my bed amidst the debris and read through the script. I was to be in one scene:

Scarborough, old geezer, once a detective, comes out of the MacDonald's. Donna goes up to him.

Donna: You done it now ain't you?

Scarborough: Who are you?

Donna: You know who I am, you old shit.

Scarborough: Go away.

Donna: You been trying for fucking years.

Scarborough: Get lost. Or I'll....

Donna: Or you'll what? Nothing, nothing at all. You're all fucking corrupt!

Donna walks off leaving Scarborough scowling.

And that was it. Scarborough, old geezer? How old did Arnold think I was? Anyone under the age of twenty sees everyone over thirty as past it, but I was no old geezer. I read the rest of the script which was incomprehensible. Maybe I was past it. In his note Arnold had asked me to wear an old raincoat. I didn't have a raincoat, old or new, and didn't know anyone who did unless they were old geezers splashing through puddles in galoshes. Old geezers? The word acting came to mind, the ball began to unfurl, the knot in my gut loosened; is that what acting meant? Being something you're not? An old geezer? Me? I had a longish anorak from the last century which would have to do. Once a detective? What did that mean? How long ago is once? At my age I'd still be a detective. Old geezer again. It was beginning to occur to me that when Arnold said he was desperate he meant me. And what kind of detective? Scarborough? Was that a clue? Was he from Yorkshire? I could do it like Tony! In fact I could ask Tony to do it! I picked up my phone but saw Annie's face again. I knew I wouldn't be able to stand her scorn, even imagining it, withered me. I switched the phone off. I could wear a fedora! Detectives didn't wear fedoras any more. I didn't have a fedora. Forget the costume! Was I going to find who I was in a costume, a jacket, a pair of trousers, a hat? Is that how you did it? I gathered myself and asked the obvious, what I was doing in the scene? What was I saying? I lay on the bed repeating my three lines: 1.Who are you? 2. Go away, and 3. Get lost, or I'll... I'd do what? Didn't a character have to finish a line? Or at least didn't a character have to know the line he didn't finish? It was hopeless; all over before I'd started.

I woke at six in the morning determined to call Arnold and tell him I couldn't do it. How could I do that? I'd be giving my step nephew-in law four hours notice and much as I didn't like Arnold and never had, it was his final project and if I didn't do it he'd fail his course and take to the streets dejected and bitter and start jacking up heroin and I'd be rejected by my sister and die of guilt. I was trapped and I knew it.

'Alright, fuck it!' I leapt out of bed. I'll do it! And if it was no good they'd have to shoot it again with someone else. But at least I'd have tried, I'd have been noble, but I'd tried. It would give Annie a laugh anyway.

I arrived on the Lewisham High Street in my old anorak. My only experience of film sets was from Hollywood. On the Tube down I'd imagined lights, cameras, action and a hundred extras. The fact that I'd had to provide my own costume should have been warning enough. There was a solitary camera on a tripod and five people all looking like Arnold, male and female, all with thick, dark curly hair and the uncompromising demeanour of youth making a film, yeah? They were kids, I wasn't, I was amateur, so were they, but I was more so. I don't know if this made my nerves better or worse. To have been the centre of attention in the dazzle of a studio would have terrified me, but to loiter and be totally ignored under the grey skies of Lewisham wasn't much better. Someone even went into the MacDonalds and bought cups of coffee for everyone but me. I thought maybe I should throw a Mae West (Annie's term for a tantrum) and walk off the set, stomp angrily down the High Street and into the sunset, but it was morning, it was raining, I'd have looked a prick and obviously not able to cut it in front of the youth of today.

Finally Arnold came up to me. I could see he was nervous and trying to be an auteur like his heroes, and wasn't quite cutting it. I felt a bit sorry for him.

'You come out of MacDonalds, the camera's there,' he said. 'This is Kate.'

Kate was stick thin, had black hair, black eyeliner, black lipstick, black clothes, and had a contemptuous black leer - although that could have been the character she was playing which was Donna the girl who was to confront me.

'Kate will come up to you. She'll stand there,' said Arnold. Kate did so.

'And you stop here,' he pointing down to the pavement. I did so. He turned to the camera and said, 'how's that?'

'Yeah, we're on a twenty-five,' said the camera.

'Right just walk it through.' said Arnold.

'What?'

'You come out of the MacDonald's and stop there.' Arnold feigned patience. 'Kate comes up to you.'

I did as I was told. I realised too late that I didn't like being looked at. Kate mumbled her first line. I could hardly hear her.

'You speak now,' said Arnold. 'Who are you?'

'Scarborough.'

'No it's your line. You say, 'Who are you?''

I stumbled through the first rehearsal and forgot my lines twice. How could I do that when I only had three?

'Anyway,' said Arnold despairingly. 'We may as well go for a take.'

'Why not?' said the camera.

They did three takes and all of them were useless. I couldn't remember what I had to say and didn't hit my mark because I didn't know where it was.

'It's there,' said Arnold. 'That crack in the pavement.'

'The pavement's full of fucking cracks, Arnold!'

A girl, I reckon to be aged about thirteen, chalked a line on the paving.

'Like a detective,' said Arnold. 'And not from Ireland.'

Not from Ireland? What was he talking about? I realised he was right. For some reason my heritage was insisting on asserting itself and I was giving it the full Dublin.

'Christ, can't you get an actor?' said Kate/Donna who had probably been one herself for about five minutes.

'For fuck's sake,' said Arnold.

They all looked at me with the utmost contempt. I can't say I blamed them, I was wrecking their film. Maybe I would have been better off facing Annie. 'I don't know who I am!' I whined.

'Well fucking make it up,' shouted Arnold, losing it. 'That's what actors do!'

There was something about the scorn from this twenty something Spielberg, something about the blaze in Kate/Donna's eyes, the dismissive shrug of the clown behind the camera, and the sound boy was giggling. All of it was pushing me into a place I hadn't been in for years, even in the classroom.

'Alright we'll do it again,' I said through gritted teeth. I turned round and walked back into the MacDonald's, clenching my fists as I felt the bile rising, the nervous ball unfurling. I came out again fast. I didn't stop on their fucking puerile chalk mark and when this black-haired nobody called Donna - and I fully accepted her as Donna now, although it had been the actor called Kate who'd pissed me off - yelled at me. 'You done it now, ain't you?' I snarled back, 'Who are you?' It was a good question. I had no idea who she was.

'You know who I am, you old shit.'

I didn't like that, especially the old. 'Fuck off! I shouted, which wasn't the script but I didn't care.

I saw her recoil and was delighted. She came back with venom. 'You been trying for fucking years!'

Then came my masterstroke. 'You don't fuck off, I'll stick a spike up your cunt!!' It came out in a gale of pure rage straight from the my gut. I could feel my face contort and my body shaking. I wanted to kill her.

'Alright mate,' she said, and stepped away from me looking scared to death and I was ecstatic. You're all corrupt anyhow.' Then, confused, she walked away from me in the wrong direction.

'Cut!' said Arnold.

The sound of his voice brought me back to reality. I was standing on Lewisham High Street screaming like a raging alcoholic at a girl I didn't know. 'Sorry,' I said, 'didn't mean that.'

'Brilliant,' said Arnold. 'Thanks uncle, that was perfect.'

Uncle? Now he's calling me uncle again. 'No, They were the wrong lines.'

'Don't worry about it,' said Arnold. 'It was fucking great. Didn't know you could act. Thought you were just a teacher.'

'Don't I get a close up?' said Kate/Donna, miffed that I'd nicked her scene. I was standing aloof now, weirdly straight and tall as if I was waiting for my dresser.

'No I got it all on the wide,' said Arnold. 'Pack up, let's get down to the museum.'

And that was that. I'd done it. My first stint as an actor. I watched as they loaded their gear into an old van. I was shaking and shocked like a minor earthquake had erupted inside me and released a wave of feelings that I didn't know I had. 'That was great. Didn't know you could act," Arnold had said. And I hadn't either. I didn't know whether I was delighted, or terrified, or appalled. It had all been based on a hatred for that girl Donna and also a compassion for her; an entanglement of feeling so strong and electric that I couldn't discern the one in the torrent of it all. I wanted to kill her and love her at the same time. All me somehow, more exhilarated than I'd ever been. That old nervous ball, had for thirty glorious seconds been transformed into a glorious energy which I'd never known and had no clue as to its origin unless it had something to do with the wildness I saw in the kids. But one thing was for sure, I wanted to do it again.

# 8

I spent the next couple of days in confusion, rocking between excitement and shame. Finally the bubble burst leaving just a few damp patches on my psyche, but the thoughts remained, whispering in my mind like stray clouds, in the unexpected voice of Ireland. Where'd that come from? I'd been born in Dun Laoghaire to an Irishman and his English wife but had no great yearning for the old country. We'd moved over to London when I was eleven and I'd grown here. None of it seemed much different to Dublin. My childhood horizons were narrow; dirty streets, muddy football pitch, a school slabbed up in the sixties with low flat roofs and yelping boys fighting at playtime. I'd been a fierce-accented Irish wean who'd changed within a fortnight into a Kilburn kid so I wouldn't be seen as too different. Ma smiled at my effort but Pa was stoney. He called me a traitor once after a football game, but was I to stick out like my ears and be persecuted for being a Paddy? I lost my virginity to a Queens Park girl called Jenny Marshall behind the pavilion in Gunnersbury Park and considered myself well and truly home. When I went back to Cork to see the grandparents I didn't feel any particular pull and was pleased to get back. The only time I admitted to Hibernia was when the football team played and I became mad crazy waving a plastic harp in front of the pub TV doing a jig after too much of the black stuff.

This voice that had come out of me in Lewisham must have come from memories I didn't know I had, or from the old man, or from an ancient family buried in the mists of time. How far back do we go? Does this mean I'm still a Catholic? Once an Irishman...? Deep in my soul can I speak Gaelic? I'd released a deep-rooted primitive energy which thrilled and at the same time terrified me as - panic-struck - I realised it had all been recorded for posterity. The thought of watching myself in that state, as surely I would when Arnold had his grand premiere, filled me with humiliation and shame. I made excuses in my head to avoid attending; illness, a school event, an emergency trip to Angola, anything, to avoid witnessing my own rage expressed on the silver screen in front of all who loved and saw me as entirely something else.

My state was such that I even sat with a pile of essays from Year Twelve. I'd asked a class to write about leaving home and what it would mean to them? A bright girl called Angela Griffiths wrote, 'I wouldn't be putting a coat on to go out, I'd be taking one off.' That summed up what I was feeling myself, except I wasn't sure which coat was which, or even what I was wearing in the first place.

Accidentally it seemed I'd embarked on an exploration of the actor's psyche - or more exactly my own. Had I been so shocked out of myself by the experience that I'd actually become myself, or more of myself, or some other self I didn't know about? Was I, Francis Riley, no more or less, just a repository of an unknown past which could leap out and bite me anytime it felt like it? And so what was that past? Could I ever know it? Could I ever leave it behind? And if I did, what would I be? Empty? 'You'll have to find your character now,' said Annie. What character was that? Myself, or one I'd have to make up, or conjure out of thin air, or take from some person I'd seen on the street, or in the pub, or at school? Was I supposed to imitate someone else like Alexander had said he did? Or were all those characters already there inside myself, waiting to be stirred and shaken into life, to come roaring out of me like some mad menagerie that had been slowly and silently waiting for its moment for all the years of my life?

I thought about all those actors I'd condemned for their superficiality over the years. What about their emotional liberation; all their immediate and unembarrassed laughter and tears? I'd said they were just attention seeking, but I couldn't deny the sheer freedom of being able to show feelings the rest of us took years to realise and release. Compared to them I felt as if I'd been boxed in by my own inhibitions all my life. They were free (that word again) and I wasn't.

Annie called me. I'd never heard her so enthusiastic. 'What happened to my shy little brother? Arnold said you were brilliant! He thought you were going to smash up the MacDonalds. He hasn't seen so much rage on screen since de Niro in Raging Bull.'

'Oh you know,' suddenly bursting with pride. 'I just did it.'

And that was the truth of it. But I was worried that I hadn't been responding to the demands of the script. I'd forgotten completely in that moment that I'd been in a film at all. My temper had been caused by Arnold's dismissive attitude and the contempt of his crew. Was it possible that I could do anything other than go slightly mad? How many scripts needed that?

Anyway it was enough of a buzz to set me up for Abebi

# 9

The psycho conference wasn't held in the university refectory as before, but in a small function room on the first floor of the admin building. It had a long balcony running along one side overlooking the front drive and grounds of the university. I was happy that Theo Skinner, relegated to more cramped premises, clearly didn't have the same pull as Alexander the great. And he didn't have canapés either, just a couple of tables along one wall serving red and white with a few paltry bowls of crisps saved from the previous reception. I put on my one suit as I'd promised Miriam. It wasn't much, a conventional dark blue with a stain on the cuff and one in the middle of my back which I hadn't noticed - ok if I didn't stand too much in the light. I had no plastic lanyard with my name and university displayed - which meant I'd have to do the English teacher, friend of Miriam Diamandis, routine every time I met someone. Not that many of them would be interested in me; I was just another body in a dull suit looking lost in an anxious room.

Skinner was standing at one end, barely visible over the heads of the throng, giving a speech extolling the exciting future of Barr-Lyon University, especially, mainly, the psychology department. 'We're as yet small but dynamic.' He looked forward to the 'eminent and essential.' speakers at the conference. Then a couple of awkward witticisms and he smirked like a snake as he received his applause. Not impressed, I took a glass of red from the table and scoured the crowd for Abebi. I hate events like this. I stand around not knowing who I'm supposed to be and hope someone will show up and tell me. Generally I end up going home none the wiser thinking maybe the next one and I'll find out. The attendees broke up into small groups chatting and laughing too much, or trying to appear 'eminent and essential' as they nervously introduced themselves - but no sign of the gorgeous professor.

I could see Miriam had made a bee line for Skinner on the other side of the room and was standing talking in all her Hellenic animation to a tall blond man in a leather jacket who looked like Max Von Sydow. As she was the only person there that I knew - I didn't count Skinner - I decided to join their group. Miriam, always good for the first thirty seconds, introduced me to Max, who turned out to be Lars Jensen from Goteborg.

'This is Francis Riley. He's an English teacher.'

She didn't actually say just but the implication was clear enough; he isn't a psycho scientist, wouldn't know cognition from ignition, he's not important, ignore him. Which after a brief nod, Lars did.

I was number seven in a circle of six. I was turning into Tony, counting everything. They were all reminiscing about other conferences and mutual acquaintances, none of which I'd ever met. Miriam was happily leading the conversation as ever, which was why Skinner wanted her by his side; never a dull pause when she was around. I noticed that the circle was slowly drifting away from me. I took a pace forward to keep up but the ring continued to travel slowly but inexorably away from me towards the centre of the room. I felt as if they were some kind of lifebuoy that I could hang on to if I didn't want to drown in my own nonentity. After three or four steps keeping up with them I decided to stand my ground and let them disappear into the pool of the bigger crowd. I reversed, took a pace behind, and then a few more, until I was standing with my back to the wall which was appropriate enough. I looked around and still couldn't see Abebi. I thought I'd have another drink and if she didn't show up I'd leave. As I turned towards the booze table I walked straight into her, spilling her glass down the front of her dress.

'Oh no, shit, oh no...' It was at times like these I wished I carried a handkerchief to rescue wet women like all the real men in the films. 'I'll get a cloth from the bar.'

'Don't worry about it,' she said. 'It's only water, lucky I got a black dress.'

'Not too much damage?' I said. 'I mean it won't show up, will it? I mean...'

'I'm soaked.'

'Oh Christ, that's terrible.'

'Aren't you the guy from the pub? Spurs?'

'Yes, yes that's me, Spurs, right. You too, right? Ah...?' She was looking around the room. I couldn't let this go. It could be the chance of a lifetime. 'What do you think of the new signings?'

'What new signings?' she turned back to me with no trace of a smile.

'Spurs.' It was hanging by a thread.

'How should I know?'

The thread snapped but I immediately forgave her. How could a woman from Baltimore know the latest? 'Ah well, doesn't matter. Let me get you another drink.'

'Abebi!' Skinner turned from the pack and called across the room. 'Come, come, let me introduce you.' The bastard, always there ruining everything with his tiny-toothed smirk. He stepped towards us, ignoring me, but with his arm out in welcome to Abebi. She gave him her most appealing smile and before I could get her a drink or our conversation back to something I knew about, she'd gone. If my glass hadn't been empty I'd have thrown its contents over the back of Skinner's head. Instead I watched as the light of my life was drawn into the jostling darkness of the Skinner inner circle. I wondered about following her, but the group had now expanded to more than a dozen happy, yappy, competing psychos who would all completely ignore me.

'Fuck it, damn, bollix and fuck!' I stomped angrily back to the drinks table. Another Francis fuck up and I'd played directly into the hands of that snide shit, Skinner. I picked up another glass of red wine, grabbed a few soggy crisps and looked over the crowd. At least from there I'd be able to gaze at her uninterruptedly through the nodding heads. The pack shifted and her image came and went. After a minute or two she disappeared from view behind Miriam and Skinner. I gave up and went out onto the balcony for a cigarette.

How could I have trounced myself so badly? How could I have been such a useless tool? In the history of our relationship I'd spoken about four sentences and three of them had been to apologise for soaking her. I was tempted to leave right there and then, relegate myself from the premiere league and give up the whole shebang. Why bother, Francis, why bother? Let's face it there's nothing here for you. You're out of your class. I took an angry drag on my cigarette. Got to give up smoking. I could hear Miriam. Then I remembered Alexander, 'Everything's an act.' What kind of act, Alexander? I didn't know. I was out of my depth. How many acts were there anyway? A million, anything, everything, the world was my ostrich and there I was with my head in the sand. What was I supposed to do? Walk back among the psychos, shove my way through the crowd, bedazzle her with a charming grin, crack a joke, shoot a deadly glance at Skinner, turn back to her with that old movie star deep look and crooked grin and leave with her hanging on my arm?

I stood leaning on the wall as far away from the door to the room as possible and looked out over the university lawn. I saw Tony's pink arse bobbing on a blue coverlet. There was Alexander himself strolling purposefully towards the rotunda considering a sonnet. I heard Miriam's laughter, lit another cigarette, heard Miriam stop laughing. I wondered what I'd do for a holiday, then I heard Abebi say, 'Ah, there you are, got a smoke?' I turned. She was standing by the door. 'A fag, don't you call it?' She laughed. 'Don't say that in Baltimore.'

I unsagged my jaw, scrambled for the packet, dropped it

and picked it up. 'Sure, here. Please.' My hand was shaking. She took the cigarette with slim, precise fingers, held it to her mouth and towards the flame of my lighter. She didn't smoke much I could see that, and took a clumsy drag and blew the smoke out through her nostrils. 'Sorry about the Spurs,' she said.

I thought she was referring to our end of the season plunge. 'Oh next year, don't you worry..'

'I was kidding you. San Antonio Spurs,' she said it with a grin. 'They're a basketball team. My old man played for them a hundred years ago. Couldn't resist it.'

'Well you had me there.' I tried a laugh but was confused. What was she? A joker? Didn't you only kid people who were on your wavelength or was that just the English? I remembered the Indian woman who'd received the honorary doctorate. She'd confused me too and wasn't English either.

Abebi stuck her cigarette in her mouth, raised a leg, straightened it, then put her foot up onto the balcony rail, stretching forward showing the bottom of her thigh as the skirt of her dress rose up. 'God, I'm stiff. Still haven't got over being cooped up on that flight.'

I wanted to run my hand along her calf, under her silky thigh and slowly up over her buttock. Was she showing me something? Don't be ridiculous. I tried to convince myself that it was perfectly normal to practice calisthenics on a university balcony at a psycho-conference. I wanted to sound matter-of-fact. 'Your old man still knocking them out of the park then?'

'That's baseball. He was was a basketball player.'

'Oh right, the hoops and all that. I know it. I was in new York once, saw the Giants.'

'They're baseball too.'

'Oh sure, they played the Boston Red Sox, baseball too, of course. Loved New York. How is your old man by the way?'

'He's dead.' Abebi shifted and put the other leg up. My

caress resumed but this time started higher at the back of her thigh. 'Sorry to hear that. So's mine. I mean my mother.' I tried to lean insouciantly against the wall. 'Of course New York's a great city. United States of America..'

'That's where it is.'

'Absolutely, we all know that, ha! Know Kilburn? It's in London. It's where I know. Used to know. I don't live there now. I read a lot as a child. I mean about...' I couldn't take my eyes off her legs and the various curves of her backside.

She gave me a strange look as she brought her leg back down and put her hands into the small of her back as she arched backwards 'What was your name? Francis? Was that your name?'

'Oh yes. Still is.'

'So what did you read?'

I had no idea why I'd told her that I read a lot. All I wanted to do was put my arms round her. I inched to one side on the wall somehow thinking that if I moved laterally it would bring me closer to her. 'Oh you know. About New York. I teach Jane Austen among other things. You know Roddy Doyle, he's an Irish writer?' Oh Jesus. What had Roddy Doyle got to do with anything? Where were all those great thoughts I'd told Miriam I had? All I knew was that I had to keep her out there, away from Skinner. 'Oh yes, wonderful Irish writers, not Jane Austen obviously.' What was all the fucking Irish? Maybe it was some kind of language of distress? '....she was great anyhow.'

'Who?'

'Er...Jane Austen.'

She gave me a bemused look. 'What's she got to do with New York?'

'Oh nothing, just chatting.'

'Thought you were a sports guy?'

'Sport, love it. My old man bought me a telescope once.' What? Why was I talking about telescopes? 'I mean, ah, so I could watch it from a distance.'

'You watched sport through a telescope?'

'No the stars, in the brief time I wasn't playing anything. Football mostly, you call it soccer, I say tomahto and you say...ha!'

'Sure, cultural dissonance.'

'Amazing, And we think we speak the same language! Ha! See the old man was, still is, an amateur astronomer, saw the future in the heavens.'

'Isn't that astrology?'

This was getting so bad I couldn't believe it. 'Oh sure, that's right, but you never know.'

'Know what?'

'What you see up there in the dark black skies. And we thought we knew everything. We used to watch the football together.'

'You and your father?'

'That's it, that's what I've been meaning to say.'

'The Spurs?'

'Exactly. It took a while, but we got there in the end!'

'Sure, Francis. I think I should go back in. Can you take this?' She gave me her cigarette butt.

'Thank you.' She was walking away. It was hopeless. I called after her. 'Ah, professor.'

She turned back, 'It's ok, you can call me Abebi.'

'Look I'm sorry. I'm really... I've been talking a load of rubbish. That's not me. I'm not like that.' I realised I was earnestly bending slightly forward to convince her. 'It's you. I don't mean it's your fault.' I looked at her like a helpless puppy. 'I'm quite sensible really. Sensible usually means boring doesn't it? I'm not. Well I am sometimes quite sensible. Sorry. Just I couldn't stand it in there. Anyway, sorry.'

She waved a playful, all knowing finger. 'I got it. Doctor Skinner?' she said it with a smirk. 'You don't like Doctor Skinner, do you?'

I was amazed. She understood. Somehow I'd broken

through. 'How'd you know that?'

'There are a million Doctor Skinners, Francis.'

I could have hugged her to my broken breast. 'You know him?'

'I met him a year ago at one of these conferences in New Orleans. They're all after the same thing.' She crossed her arms over her chest and stood with one hip thrust to the side.

What thing? What was she saying? That I was after the same thing too? Or was I in some other category that existed outside of the usual male obsessions? Did she mean that I was just a friendly face, non threatening, irrelevant - or was she saying I was pathetic?

'You get the airfares anyhow,' she said. 'Baltimore can get pretty samey.'

'Oh sure.'

'You've been there?'

'Ah? No.'

She hadn't left. She was still standing there.

'But you've got London. Where's good?'

My holiday plans instantly reverted to a staycation. 'Ah Buckingham Palace.'

'Come on Francis, you can do better than that.'

'I will, I can. I can show you. Look...I'm sorry. I've sounded like an idiot. I was nervous.'

'I know,' she said and smiled. 'I'll tell you something, you're the nicest guy I met since I been here.'

I was holding a cigarette butt in each hand not believing what I'd just heard.

'There's always the West End.'

She went to the door, then turned back, 'Why don't you come and hear my paper? It's on Saturday, four o'clock. Same place. It's called The Truth we Tell.' She laughed and disappeared into the room.

I breathed in deep. Was she joking again? The Truth we Tell. Was that a comment on me? Like somehow I'd shown her the truth about myself, I'd allowed the cover to slip and there I was in all my unadulterated idiotic but somehow decent and charming glory? And having seen the real me she'd thought I was the nicest guy there? I was nicer than Skinner, who let's face it she'd been very offhand about. 'They all want the same thing.' Well Skinner did, that was for sure. Who would trust a Skinner? And how could you not trust a Francis who'd just shown you the worst of himself and then said it was because he was nervous, and more than that implying nervous because of her? What an admission that was, what a truly, heroic piece of self-effacing honesty! How could she not think I was the nicest guy? I was beginning to think it about myself. This wasn't Francis the dumbest man in town, this was Francis the fucking saint! That's what Abebi thought. As Alexander had said, 'There's the world, use it.' Well I certainly would. There was nothing that could stop me using it. She'd invited me to hear her paper, hadn't she? There would be a drink after it and Miriam or Skinner couldn't object to me going, the Professor had asked me personally.

It was all too much, enough for one night anyway. I could only make it worse. I went back into the room and tapped Miriam's arm with my wrist as I was still holding the two cigarette butts. I was actually considering keeping Abebi's because it had a trace of her lipstick on it.

'Where've you been?' said Miriam

'Having a cigarette.'

With Professor Musa? She looked down at the butts in my hand. 'What are you doing with those?'

'Ah? Looking for an ashtray.'

'Well you won't find any in here. This is a no smoking building.'

'Ah sure, I'll take them outside.'

'You've just been outside.'

'I mean the real outside, not the balcony.'

'Did you have an interesting conversation with the professor?'

'Oh yeah, great.' I looked round and saw Abebi talking to Max Von Sydow and knew I had to get out of there before my exhilaration was destroyed by jealousy or eviscerated by Miriam's probes.

'Ah well, I was just on my way anyway. Talk later, Mitzy.'

I took a last look at Abebi and smiled at the back of her head, then swerved quickly round fifty psychologists slowly drinking themselves into a profound analysis of their careers and went out through the door.

As I walked past the rotunda, I threw my butt away and put hers' into my pocket. I'd make a decision on that later, probably throw it away let's face it. Then I strode slowly and purposefully across the lawn like Alexander Hudson might have done. A sonnet came to my mind. Shall I compare thee to a Summer's Day? I could probably have done better but it would do.

# 10

I woke up full of energy with Abebi on my mind. Our one-smoke tete-a-tete on the balcony had brought her into focus with her obvious attractions becoming more rounded as it were like the sweep of her thighs and how I could hold her from behind with her buttocks pushing back into my groin, and obviously she was bright, sharp and confident too. What else would she be, she was a professor. I had to remember not to be intimidated by that. Did I like her more or less as my infatuation grew - amongst other things? Like? Strange word in the circumstances. Yes I did like her, there was something nice about her. She was friendly. I liked that a lot. It made me feel better, not to say safer, although I had to admit to a disturbing, if not neurotic, crisis of confidence as I spoke to her. I hadn't been able to quite place myself, like who is this Francis Riley standing there on the balcony outside a conference I should never have been at? 'You'll need to find your character now! ' Annie's cackle again. What character? The lover? That's the character I wanted to be, but that was a category, some kind of stereotype, and anyway to be a lover you had to be a man first, and who was the man?

I was staring up at the crack in the ceiling above my bed which was beckoning me in. I'd been there before. It went nowhere. To hell with it. I refused to ruminate further. Abebi had invited me to her party even if it was a lecture I wouldn't understand. Sure I'd be there with fifty other people but I'd find a way to stand out, to stride forrard, to become the man I am! This was a moment to cast doubts aside. This was a time for action!

I leapt out of bed. I was going to put a few things right. What? How? I sat thinking about it. I wasn't entirely sure of the problem so the solutions were vague. I realised I was staring down at the jumble of my life yet again. My eye followed the trail of tech leads, socks and dirty glasses to the open door and beyond. I could imagine it going on forever, and realised that was the problem. My life was full of junk, all floors, all rooms, all surfaces, junk, junk and more junk. And how could that interest a professor of psychology? It was all distraction, evasion, the grand cover up of what I really was. Abebi would require a clean, analytic mind. I snapped to mental attention. I knew exactly what I was going to do. I was going to clean my flat. I wouldn't be seeing her again until the next day but I was going to begin now because if this was to be life changing, good habits took time to settle in. And I had twenty-four hours.

It needed to start with the personal and that meant body hygiene. I took a long shower and thought I'd get a haircut later. I put on clean underwear and a shirt promising myself that I'd change both again before I saw her. I gathered armfuls of clothes and hung them in the dark place they'd forgotten, my wardrobe. Another pile went into the washing machine, dishes that had lingered for days in grease and grime found their way into the sink, emerging ten soapy minutes later shined and stacked. I even mopped the kitchen floor and cleaned the windows. I couldn't remember the last time I'd done that.

In my bedroom I cleared out a couple of drawers and took down boxes that had stood dusty and undisturbed in the bottom of a cupboard for years. They were full of rubbish from my university days; nothing academic, I'd never felt the need to keep any of that. But there were other mementos; a photographic album showing a holiday I'd taken in Spain with Dolores. Oh Dolores. I took some moments staring into her Spanish eyes, remembering Granada days and Alhambra nights, red wine and tapas, fierce fights and sharp nails, spitting insults and wild sex. I'd been an erection on legs. Those were the days.

There was a box full of loose pictures; of me resplendent and proud in mortar and gown at my graduation with Ma, Pa and the sisters, a shower of snaps of old friends and gone friends; Larry, Petra, Ali, Steve; all faces I couldn't recall even as I looked at photos of them. Ha, here's one, a memory! His name was Richard Head and he called himself Dick. Dick Head! You can laugh once but that's it, he'd said. So we shut-up.

I found an old photograph of Giselle, a French girl with a big nose I went out with in... well, France. Where in France? I had no idea. What did we do all day, where did we stay? I didn't know. I remembered a cafe somewhere, Ricard clouding with ice, cognac biting; and back in the UK pint after pint in amorphous pubs up and down the country all merged into one long wet booze-soaked bar of noise and laughing my head off in recollected scraps like entrails trailing in the water of my mind.

If I forced myself I saw old faded love affairs. I was waiting for a romance I didn't believe in or more likely was waiting for it to end. I was in a relationship, I was out of a relationship and didn't really know the difference. I'd been hurt and hurtful but the details escaped me. This is my life. What's it doing in my wardrobe?

I wondered how many hours had gone uncounted and were now unknown? What had I done in the last twenty years? I could answer that only in places of work, or where I'd lived, or in the few intense feelings I still had involving deaths, births, the odd Christmas or vacation, or maybe a birthday. But the detail? Where had I been on the fifteenth of July nine years ago, or at Easter twelve years ago? What happened in 1995, 96, 97, 98? Or 2002, 03, 04? How had I felt living in Southampton? Or Coventry? The cities were a blur like cities everywhere. What clothes had I worn, where had they all gone? What happened to that orange shirt? I'd liked that orange shirt. What bin had I thrown it into? Where had all those millions of seconds gone? Where was I? What was I?

This was my life and I didn't have a fucking clue about any of it. It was all nothing more than the tiniest fragments of disconnect residing somewhere in the great fog of a past that had made me what I am. It was my great treasure chest of joy or despair and everything else; my box of self all lost and forgotten and I could never have it back, except it seems by accident in a roaring Irish accent I never knew I had.

I sat on the floor leaning against the wall by the bedroom door and picked up a few old exercise books from the time I'd fantasised about being a writer; a few starts and half starts, some bizarre ideas but nothing I could understand now. I glanced through them. They were all crap. At the end of one book was a poem. It was almost illegible. I must have been drunk and from the handwriting I guessed around nineteen years old. It was entitled, Me.

There's a lack of cohesion
That's causing a lesion
Between myself and me.

My brain keeps growing
With additional knowing
But has no identity.

Maybe it's the fashion
To keep your passion
Under lock and key.

If that's the case
I'll exist in space
And have no integrity.

But I don't like that much
Seems this mental crutch
Revolves round futility.

So I need a device
Something very concise
To set myself at liberty.

And that was it. TS Eliot it wasn't but amazing it was. Amazing that I should have written such a coherent description of what I was then and still was now. My lack of direction, no centre, life as a continuous search for something unknown. And not much had changed. I still needed this device whatever it was to set myself at liberty.

There was only one thing for it. The past was a blur, my mind incapable of organising it, let alone my present. All that was left was my body. I could at least recognise that. Why not get fit? Why not take a walk along the river? I remembered the teenage Angela in her essay on leaving home; You don't put a jacket on you take the old one off. So I went out in my T-shirt to begin my new day with the thought of Abebi somewhere at the end of it. Was it another romance that would fade? Probably. But there was always hope. I'm with her in Californian sunshine. I can feel the heat of the day, the glow of health, the white of her teeth, her hand in mine as she walked by my side, bright and joyous, on a perfumed path through an orange grove. The sun is high, the sky is blue... Did I mourn my lack of remembrance of things pissed? Not a bit of it. I was going to celebrate the remembrance of things future,

The day was damp and there was a warm drizzle on my face. I was soon soaked, maybe the T-shirt hadn't been a great idea. I obviously still need to think about the new jacket. My trainers squelched on the path, raindrops flicked up little spurts in the puddles and caused whorls in the grey river that was slowly passing me by. The water seemed to know where it was going anyway. The trees dripped on my head, the summer rain relaxed me like a warm bath. I walked for two miles getting fit, then returned to my flat and stretched a couple of times holding onto the top of the fridge. I stood tall, my feet planted square on my pristine kitchen floor and took a couple of deep breaths. I felt well, my horizons were broad, my future limitless. I had begun.

I cooked a meal on my sparkling stove, collapsed in front of the TV on my newly recognisable sofa and watched a rerun of an old Michael Caine film, Get Carter. Threatened by the Geordie mob Caine emerged from the terraced house of a woman he'd taken up with. He was stark naked with nothing but a shotgun in his hands, lethal in pink. What a man. What a winner. Who was this Michael Caine? Whatever role he played, whatever film, Michael Caine was always Michael Caine. Was that the real Michael Caine, or had he invented it? Had he created himself from his past and over the years constructed the look, the sound, the rhythm, the image, the Michael Caine brand? Impermeable, indestructible, nothing more, nothing less. What was his device that set him at liberty? How did he do it? Abebi wouldn't have stood a chance with Michael Caine that's for sure.

# 11

On the day of Abebi's paper I had a haircut which didn't seem to make much difference and not having too many options put on the same suit as I'd worn for the gala. I walked quickly and confidently out of my flat, had a couple of solitary pints in the Calf and considered my strategy. I quickly realised I didn't have one but that wasn't going to stop me. I walked on up to the university.

The reception room was filling up with earnest psychos. Abebi's fame had obviously spread through the conference. Or was it her looks? Or was it the title of her lecture; The Truth we Tell? It was catchy I had to admit and sounded a lot more interesting than The Primitive Consciousness, or The Dilemmas of Neuropsychiatry which constituted the opposition for the day. These psychos, would they ever learn? The point was to be clear and show the world - represented by me, who didn't know anything - what you were talking about. Wasn't it?

Abebi was to give her paper from a small raised platform that had been erected at the end of the room. I found a seat a few feet from the front to one side as people continued to arrive and the room filled up. It wasn't long before they were standing shoulder to shoulder along the walls.

On the button at four o'clock Skinner came up onto the stage dressed in a smart blue suit. I could see Abebi standing to one side with her hands clasped in front of her and her head down as if she was considering what she was going to say. Skinner introduced her with his usual obsequious charm. 'Professor Musa, graduate of UCLA, A PHD from Boston, associate professorship at the Mid Western University, and author of the best selling book, The Truth we Tell.

A book? I might have known she was selling something. Why might I have known? Why was I always so suspicious? Where was the font of generosity I sought within? The backslaps of approval, the hail-fellow-well-met, and smiles for all? I shook myself to release the angst and stretched my face in my broadest grin as Abebi came up on the little stage dressed in a straight grey skirt and white silk blouse. Her hair was pulled back behind her ears. She wore rimless glasses and looked terrifyingly and beautifully professorial. And sounded it too. She smiled and thanked everybody for coming. It was as if she was welcoming them to a conference they'd only attended in order to listen to her. She stood erect and easy in low tasteful black heels behind the tubular steel lectern and held up a copy of her book which she said was on sale at the information desk in the main foyer. I saw that quite a few members of the audience had already bought a copy and were sitting with it snugly in their laps. I wished I'd done the same, not just because I wanted to read it, but because I wanted to show support for what I now considered to be my professor, and I could have got her to sign it afterwards in what I imagined was going to be an evening of warm and intimate conversation when I would be strong, confident and not nervous.

Abebi pushed her hair gently back, smiled and began. The Truth we Tell didn't seem to be about truth at all. In fact the reverse. She began by describing every kind of lie; of error, of omission, exaggeration, circumlocution, equivocation, grand lies, weasel words, half-truths, false compliments, flattery... it was a long list. She gave examples of several of these lies in relation to how we behave. According to her there was nothing we did that wasn't some kind of cover-up. It was all lies, a great web of them disguising everything we do and hiding the real self. Add them all up and you have a human being - like myself, a man who probably dipped into his larder of lies every time he opened his mouth. I couldn't say I disagreed with any of this although there were moments, not too many admittedly, when I felt that I'd been honest in the daily slog. Others may have disagreed. Liar, truth-teller? Hmm? The jury was out. But the prosecutor hadn't finished. She went on to say that out of all this develops your personality, which is a weaving together of this basic fabric of falsehood. The more she spoke the more I decided to agree with her. I mentally added one little lie to the next as I calculated the extent of my entirely deceitful life. How had it come to this? How did I get to be such a liar? She had no answer to my question and avoided any theory about the origin of these falsehoods. Rather she talked about our acquired personality which apparently you acquire more of every second as the lies pile up. I wanted to know if this meant we could change it but she didn't mention that either. Instead, she said that every lie fills a truth shaped hole and in 'examining them in their particularity, and our need to tell them at any given moment, can give way to a precise analysis of the truth we're hiding.' Wow! She gave the example of a child saying I hate you when she means the reverse, the pretence of enjoyment, the adoption of despair when necessary, and so on. In other words the lies we use are an indication of the Truth we Tell.

I didn't know whether anything she said was new, or relevant, or finally even, to be honest about it, if it meant much to me. I could go along with it in my head, but beyond that was a different matter. Not that any of it distracted from my longing to hold her - although I was marginally aware that the three pints I'd sunk in the Calf and the swift scotch I'd tossed back before leaving home might have slightly blunted the sharp knife of an intellect already distracted by the almost painful bulge in my trousers. But, what the hell, she'd stated it all with such confidence that I couldn't see that anyone would have any doubts that she'd just told the absolute truth about lying, or the absolute lies about the truth. Confusing she may have been, but fuck me she looked great.

I was tempted to ask a question at the end but didn't have the nerve. She left the stage to loud applause and was soon surrounded by a small crowd of admirers including Miriam and Skinner. Someone produced a bottle of champagne and half a dozen glasses which were clearly not enough to include me. But, undeterred I slid my way into the pack around her.

'That was great,' I said, 'I'm hoping to get the book.'

'Hoping?'

'I will get it.'

'The Truth we Tell.' She laughed. I didn't know if there was an edge to that. Skinner obviously did. 'Will he, won't he?' A couple of others sniggered although I was pleased to see that Miriam didn't.

'I meant it,' I said.

'I know you did,' Abebi said, and she touched the outside of my left arm which could have meant anything but I decided it showed a familiarity at least which would shut Skinner up. 'I'm pleased you came, Francis,' she added. The smirks turned into a kind of frozen condescension.

'Why don't we get something to eat?' This was Skinner again. He didn't seem able to let me complete a conversation with Abebi.

'How about a pizza?' I spoke up, buoyed by Abebi's support.

Miriam gave me a worried look. How could I think I was in any position to set the agenda for the psychos?

'I think we can do better than that,' said Skinner.

There was general agreement around the circle which I'd seen now included Max Von Sydow.

'Oh but I love pizza,' said Abebi.

She'd ridden to my rescue again! Suddenly everybody loved pizza and I imagined she loved me too.

We all went to Guiseppe's just down the road. Skinner monopolised Abebi every step of the way with Miriam keeping up gamely. Once in the restaurant she sat to one side of the American with Skinner on the other and I could see her slowly drawing Abebi into her confidence at the same time as keeping Skinner happy with flattery. I watched with a kind of awe as Miriam practised her art. I'd noticed before how she latched onto women I was attracted to and turned them into her best friend. I sighed. Not only would I have to keep Skinner at bay but Miriam too.

The restaurant was dimly lit, packed and noisy as Italian restaurants should be. I was relegated to a far corner of the large square table in the middle between a German woman I think was called Jericho, and a Japanese who didn't speak English. Jericho was soon engaged in an intense conversation with a man to her right; the Japanese smiled, nodded and said nothing. I kept my mouth shut as the usual psychobabble ricocheted round the table, devoted myself to the red wine and disappeared into my head. We'd been in California for a number of years and had two children and a large hairy dog called Django who accompanied me every morning as I jogged along the cliffs before my daily routine with a fitness trainer. By this time I'd published several books and was often asked to sign them in expensive restaurants, not pizza houses. There was a big Californian actor called Brett Redford with cowboy boots, a silver buckle on his belt and a stetson, so maybe he was Texan. He wouldn't leave Abebi alone. I told him politely to take a walk, buddy, but he wouldn't so I had to decide whether to slap him in the mush or win a Pulitzer prize. I decided on the Pulitzer and walked into a famous LA brasserie with Abebi while the Californian/Texan skulked in the corner and the rest of the diners stood and applauded. The rest of the table in Guiseppe's were ignoring me so I tipped back the last of my glass and went to refill it. I saw that I'd finished the bottle in front of me as neither Jericho or the Japanese drank. Things were getting a little unfocussed.

The plates were cleared and Abebi got up heading for the bathroom. I watched her go as she went round the other side of the table and didn't glance at me, but on her way back she took a different route and I felt her hand touch my shoulder. She leant down and whispered in my ear, 'I could really do with a cigarette.' I thanked God I was smoker. See Miriam you don't know everything. She went back to her seat and picked up her jacket which was hanging over the back of her chair.

'Thank you, you guys, it's been great. Sorry, I've got to get back to my room and start thinking about Baltimore.'

'Oh no, have another drink.' Skinner looked stunned. All his best laid plans were coming to nothing.

'Sorry, Theo, need to go.' She smiled and pulled on her jacket, then reached for her purse. 'Oh, should I leave something?'

'Absolutely not,' said Skinner recovering well. 'It's on us.' And as if his disappointment was too heavy to let pass, he turned on the sucker across the table. 'Francis you can pay, can't you? It was your idea!'

There was big laugh. I could see that I could easily become the butt of the evening. Added to that Abebi was leaving and she'd told me what she wanted. The alcoholic fuse that was fizzing through my veins flared. I stood up. 'Nope, 'fraid I have to go meself. Stack of marking to do.' If they were going to throw my occupation into my face they could have it right back. 'I'll walk you to the university,' I said to Abebi, 'it's on my way.'

I couldn't believe I'd done it. It was as if I'd just signed their star player. There were a few looks around the table. Miriam went from hostile, to wryly amused and back again.

'My contribution.' I threw a twenty onto the table. Then another. 'For the professor's dinner and as a mark of my admiration for her book which I haven't read but will do so as soon as possible. Goodnight.'

'It's been a privilege,' said Abebi. 'And so great to meet you all. I mean it, truly wonderful.' She gave the table a small wave and a big smile, then turned and went to the door followed by me, feeling the prickle of silence behind and imagining Skinner's face and Miriam's gulp.

'Wow,' she said as we got outside. She stretched her arms wide threw her head back and looked up at the sky, the size of her freedom. 'Done it, earned my ticket''.

'Your ticket?' I gave her a cigarette.

'Plane fare,' she said. 'That damn book gets me round the world.'

'Ah, would you care for a celebratory drink?' I said, delighted at my triumph in getting her out of the restaurant. Before she could answer I said, 'I know a nice little place.'

'The same pub as last time?'

'Oh no, they'll all be going over there. I mean, if you prefer to be with them, I don't mind.'

'No let's go somewhere else.'

She didn't want to be with them. She wanted to be with me! 'This way,' We walked quickly away from the restaurant and down the lamplit High Street. It was almost as if she was happy to be with me.

## 12

She tossed her cigarette end into the gutter as we came to the end of the alley which led to Alexander's club. I could hear her feet tripping down the narrow stairs behind me as we descended into the darkness below. I was playing it by ear with no idea what would happen next. What I hadn't predicted was that as we came to the door at the bottom an old man in a suit who looked like he'd been there forever seemed to appear from inside the wall preventing us from going any further. He said, 'Members only, sir.'

I had to think quickly. Abebi was behind me and I wasn't going to fail now. 'I'm a friend of Sir Alexander Hudson. I was here with him the other night, you may remember?'

The old man whose sallow face seemed from beyond the grave weighed me up. 'Ah yes sir, of course.' He stood back holding the door open for us and we went through into the club. It was as dark as it had been before, but with fewer drinkers. I noticed some of the same shadowy figures sat beneath the velvety walls or stood at the small bar. There was someone playing the piano in a far corner. I saw for the first time faded pictures of actors dim on the walls and that the carpet was black with grime and melting into the floor. It was like something out of the old times when men came together on the quiet.

'God,' said Abebi. 'Did you say, Alexander Hudson? You mean...?'

'That's the one,' I was gaining confidence again now we'd been admitted. 'It's not much of a place as you can see. But it's private anyhow, and no-one else knows about it.' I nodded back to the entrance as if to say there won't be a hoard of psychologists joining us. I wanted to add, stick with me, if you want to see the real London, but felt that was maybe going a bit far.

'But you know him, Hudson?

'We were here just a few nights ago. Over there.' I indicated the table I'd sat at with Alexander, which was now conveniently free. I staggered slightly as we sat down but so much that she'd notice. 'He sat right there and told me his life story. It was pretty interesting.'

'Alexander Hudson, wow.'

The girl with the longest legs in London came over and said, 'Hullo, sir,' which made me sit up straight like the known figure I obviously was. 'What would you like, Abebi?'

'Can I get a daiquiri?'

'Anything you like, I'll have a large scotch.' I was forgetting the beer in the Calf and the wine in Guiseppe's; tonight I'd have anything I wanted. The girl walked on her legs to the bar.

'And thank you for getting my dinner,' said Abebi. 'Really appreciate it.'

'My greatest pleasure.' I felt I was running up the mountain, my knees brushing the heather, my lungs bursting, heading for the summit - but not there yet. I wondered what Tony would do next.

'You're going tomorrow?' I was trying to sound as if it was just a casual enquiry.

'Only into London,' she said. 'My boyfriend is there for a few days and I want to spend some time with him before I go.'

The summit suddenly seemed a long way off, the mountain was crumbling and within seconds I was contemplating a torrid summer with a sad pint or two in the Calf, maybe a weekend with Miriam in the Dordogne, or see the old man in Cork? Oh no. The girl brought the drinks. I tossed down the whisky in one and asked for another as Abebi sipped the daiquiri. The hot rasp of the scotch burned the back of my throat.

'Oh I'm sorry.'

'That I'm leaving or I've got a boyfriend?' she said it with a grin.

'Ah well, being as you're asking. Both. Is he another psychologist by the way? Just wondered.'

'Nope. He's a chemical engineer. He's from Amman. That's Jordan.' She took another sip of her drink.

'Then you're immediately back to the States, are you?' I could feel myself sitting further back into his seat, the velvet scraping the back of my thighs and making my arse itch.

'Maybe I'll stay on a while.' She smiled at me over the rim of her glass. 'And maybe I'd like to see Buckingham Palace.' She laughed.

'Or there's a good pub in Kilburn!' The summit was becoming visible again.

'Or maybe I'll just go home,' she replied.

I took the plunge. 'Can I have your number? I mean, in

case you decide to stay?'

'Sure,' She pulled out her phone and my buttocks ceased to bother me. I'd have something at least in concrete, or digital, and supposing she did stay on? Obviously she was bound to have her own world including a boyfriend. I couldn't exactly expect a woman as beautiful as this to arrive on my doorstep unencumbered. I began to feel another surge of optimism. I knew the truth now and like a man I would deal with it. I ordered a third scotch and felt good as it went down and asked her about her father. She told me about the shelf full of medals and trophies he'd bequeathed to her when he died.

'Shortest guy on the court,' she said. 'He used to go through their legs, never dropped the ball.'

Something about not dropping the ball triggered thoughts of good old Tony again. 'Just put it on the table, go on you can do it.' I lowered my head down to one side and assembled my face into what I hoped was a sophisticated mischievous grin. 'You've got great tits.'

I'd followed instructions, done what was necessary, my mind was blank and I had no idea what would happen next. I vaguely remembered what Tony had told me. I said, 'If you want to move away, we can talk later.'

'Move away?' She looked puzzled. 'Where do you want me to go? Stand by the bar?'

I didn't know the answer to that. Tony's theory seemed to have collapsed hardly before I'd put it into practice. And my own brain wasn't helping. 'Ah, I mean.'

She looked at me with an amused glint in her eye, waiting for an answer. 'You tell me I've got great tits and you want me to go? Where? Back to the university? Baltimore?'

'No, I don't want you to go anywhere. See there's this friend of mine who had this idea. I mean he's not such a close friend...'

'What about him?'

'He had his heart broken and wrote a book on arithmetic

for ten year olds and he said you should always put it out there.' I waved to the girl for another drink.

'Maybe you've had enough.'

'Sure.' I held up my palm flat cancelling the order.

'So what are you putting out there, Francis?'

The girl came over anyway.

'Can I have another?' I wasn't sure if I was asking permission of the girl or Abebi.

'Ok I'll have another one too,' she said. The girl returned to the bar.

'You want another one?' I said, trying to work out whether that was a good sign or not.

'Yeah I think I will. I'd like to know what you're talking about.'

'I'm sorry, Abebi, I'm really sorry.'

'Are you asking me if I'm interested in sex? Now? Tonight? The answer's no.'

'I'm really sorry.'

'And what's all this about arithmetic?'

'It doesn't matter.'

'Tell me Francis, as you're being so honest.' She suddenly laughed. 'As you're being so fucking stupid.'

'I am, I am, I'm sorry for being so fucking stupid.' I could feel my head was beginning to loll. 'How'd you get to so interested in the truth anyway?'

'What?'

'Like your book.'

'You talking about books now?'

'I think it could be safer, you know? I mean, you got a boyfriend. Sorry about that. I don't mean sorry you got a boyfriend. Well maybe...' The girl brought the drinks. 'Last one.' I took a sip. 'Look I know you won't never want to see me again ever, I understand that. I get it, but I just wanted to say..'

'I got good breasts?'

'No, it's more than that. I didn't mean...'

'Maybe it was just a compliment?'

'Oh sure. It was that alright.'

'Thank you.'

'What for?' I looked up at her with sad eyes like a beaten dog.

'Thank you for the compliment, Frankie. Frankie? Isn't that what that woman calls you?'

'Miriam?'

'Sure, the one who's always hanging around Doctor Skinner.'

'She doesn't always hang around him.'

'She calls you Frankie. So can I call you Frankie?'

My head was spinning. 'You can call me anything you like. And frankly I wouldn't blame you.' I tried a laugh, it was more a squeak.

'Frankly! Maybe I should call you Frankly! My friend, Frankly.'

'Your friend,' I said. 'Your very good friend. Even if you have got this fellah from Jordan. I mean Frankly is the name and Frankly is what I am.' I tried to laugh again.

'Listen I think it's time we went home, don't you?' she said.

She took my arm and helped me up the stairs. She stopped me swaying too much as we walked to the university hall of residence.

'Can you get back home ok, from here?' I asked.

'It's just there,' she said, pointing at the door three yards away.

'Absolutely.'

'How about you?'

'Oh sure. Always know the way home.'

I was vaguely aware of people passing us and going quickly up and then disappearing into the darkness of the building. She kissed me on the cheek. I wanted to hug her. I wanted to pass my hands over her body which was standing so close to me.

She said, 'you've got my number?'

'Oh yes.' I patted the phone in my pocket.

'Good night, Frankly.'

'Night.'

She walked towards the door and turned back with a smile as she went in. I waved and was suddenly aware it was very quiet although the night seemed to be singing. I looked up at a starlit sky and wondered about going down to the Calf where I knew Miriam and the others would still be after their pizza, then shook my head in wonderment as to how stupid the idea was. They'd all look and ask questions and take the piss out of me. And I wanted to celebrate. I remembered she called me Frankly and called me fucking stupid and you couldn't get much better than that from a professor of psychology.

I wandered away into the night, walking with her down Park Lane through the big swish of London cars and money. We went into the Hilton Hotel and I was dazzled by how bright it all was. We were going up in the lift. She came into my arms and we kissed, a long, loving, warm kiss. I could feel her sucking on my tongue and I slid my hand over the firm curve of her backside and pushed against her. She could feel my erection and said, 'Oh is that for me?' 'Who else, baby?' I said. The lift doors opened and I was back in my flat, on my bed, looking up at the crack in the ceiling which kept curving from one side to the other as I stared at it.

## 13

There was only one thing for it, a bite of the dog and a talk with Tony in the Calf. It was around two o'clock and the place was half empty and hazy in the low light coming through the bottled glass of the front windows. The sounds were muted, a scuff of the foot, whispered conversations, the occasional chink of a glass, an English pub in the afternoon. The quiet of it suited my mood. I sat with Tony in our usual corner. We were on our second pint and I'd told Tony what I remembered of my conversation with Abebi. I could hear that my voice was low and dull. I felt disorientated; the hangovers were stacking up the one above the other like doom-laden clouds and they were sinking slowly over my aching head and leaving my heart in limbo. I had no real idea of what I'd done and what would come out of it. All I knew was that there was still, somewhere deep, a terrible desire for this woman I knew I was in love with.

'Have I destroyed it?'

'You actually said, "You've got great tits?"'

'In so many words.'

'What words?'

'Those words.' What was the point of denying it? The past was written in stone. All that mattered was now and what she would think of me in the cold light of day. I took a long slug of beer in a valiant attempt to drown the memory. 'And it was all going so well. I'd got her out of the restaurant and down to the club like I was some kind of hero, then I thought of you and what you told me and it seemed like a good idea at the time.'

'There's a time and a place, son. It was important that you gave her the space to make up her own mind. How could she do that when she's rammed up the corner with your hot breath all over her?'

'Don't! I know it.' Maybe talking to Tony was a bad idea. I could have just as easily flagellated myself in front to my bathroom mirror. 'You're supposed to be my advisor, Tone. My very own Cyrano.'

'Who?'

'Except your nose is shorter. Would you stop looking at me like I just shat in your pocket? I need a smoke. That's where it all started, giving her cigarettes. Miriam's right, I should give it up. Look where it gets you.' I took another swig of bitter as a temporary substitute for the craving. 'She handled it though, didn't she? Abebi, I mean. Matter of fact I think she was laughing at me. Is that a good sign?'

Tony looked worried. I don't think he thought being laughed at was a good sign at all.

'Well, she didn't punch me in the face.'

'I give it to her, she sounds like some woman. Maybe just the woman you need, Frankie. What was the last thing she said?'

'You've got my number?'

'Like she wanted you to have it?'

'Or wished she hadn't given it to me.'

'Wait a minute.' Tony placed his palms on the table either side of the table. The only way to solve any problem as far as he was concerned was to face it square on, the Northern way. 'Let's look at the facts, Frankie. Go back to the beginning. This club?'

'Called Jonny's. There's a sign by the door about the size of a postage stamp.

The door?

The sign. Now is not the time for levity.

'Right,' Tony said, 'you're in Jonny's. She tells you she has this boyfriend, a chemical engineer, so he's a scientist.' This seemed to interest him. His brow furrowed behind the rim of his glasses. 'He's a logical man. So she's attracted to logical men.'

'Which rules me out.'

'Did you say Jordanian? Maybe he's rich?'

'So does that.'

'When you said "great tits", which by the way is better than big tits which isn't very flattering, anybody can have big ones, and at least you didn't say bazookas.'

'Oh fuck off, Tone.'

'And she laughed?'

'Not right away.'

'Were it a fond laugh?'

'Could have been. Look I was off my head.'

'And she called you "Frankly." And says she likes you.'

'And I was fucking stupid.'

'She's obviously intelligent.'

I felt like smacking him - I wondered why I was always wondering about smacking people. I never had and never would. Anyway if I was going to get anywhere Tony was my only chance, other than time, and I didn't have any of that. Abebi was leaving for London that day and I had no idea how long she'd be there.

'Listen, I know I fucked it all up but the truth is she did have beautiful breasts like she had beautiful eyes and hair and I really thought she was something else and I wanted to tell her. She really got to me, you know? I just wanted to tell her that, Tony.'

'Well you did.'

'Yeah, but I didn't get round to the eyes or hair and I didn't want to tell her like some bullshit merchant.'

'Are you talking about me?'

'Your advice was bullshit.'

'Only because you took it the wrong way.'

'Anyway I wanted to tell her what I felt about her, what I really felt. Like when I told you about my acting, when I was roaring in Lewisham. I was mad and I admit it, but I spoke, didn't I? I actually spoke what I was feeling, even if it was just some fucking rage.'

'From the heart, you saying?'

'I don't know where it came from. Anyway I spoke. And then I met Abebi and under the rules of normal life I'd have just clammed up but because of your advice which I admit I got all wrong and because I was half paralytic, I wanted to speak again. There was some power in me. I wanted to tell her how I was feeling.'

'You alright, Frankie?'

No.' I rubbed my eyes. 'I'm feeling a bit upset to tell you

the truth. Actually, Tone, to tell you the real truth I'm feeling actually terrified for some reason. My gut's shaking away down there, my legs feel funny.'

'Just the booze from last night.'

'Maybe. I think it's something else.'

'You're going a bit deep here, son. I've noticed you've been doing it a bit too much lately'

I couldn't speak. Tony squeezed my arm. 'I'll get another one.' He went to the bar. I felt like I was floating and everything around me was floating too and it all floated around as I tried to touch it and it floated away, and even if I got a half grip on it and brought it to my face I still didn't know what it was. I looked down at the table. There were six beer mats. I counted them and ran my finger into a couple of tiny puddles spreading the spilt beer and wondered what shapes I was making.

I remembered reading a book by Erica Jong called Fear of Flying about a woman who attended conferences and occasionally picked up men, or men picked her up, and they had sex. This woman fantasised that she and the man would be wordlessly transported to a bed and have what she called the zipless fuck, where you just slid into someone, went straight through them and out the other side again with nothing spoken. Just the joy of sex without anything else. I wondered if it was possible that this could have happened with Abebi but then decided I didn't want it anyway. What would have been the point? I slid the beermats around the table. For years I've existed more or less in a kind of purgatory spending pointless months and years searching for her, the one who would release the love, the life, and undeniable possibilities within myself. Who didn't have hopes like that? It wasn't sex, or it was, but that was just the beginning. There was something bigger, a desire for the ultimate; a thing so powerful I could only touch it in my dreams. Either she existed and you couldn't touch, or you could touch and she didn't exist. Schrodinger's cat-woman, except her mystery wasn't boxed; she came and went according to whim and I was left on a cold morning with a huge erection in an empty room. I stared at the wet pub table. I'd behaved like the worst kind of antediluvian prick. Tony's an ape. A pint appeared in front of me. Tony was looking concerned.

'Did you actually ever say to any woman that I think you've got great breasts?' I asked him.

Tony sat down, 'A couple of times, mebbe.'

'Did it work?'

'Mebbe'

'What do you mean, maybe? Did it work with Miranda Vee?'

'Didn't need it. Couldn't get a word in edgeways. She wanted it more than I did. See, we both got what what we wanted, Frankie.'

It wasn't quite zipless but near enough and it was all too much for me. It was all bullshit and nothing to do with with what I was talking about. I took a sip of the new pint and stared at Tony who was looking out of the window with the sun gleaming yellow on his forehead making him look like something out of an old master with the dark wooden wall behind him.

'You may think you're a genius, Tone, and I'm an eejit but I'm not. Matter of fact I'm no eejit. I've read hundreds of books. I've read thousands of books, How many have you read? Five? So you can fuck off, you don't know anything.'

'Called the university of life, pal.'

'What's it about your life that's so clever? Getting mud up your arse on a rugby pitch, teaching numbers to numbskulls? Fucking loads of women?'

'Well I've got you there, son.'

'Doesn't mean anything. It's just another numbers game, Tony.' I could feel tears coming to my eyes. Finally something of what I meant to say was coming through.

'Sorry, son, didn't mean to upset you.' I could see that he

sensed he was in dangerous territory. 'And I don't think you're an eejit. What's an eejit anyway?'

'It's Irish for wanker.'

'Well you're not one. Sorry I've been a bit big-headed. I admit that. Just you know, showing off and all that. It's what we do, don't we? Anyhow, sorry.'

'You've got to feel something, Tony.'

'Course I do.'

'What?'

'I don't know.' Tony took a long draw from his pint. 'Don't want to talk about it.'

'What? Come on, tell me something that's fucking useful.'

'What's useful?'

'How you fucking feel!'

'About women?'

'About anything!'

'Alright, Francis, if you want to know, I feel a bit lonely sometimes. Alright?'

'This is like getting blood out of a stone.'

'I deal with it.'

'How?'

'I meet up with you, don't I? Watch a game on TV. And you know... women.'

'And that makes you feel better?'

Tony shrugged his big shoulders, 'Mebbe.'

I could see we were on the brink but didn't have the words to jump. We never had the words. How could you have the words for something that you weren't even sure was there, like some mysterious sickness that melted away as soon as you looked at it and then reappeared the moment you thought it was gone, just leaving you anxious and not knowing what to do. We were paused, looking down at our nearly empty pint glasses as the froth slowly slid down the sides and evaporated in what was left of the beer. What else was there to say? After a while Tony looked up, 'Spurs doing well.'

'Better than Wednesday.'

'Everybody does better than Wednesday.'

So that was that. But whatever we talked about didn't matter. Abebi was gone with her cases onto a train and then she'd disappear into the underground and come up and out and straight into the arms of the Jordanian. I realised I didn't know what his name was, and imagined him as some kind of Omar Sharif with a sad smile and a head-dress shimmering wealth in desert sands. I thought of Michael Caine. What would he have done in Jonny's? He wouldn't have said what I'd said that's for sure. I wondered what mature men said in mature conversations? Talk about property prices in Geneva? And what had I done? I'd sat there on the velveteen banquette with an itchy arse and imagined I was running up the mountain through the heather. Where'd the heather come from? As usual, no answer. All I could think of was to call Abebi and make a proper sober apology. At least I could do that. Ideally I wanted to catch her just after the Jordanian had left London, but before she returned to the States. The problem was she hadn't said how long her boyfriend would be with her. I thought about it and decided on three days. I'd call her then. I felt better with the decision made. We talked about the Spurs again and Sheffield Wednesday.

## 14

Annie only ever invited me to dinner as some kind of makeweight when someone had pulled out, but after my triumph in Arnold's film I'd gone up in her estimation. And she'd invited Miriam too which just showed me how much I'd risen. Mostly Annie and Miriam fought over me.

Although I knew that my sister took Miriam's point that I was a not bad-looking, reasonably-bright nonentity, she didn't like what she considered to be Miriam's condescension to a member of her family. And Miriam objected to anyone defending me that wasn't her. I was the bone of their contention. If nothing else it indicated a degree of jealousy over me which maybe I should have been flattered by.

I'd waited thirty six hours now of my three day deadline to call Abebi and was beginning to feel alright about it although I felt guilty about my outburst to Tony. I knew that the Sheffield man of steel had a soft heart and couldn't help what he was. Maybe that disappointment with the girl Debbie from up there in his Yorkshire past meant more than he'd said. Who knew what went on in the deep recesses of the human heart? Why was I all of a sudden getting so philosophical about everything? Maybe it was because the skies were clearing too about my own feelings for Abebi. At least I was beginning to see the funny side. It could have been out of a bad film; the drunken, besotted, bonehead lover following rules he didn't understand, committing lover's suicide. I'd been a prat sure, but that was yesterday and as they said in another film, tomorrow is another day.

Miriam was already at Annie's when I arrived. She was wearing a bright printed summer shift although it was still mainly her habitual black. She was leaning against a counter in the kitchen with a glass in her hand talking animatedly to none other than Miranda Vee. I wondered if she recognised me as the witty intruder by the bedroom door wanting a mathematical analysis of her intercourse with Tony. Whether she did or not she gave me a bright smile and a lip-sticky kiss on the cheek. I grinned in recognition but she didn't respond. I handed over my bottle in its Sainsbury's bag to Annie.

'Oh no, I hope it's not Retsina,' she said.

'He likes it,' said Miriam in the same way as she might have remarked on a baby clutching tearfully at his battered teddy. 'It's because it's Greek.'

'It's usually Chardonnay,' said Annie.

'Oh no, he hates Chardonnay.'

It amazes me how my smallest traits seemed to stick in people's minds for forever and became the sum total of who I am. He's a Chardonnay drinker, he hates cabbage, he always wears blue, he prefers to sit not stand, he doesn't like Camden, none of which I give a toss about. But there you have it, five facts, that's me, beginning and end. I let them get on with it.

A tall and serious looking man with a dark fringe and wearing an immaculately pressed pale blue silk shirt came in to the kitchen. Miranda told us that he was her boyfriend, Harry.

'Nice to meet you,' I said. 'Been together long, have you?' It was a mischievous question but what the hell.

'Three years,' said Harry.

Miranda gave me a quick and wryly plaintive glance. She'd recognised me as the Peeping Tom alright. I thought of her painted fingernails scraping Tony's pink arse and was on the point of a grin and a raised eyebrow when I noticed the look of brave resignation on her face and adopted a serious look on my own. I turned to Harry, 'You an actor?'

'Do I look like an actor?' Harry was obviously happy at the insight. What else could he have been, with his face tilted to the light, his right arm carelessly draped over Miranda's shoulder and with his left hand insouciantly fingering a fridge magnet. He gave me a brief resume of his latest job and the one he was about to go up for. Miranda now confident that I was somehow her accomplice, enthusiastically elaborated on Harry's role before the last one and his bright prospects after the next. The whole thing took about ten minutes and I reminded myself not to ask stupid questions.

'He's such a wonderful actor,' said Miranda, bringing it to a conclusion. 'I couldn't be with him if he wasn't. I mean, how could you go out with a bad actor? That would be absolutely impossible!' She put her arm round Harry as if to protect the fragile vulnerability of his awesome talent. He looked to me like an arsehole. But I quite liked him too. The trouble with actors was that you never knew who they were. Sometimes you liked them, sometimes you didn't.

Paul came in from the patio. 'We're eating outside,' he said. 'It's still summer, just about.'

He led us out to a beautifully laid table strung above with strings of tiny yellow lights. There were two men already seated. I recognised one of them from some other event at Annie's, as Louis Foster, Paul's agent, a small man who exuded a careful, dapper energy. He had tight, thick, black hair that was probably dyed; was sharp in his face and moves, and wore an expensive well cut suit with a pink shirt. The man next to him was his husband, Jayesh, a middle-aged Indian in a lurid orange kaftan with a puffy face and bright smile who I liked on sight. I sat opposite them with Miriam on my left and Miranda to my right, facing Harry. Paul placed a huge platter of Italian cold meats in the centre of the table with a couple of salads.

Hardly had we begun eating when Annie piped up. 'I have to tell you Louie... ' She grinned at the agent and pointed her knife dramatically at me. '...about my little brother!' She launched into a long and extravagant description of my acting debut. 'I've seen the rough cut,' she said, 'there was fire in his eyes, absolutely terrifying, I didn't recognise him!'

Even Miriam was impressed. 'He's not that violent.' Her eyes widened. 'Are you?'

'Ah well,' I said, not sure whether I was or wasn't.

'You should take him on.' Annie laughed to Louis. It was half a joke. and he knew it. Why would an established agent like him want anything to do with an inexperienced unknown like me? But amusing hints were Annie's way of getting things done. Louis nodded and smiled. He'd obviously heard all this before.

'I'm no actor, sure,' I said, stuffing my mouth with

prosciutto.

'Oh, it's raw, I'll say that, but it's real,' Annie said. I didn't know whether she was talking about the ham or my acting. It could have been both.

'It wasn't bad actually' said Paul tentatively throwing his weight behind his wife's view. 'You should get some training,' he added, giving a professional gloss to his opinion. 'Learn how to control that energy.'

'I'm a bit old for getting up in tights in some drama school production of As You Like It,' I said.

'Never too old, darling,' said Miranda. 'I should know!' She roared with laughter.

'Oh come on,' said Harry blowing her a kiss across the table.

'Oh thank you, darling, it's so wonderful to be believed in!' Miranda blew the kiss back.

'Absolutely!' said Annie. 'What are we, if not friends?' A momentary tear formed in her eye.

Miranda gave me a conspiratorial smirk. For a second I thought she was flirting with me. Then I felt her knee against mine under the table and knew she was. Must be terrible to still be a teenager aged forty-eight. I moved my leg away.

Annie cleared the table and Paul brought out more dishes and wine was poured including my Retsina which everybody seemed to like except Annie. 'Tastes like petrol, darling, but who cares? Can someone pass the Barolo?'

Louis gave a funny report about a fringe show he'd seen recently and Paul with a rather dubious link related his own tale about a fringe actor who he'd worked with on The Lord of the Rings, which magically segued into the hilarious story of him being made up as the wrong Hobbit. Miranda followed with another fringe anecdote, then Annie, and finally Harry, whose small stage story mysteriously ended up with him appearing as a second lead at the National Theatre. I noticed that Jayesh, Louis's husband, was smiling at me. The Indian leant forward over the table and said, 'Perhaps you have a hidden talent, Francis?' Louis glanced round at his husband who looked at me with raised eyebrows. 'Annie's no fool,' he said.

'Oh I'm no actor.'

'But you have something, I can see it in you,' said Jayesh. His look was so penetrating and bright, his smile so warm and welcoming, that I wondered if I hadn't just been pierced by some mystical insight. Whatever it was the whole table went quiet and looked at me, even Harry, who was about to relate his second entrance onto the Olivier Stage.

'But it's nice of you to say, Mr Jayesh,' I said.

'Oh just Jayesh,' he said with a smile.

'But you know, I sometimes wonder.' I said. 'I mean I hear all these stories and they seem very funny and attractive to me. And glamorous, you know, like Paul shooting a film in New Zealand, sounds pretty good. And Annie's always going on about it. I sometimes wonder...' I sometimes wondered what? I didn't know how to finish the sentence. 'Maybe I'd love it.'

'We are all many things,' said Jayesh, 'and all of them are in ourselves. Not out there.' He gestured to the garden and beyond. "See within, my friend, that's my advice to you and maybe you will find everything you are looking for.'

'Thank you, Mr... er Jayesh.'

There was something about the simple way he'd said it that made me feel humble. I didn't know much about the Orient and Eastern ways, other than a few creaky months practising Yoga with Dolores in Granada, and I wondered about asking Jayesh for some sage advice about Abebi but for once kept my mouth shut. Harry resumed his story and was about to go up for the lead in a major production at the National which he missed by a whisker, when Paul butted in with another anecdote about himself because after all it was his party and he could boast if he wanted to. The rest of the dinner passed in good spirits.

Miriam was more than usually supportive of me, 'See,

perhaps everything isn't so miserable,' she said. Miranda stopped rubbing her knee against mine and directed her attention to her boyfriend. I felt good, better anyway than the idiot I thought I'd been, and decided to cut things short and call Abebi the next day. May as well get it over with.

As Louis was leaving with Jayesh he handed me his card and said, 'Give my assistant Annabelle a call. She does commercials.'

'I don't think I'd be very commercial.'

'Ads,' said Louis, adding. 'On TV.'

'Ah sorry.'

Louis grinned. 'But don't give up the day job,' He went out onto the street with Jayesh who gave me a friendly wave and another big smile as they got into to their taxi. I put the card into my pocket. Suddenly an acting career was ahead of me with Louis as my agent and Hollywood beckoning. I remembered that feeling I'd had at the end of Arnold's shoot. I wanted to do it again and again. Maybe I'd have a few stories of my own to tell.

Not long afterwards I was sharing a cab with Miriam.

'So you're going to be an actor?' she said.

'I should fucking coco.'

'I can see it in you.'

'Not in a million years.'

'I always believe it when things like that happen.'

'You mean Jayesh? I don't think he knows much about the acting business.'

'Louis Foster obviously adores him. And anyway I think you'd be a very good actor. It runs in the family doesn't it?'

'Only Annie.'

'Try and be a bit more positive, Frankie.'

'Alright I will.' And sitting there looking at the suburbs quietly passing through the night I thought I might as well be. Who knew about Indian mystics? Maybe they tapped into sources that no-one else knew about.

'And anyway Abebi would like it,' said Miriam.

I glanced at her. She was staring out of her own window now. Ah Miriam, sometimes you show yourself so vulnerable.'

# 15

The thought that Abebi would be impressed by me as an actor had been festering in my mind like so many other broken notions, but now Miriam had spoken it filled me with a ballooning optimism. Actors always got the women didn't they, with their laughs and energy and stories? Maybe I could be the same? Was it the job itself that did it, or was it the natural personality of those that undertook it? Yet another one of those chicken and eggs. If I became an actor would I mysteriously absorb those qualities and entirely change my personality, or could I never become one because I didn't have them?

'Maybe actors liked their freedom.' I remembered again what Miriam had said. Was that the clue? Did I need to become free in myself to become a laughing, energetic story-teller who could project any persona I felt like? Could I be like Paul and smoothly shift from a story about a fringe actor he'd bumped into on the street into a hilarious anecdote about himself on the set of a major Hollywood movie? Essentially I'd have to stop being such a miserable bastard breaking out every now and again in drunken outbursts of embarrassing incontinence. 'It's all in the mind,' I heard Jayesh. 'It's all in there you know?' I could hear myself telling Miriam. 'I run marathons while you take a walk in the park.' I poked my forehead with my finger as I thought it.

I was in my kitchen watching the kettle waiting for it to boil. Extroverts are just people who need people. Introverts like me are self-sufficient. We deal with our own needs and don't need everybody else to know we're alive. And you didn't have to be extrovert to be in the films anyway. How about the strong silent type? It never hurt Clint Eastwood. All you needed was charisma, deadly charm, intense emotional intelligence, a packed interior energy just waiting to be released. I glanced at my reflection in the window. What would Alexander say? What would Tony do? They'd tell me to play the horses, take the chance and go for it, wouldn't they? All I had to do was believe in myself. Alright then, so I would. I picked up Louis Foster's card from where it was lying on the counter top next to the kettle which still hadn't boiled, took up my phone, called the number and got through to Annabelle, Louis' assistant.

'Mr Foster suggested I phone,' I said. 'He told me, I was commercial, no, I mean...'

'Oh yes he mentioned you.' Annabelle cut through. She had one of those sharp, cold middle-class voices.

'My brother-in-law is Paul Cross.' I hoped that the mention of my once famous brother-in-law would warm her up.

'Jayesh liked you. Louis told me. Do you want to come in and I'll look you over.'

Look me over? Like a car, or a piece of furniture? What was I, some object for sale? Perhaps that's exactly what I was. I remembered Annie talking about being handled by an agent and used by a director as if she was something they tossed around between them. I didn't like any of it much but thought I'd better get used to it; this was the game and I wanted to play it. 'Ok, I'll be brushed up and ready for inspection.'

She didn't catch the irony. 'We're in Lisle Street behind Leicester Square.' There was a pause as she checked her diary. 'Thursday, five o'clock?'

'Ah yes, I know Leicester Square,' I said proving my cosmopolitan credentials.

She gave me the street number and rang off. It was that

easy? Thursday was two days away. I was still looking at my phone. Annabelle had said Jayesh liked me. Obviously the mysterious smiley Indian had all the clout that Miriam had instinctively recognised. Although I could recognise Jayesh' influence over Louis Foster it didn't mean that he would know a good actor from a Banshee, or more to the point whether I could be one. But one step at a time. I was going in to see a theatrical agent. It was serious. I began to panic. I called Annie.

'Don't thank me,' she said. 'You're my brother.'

'Well thanks anyway, big sis.'

'You'll need photographs, darling. And I don't mean holiday snaps. It'll cost you.'

'Will it?' More panic. 'How much?'

'We use John French. He's local anyway. Can be four hundred, but as a favour, you never know.'

'Four hundred pounds? For a few photos?'

'Did anyone tell you it was going to be cheap?'

'Christ, four hundred. And then there's the fare into Leicester Square.'

'For God's sake, Francis.'

'And what do I look like for these photographs?'

She told me to take a variety of get-ups. What did that mean? I didn't possess a variety of get-ups. Marks and Spencer didn't do get-ups. They did trousers and jackets and pants and socks. All I had was my suit which I hadn't worn for two years and this would be its third outing in a week. And what else did I have? Jeans, variously black and blue, a washing basket of T-shirts, the black top I wore practically everyday to face thirty kids, my black jacket... I realised I didn't have any clothes, or anything that a theatrical agent would recognise as clothes. And what are you supposed to look like for a photographer? I called Annie again. She was uncompromising. 'Look if you want to do it...' I could see her pride in her little brother was wearing thin.

I sat on my bed staring up at the variegated jumble in my

wardrobe. I realised that I'd had most of the stuff in there for over ten years and none of it stood any chance of dressing me up for a new career. I was going to have to kit himself out from top to bottom. And that was going to cost me.

I should say I've never had an easy relationship with money. I don't like the stuff, it makes me nervous. It was probably because I'd never had any. And when I had I either got rid of it as fast as I could or hung onto it as some kind of lifeline - and then got rid of it as fast as I could because having a lifeline seemed to imply that I was frightened of a life without it.

Either way the fact of the matter was that I had about four thousand tucked away in a savings account which was supposed to be for a deposit when I got round to buying a flat which I should have done years ago but never had. Four thousand after eighteen years teaching. How impressive was that? I blame Tony and the Forlorn Calf. But I did have a credit card with a three thousand limit! I could use that and pay back what I'd spend today over a month or two, which meant I could convince myself that I hadn't spent anything, which meant I needn't touch my savings, which meant I would still have the lifeline which I didn't want anyway.

I thought it through. Four hundred for this photographer and another five or six hundred on the clothes I'd need, which made a grand. No problem. No, wait a minute, no need to be stupid. I'd make it eight hundred for the clothes and the photographs. Maybe seven fifty? No, stick at eight. I'd invest that much in my new career. But no more. That was it. Then I remembered the glory of Arnold's film and didn't care how much I spent. I'd go the full grand. Wow, I was going to spend a grand! I was getting excited. An actor I would be!

I called John French who sounded sympathetic. which at four hundred for a session didn't surprise me. He said someone had cancelled and I could see him the next day in his studio, so that I only had this day, this very day, to go and spend six hundred quid on clothes! I panicked again. What clothes? Maybe I should ask Annie to go with me? No, far too scathing. I'd be a wreck before I tried on a jacket. Or Miriam? No, she never wore anything but black and that included a summer dress with flowers on it. Come on, this was my chance to break out and find the new me who could be anything. I'd be independent. I'd buy clothes on my own!

I was about to go into the High Street to begin the creation of my new self when I had a brainwave. I was going into the city on Thursday which was five days from when I last saw Abebi. If she was still in London I had the perfect excuse. 'Hi Abebi, how are you? Oh yeah I'm great, got a lot to do at the moment, you know? Listen I'm coming into Town to see my agent. Oh didn't I mention it to you? It's Louis Foster, yeah he's pretty well known...' How could she refuse? By being in Baltimore, that's how. I refused to believe it. It was all going so well, I was full of it, the energy was roaring, there's a tide in the affairs of men. I'd have an agent, new clothes. I picked up my phone and paused. To actually speak to her would have been too much.

I sent her a text; Hi, you still in town? I'm gonna be in Leicester Square seeing my agent, Thursday. Fancy a drink around seven? Frankly. I wasn't sure about the Frankly but thought I may as well build on the one shred of intimacy we had between us. She didn't reply. I waited another half an hour, she still didn't reply. I plunged into a depression and felt the great nervous bag inside me shiver just to remind me of what a small time loser I actually was. She was on a bed in a hotel room being fucked by the Jordanian on a blue coverlet, she was on a plane, then giving her paper in New York to a packed room wearing that pale green dress. She was in her London hotel waiting for me to call. Everything was good, everything was bad, I was going insane. My intention to invest financially in myself rose and fell with my self-esteem. The thousand dropped back down again to eight hundred, then seven-fifty. Then to hell with it, I'd use the plastic, plastic didn't count.

I went down to a small boutique on the High Street and bought a leather jacket for three hundred quid. And new jeans, a pair of shoes, and a couple of shirts. I managed to spend six hundred and thirty pounds in about forty minutes, a world record. And Abebi still hadn't replied to my text.

## 16

John French, the photographer, lived in a large terraced house on a main road leading out of the town. He was a small, angry-looking man in black jeans and a tattered punk T shirt. He had long red tousled hair, a little snub nose and a round lined face that spoke of a few nights out. As I arrived he was scuttling round his cluttered studio on short legs and battered trainers adjusting a complicated system of blinds and shutters to regulate the light flowing in from the high windows at the back of the house.

He grunted as I came in and continued fiddling with his camera, hardly speaking as I took the clothes I had brought with me out of a battered holdall and laid them out on an ancient couch at the side of the room for inspection. They included my old suit with all my new purchases and at the last moment I'd thrown in the famous anorak from the Arnold shoot for luck. John French didn't look impressed. He picked up the anorak and held it between two fingers. 'So who do you want to be?' The implication being that if I wanted to be pictured in some old relic from the twentieth century then I'd got the wrong photographer.

'What? Ah? I don't know.'

'So?' he waited.

I didn't know what to say.

'Do you have an image you want to project?'

My only experience of photographs had been family groups and holiday snaps. In some of them I'd looked ok, mostly I couldn't stand them. I was either too tall or too short, too pudgy or too thin, sometimes my gut was beginning to show, my back wasn't straight, or my shoulders slumped. But worst of all there was always that wary look in my eyes and a crooked smile on my lips as if I was waiting for the shutter to click and desperate for it all to be be over.

None of this had occurred to me as I'd booked the session. Not that I didn't have hundreds of images of myself floating around my mind. These were all related to one fantasy or another; my earliest was of me beaming modestly as the youngest Spurs player ever; as I grew older I was the suave, but kindly, dashing action hero involved in love affairs that shocked the world; then the not-to-be-messed-with business tycoon; the politician and philanthropist, hero to millions; the great writer and hundreds more, all beaming, brilliantly attractive, desired and modest. Any of them could be triggered at a moments notice by a chance remark in a pub, the lies of a party spokesman, the boredom of a premiere league game, or even some tearful story from a kid in my class. None of it could I admit to John French who was waiting patiently fiddling with his camera.

'Ah well... I wouldn't mind being on the front pages.' I said it as a disarming little joke, but it probably wasn't.

'As what?' John French looked at me with fierce penetrating small blue eyes.

'Are there you have me.' I'd thought that the photographer would decide what I wanted to look like. 'I'm going to see an agent. You see?'

'What's the part?'

'I don't think it's any particular kind of part. What do you think?'

'What do I think is the part you're going up for?' John French sat on a high stool by the wall beginning to look faintly bored as he affixed a different lens to the camera.

'That was a stupid question, wasn't it?'

'Well if you don't know, Francis, how am I supposed to?'

'Good point.'

He tried to be kind, "So it's more like a general interview, is it?'

'Yes, that's it,' I said with some relief. 'So I need a general kind of photograph.'

'You're not very experienced in this, are you?'

'Sorry. To be honest, the truth is I don't know who I am. I mean who I should look like.'

'Who does?' John French grinned just like Alexander Hudson had grinned. Not knowing who you were seemed to amuse everyone. I don't see why. No-one had any answer to it, so what was so funny? Maybe they laughed because laughter was the only answer to anything you don't know the answer to.

'What do you think I look like?'

John French looked me up and down, 'You've got a good body, sort of average size, sort of nice face, good hair. I'd say you were a teacher.'

'You're joking. How'd you know?'

'Annie told me.' French laughed. 'But you're honest, I'll say that. More than most actors who come in here. They all want to look like movie stars.'

'Well, seeing as you mention it.'

'Don't worry about it. Never apologise for what you are, or what you want. Put the leather on.' French stood me up against a wall, angled his lights and adjusted the blinds. 'Moody,' he said.

I liked that. Moody it would be; the strong, silent type. And for the first time in my life I liked the camera too. Maybe it was because I knew I was performing. I enjoyed looking into the lens; it seemed to be somehow inviting me in, there was no judgment, as if it was saying be whatever you want to be, pal, I don't care. I began to feel confident. I remembered Lewisham High Street and was preparing to roar with rage.

'Keep looking into the camera.' French was talking all the time. 'Be honest, it's your strong suit, don't pretend anything.'

I did my best but after a while it all felt like play acting. Now French had mentioned it my honesty felt dishonest. How could you be honest about honesty?

French was having none of it. 'Head down, head up, turn towards me, stand square on...' The camera came closer. 'Look heavy, heavier, head down, look up.'

I began to imagine that girl, Kate, how much I hated her. That was better, I could be honest about my anger couldn't I? You could be honest about something you felt even if you were making it up. Could you? I sneered. By that time the camera was virtually up my nose.

'Put the suit on with the T-shirt. Same thing, look away, give me your profile. Now be happy. Think of something happy. Think of a beautiful woman. She wants you. She's soft, she wants all of you. She loves you. You love her.'

I thought of Abebi, seeing the curve of her waist as she walked across the room toward me, her hips swaying, her breast soft and inviting, the sharp light in her eyes, the welcoming brightness of her smile, her hair haloed by some light behind. For that one second all my doubts disappeared.

'You're the only man in the world.' My smile got broader. 'Great, great, you're a good looking man, you know she wants you. She thinks you're fantastic.' The lens was close again. 'You're going to fuck her. She's coming towards you. In your eyes. See her. See her...'

Oh Abebi, Abebi, Abebi...

The whole thing took about forty minutes. I was exhausted. I'd never pulled so many faces in my life, but something in me didn't want it to stop. I wanted to dive into the lens as John French focussed and refocussed, every swift turn of his fingers seemed to produce some other aspect of me, some other place to be, some other place which wasn't where I was.

'You're pretty cool,' he said, 'I think I got some nice ones there, the camera likes you.'

I wasn't at all sure what bit of me John French had got but whatever it was I felt excited and delighted with myself.

'Four hundred and fifty,' said John.

I wasn't that delighted, but wasn't going to dwell on it. The camera had felt like some kind of portal to elsewhere where money didn't matter, a place where everybody existed and didn't, including myself. It was unreal and at the same time it was all possible.

'Good luck,' said the photographer as I left carrying my bag of unconvincing disguises.

## 17

John French selected twenty or so shots and emailed them to me. I brought them up on the screen of my phone and I hated every single one of them. None of them looked like me at all. The ones where I'd thought I'd been ruthlessly angry merely showed me as a petulant little boy; where I'd thought I'd been softly and amusingly sophisticated I looked like a simpering idiot, and the worst were when I'd decided to show the dark, moody and dangerous aspect to my personality. I looked like a wanker.

I went into my bathroom and held the phone up by the mirror. I pulled the same faces as I'd done for French comparing the reality of myself with the images on the screen. It was worse. The actual Francis Riley was even more of a sad jerk than he was in the photographs. There was clearly no way I could show an agent any of them.

And no way I could show them to Abebi either, although the thought crossed my mind that I didn't have to show them to her at all. Why had I thought I should? When I saw her I'd be showing her my actual presence which according to my reflection in the mirror was ten times worse. Was this what I really looked like? Who was I? No answer to that. I was briefly cheered by the thought that none of it made any difference anyway because she hadn't called me back. She was probably on the other side of the Atlantic by now - with the Jordanian. So how did that make me feel better? It didn't.

I sat on my bed and looked down at the newly hoovered carpet. Oh where was the junk of yesterday? I was happy then. And now what was I going to do about Annabelle the agent? How could I show her any of these pictures? I thought about deleting them but I thought I should call John French first; it seemed rude not to.

'Hey John, I'm sure you're a great photographer, Annie says so, and Paul, but I have a bit of minor little problem here. None of these pictures look like me.'

'They are you,' he said.

That was difficult to argue with.

'I just don't see it.'

'Well who else is it?' he asked. 'Look it can be strange the first time, but you'll get used to it, take my word for it. Let me know which ones to print.'

I sat with the phone still in my hand wondering if I wasn't finally facing the horrible truth about my life and what it had looked like to everyone else; and there it all was in twenty images on my phone if I could bear to look at them again. There was only one thing for it. I called Tony and told him what had happened. 'Look don't snigger, you bastard.'

'Sorry,' said Tony. 'Just sometimes, you know, things are funny.'

'Fuck off.'

'Send them over to me,' he said. 'I'll get back to you.'

I forwarded them then called Miriam who wanted to see them too.

'I can't. I've already sent them to Tony.'

'It's called the digital age, Francis, you can send as many

copies as you like. Stop worrying. Everyone at Annie's thought you were great. All actors have terrible nerves before they go on stage; it's the same with photographs I suppose. Anyway I have to go, there's someone at the door.'

I sent the pictures to her. Christ, the digital age. I had a horrible vision of them speeding to every screen worldwide and felt my stomach contract in a spasm of future embarrassment.

I called Annie, who else; and she just laughed. 'Oh you thought it was so easy, didn't you?'

Now I knew why actors turned everything into a story; because then it wasn't about themselves was it? All their narratives were about some fantasy figure who was created by them, was them and also wasn't. What else could you do, when every step forward, every minor triumph, seemed like a step back? Get a laugh anyway. Everything was material for an anecdote, wasn't it? Even your mother's death according to Alexander. According to Alexander? The great actor seemed to have taken up permanent resident in the centre of my brain giving me a kind of guru-like overview of my entire existence. What would he say now?

Tony called back. 'What are you so worried about? These pictures don't look anything like you. They're great.'

'Thanks Tony.'

'They look like portraits of an actor. You know, like those ones you see all over the walls of Italian restaurants. Don't see the point myself. I mean sitting in the Forlorn Calf you wouldn't want to be looking at sad baby cows all over the place would you?'

'Look, I'm going through an existential crisis here.'

'The pics look a bit smarmy, mebbe like you're trying too hard, but they're ok, son. Stick with it.'

'You sure?'

'Would I lie to you? I like the one where you're pretending to be moody.'

'I wasn't pretending to be anything! I was being moody.'

'Got to go pal, there's Argentinian rugby on telly. They've got a great hooker.'

Perhaps there was a subconscious connection.

'Tone, do you have a number for Miranda Vee?'

'You're not thinking of arithmetic, are you?'

'I'll bet she's had thousands of photos done.'

'Wouldn't mind one meself.'

He texted me with Miranda's number. I called her and as Tony predicted she immediately thought I was asking for a date. I told her how great it would be to see her, it really would, can't wait, but I need your opinion on something. She immediately stepped into the part, adopting a hushed and wise tone like she'd heard somewhere on TV.

'Oh what is it, darling?'

'I have had some photos to be an actor and don't know which ones to choose because none of them look like me.'

She erupted with the harsh laughter of someone who knew all about it. 'Oh darling, of course they don't look like you! No actor ever wants to see shots of themselves; they show you up for being what you are! There's you having a whale of a time being this or being that, being glam or dramatic or moody or pretty and you're suddenly confronted by the worst question anyone can ask; who are you anyway? Who exactly is doing the showing off? And you don't know and you get so depressed and you decide that you are any one of a hundred things especially something that makes you look like Greta Garbo or Jennifer Lawrence or Julia Roberts or anyone you think you might stand a chance of getting away with; especially if it makes you look sexy and then you decide to use the one that looks most like the part you're going up for but you don't really know what that is because you've no idea what's in the casting director's mind and you get depressed again and you think; oh so fuck it I'm going to use the one that I feel like on that day, and then you panic and think it looks so horrible I can't use that one and finally you just pick one and send it off and it doesn't make any difference anyway because they're only seeing you because of what you did last week, especially if it was a success; and all the time you're screaming inside, but I'm an actor, I'm an actor! I can be anything you want me to be! And you don't know what that is and nor do they half the time! Oh darling it's so awful and so depressing I can't tell you!'

I thought she was beginning to cry. To stem the tears I told tell her about my appointment to see an agent which immediately started her off again.

'Oh darling, what are you wearing? You have to look like an actor.'

'What's that?'

'What an actor looks like. You can always tell. You've been to enough of Annie's parties, you should know.

'Well, I bought this leather...'

'Leather's alright for certain types, but it has to flow.'

'Flow?'

'It has to be soft, you see darling. Actor's don't want to seem too stiff, do they?' She giggled. ' Which is what they always are. Sorry. It was lovely to meet you by the way.'

I could see we were returning to arithmetic. 'How's Harry?' I said.

'Well Harry's a good case in point. He's very masculine, don't you think? But then he's feminine too, so he gives you the impression that he could be anything, he kind of flows from one thing to another at the same time as being charismatic. You do think he's charismatic, don't you?'

'Oh yes...'

'Well that's what I mean. Male, female, and at the same time, strong. Are you gay?'

'No, I don't think...'

'You didn't respond when I accidentally touched your knee under Annie's table, darling.'

Accidentally? I thought she was trying to sand my leg. 'I'm sorry, It must have been so slight and subtle that I...'

'Well you wouldn't expect me to be obvious, would you?

It was only for a second, but I thought you might have thought... actually now I come to think of it I am free at the weekend. How about Saturday?'

'Ah. Well, that would have been wonderful...' I could hear Tony telling me, go for it, son... 'but I'm afraid it looks like I'm away for the next few... I mean after I've seen the agent...I'm getting a train.... but look I'll call you. Can I do that?'

'Darling, of course. It was so nice of you to think of me, but I'm afraid that the weekend isn't good for me either. Harry's so demanding.'

I was beginning to feel sorry for Harry. But then thought that maybe he was as free and easy as Miranda. I'd noticed him glancing at Miriam over the table once or twice.

'Miranda, thank you so much.'

'A pleasure darling. We must always help each other, don't you think? Remember, powerful, strong, charismatic, male, female and flowing. The world is your oyster, darling. And I should change the leather if I were you. Stiffness isn't everything, is it?'

I sat back amidst the debris of tissue paper and cardboard on my sofa and ran my hand over my new leather. Miranda was right, it was as stiff as a board. I must have been trying to repeat something of my younger days when leather was supposed to be tough and enduring and definitely not flowing. All I had that could be remotely described as that would be my old suit which was definitely flowing or maybe sagging was a better word. I decided to wear a T-shirt with it and added a pair of trainers, the arty touch. At least it looked as if I didn't care too much which according to Miranda was important. And anyway it was what I was wearing - minus the trainers - the last time I saw Abebi, and, as if to confirm my decision my phone pinged a text from her. There was no apology for making me wait a day and a half. It said; Great Thursday outside the big movie theatre at 7.30. What big movie theatre? There were about six of them in Leicester

Square. I thought about pinning her down, but didn't want to look stupid by asking questions. I'd find her. Things were brightening up. I had pictures I didn't like and clothes that sagged and I was seeing Abebi. I was all set.

## 18

Louis Foster's offices were big shiny and seemed to be made of glass. I sat on a chrome and leather chair in the reception area and looked down a long corridor which had doors off either side leading to what looked like a row of transparent boxes each one occupied by a busy agent perched like a bird behind a large desk and talking like mad on the phone. Most of their conversations were hushed although there'd sometimes be a laugh, or a shout and then one of them would hang up angrily and swear at the phone. Every now and again a woman in a short skirt or a boy in tight pants would fly out of one office and into the next not finishing one conversation before they began another. Then there'd be a few minutes of silence before the next eruption. The office at the end of the corridor was closed off with blinds either side of the door. I guessed that this was where the great Louis Foster hung out: who I assumed I definitely wouldn't meet and in fact would probably never see again. Everything about the place made me tense; even the transparency of the walls seemed on the one hand to give you the impression that they were open and inviting you in; and on the other, stopping you from ever entering. You can look but you can't touch.

The receptionist, a tall young woman in orange tights and long black hair looked up at me from beneath false eyelashes under green lids. She gave me a form to fill in. It wanted all the usual personal details and then a nice little section entitled, All About You. Birthplace, then education, which clearly didn't matter too much as there was only room enough to mention my primary school. After this came a section headed training: what could I say? None. Special skills? Horse-riding? None. Weapons training? Maybe catapult? None. Athletic achievements? A runners up medal in the Kilburn Junior football league, division three? None. Accents? Ah, something I could say. Irish. Previous experience? None. Agents? None. Now I knew what none-entity meant.

'Would you like to come in?' A willowy blond with a big nose and heavily lipsticked mouth stood in the glass door to her glass box. She tucked her long hair behind her ear and stretched her lips in what might have been a smile. I followed her into her office and sat in front of her desk suddenly very conscious of the state of my trainers as they stuck out on the polished wood floor between us.

She said, 'I'm Annabelle. Hi. Louis said I should see you. Why?'

'Ah.' Commercials. Ah? Do you want this?' I held out the form I'd just filled in.

Annabelle took it and looked through it. 'You haven't any acting experience?'

'Well that's not entirely true. I did a small film. Directed by Arnold Cross.'

'Who?'

'Ah? And I... well I liked it. And my sister and brother-in-law are actors..

'And you thought you could be an actor too?'

'Yeah. Well, I don't know.'

I'd hardly arrived and could feel myself sinking through the floor. I wished I'd worn the stiff leather, maybe it would have given me some protection. I noticed a bad stain on the instep of my left trainer, then saw her shoes had a deep red shine the colour of her lips. 'Look, I'm quite prepared to forget it.' I started to stand up.

'You're going? You've only just arrived.'

'I think I'm probably in the wrong place.'

Her eyebrows arched. 'If you're going to give up that quickly then you probably are.'

'I'm just an English...' I nearly said it then Miriam said, 'You can be great.' I cleared my throat. 'No I'm not giving up. But...' But what? I sat down again and blurted, 'But it's what I want to do and so I'm going to do it. Because if I don't I'm stuck like I am for the rest of my life. And I don't even know what that is.' I had no idea where all this was going. I pouted like a defiant kid. 'If you want to you can help, but if you don't that's ok too. And you can thank Louis Foster from me. And Jayesh. Shall I go now?' I half rose again.

'No, wait a minute, please just sit down' She looked at me as if I was some sad sack clown. She suddenly smiled. Her teeth were long and white and I had the feeling could be dangerous. 'I think you're rather sweet.'

'Do you?'

'Louis said Jayesh liked you. And although Jayesh isn't in the business, Louis listens to him. We all think it's a bit odd but there you are.'

'Well, I like Jayesh,' I said. 'And Louis. They were very encouraging. Well Jayesh was.'

She had her head on one side as she looked me over. 'Do you have any photographs?'

I nearly said no, but as I was holding them in my hand it was difficult. I took them out of the envelope and put them on her desk then watched really embarrassed as she examined them one at a time.

'I don't think they look like me,' I said.

'Who do they look like?'

'I don't know. But it's not me.'

She looked up comparing me to the images that were now spread across her the desk. I could hardly bear it. 'Look I can't do the bullshit. I'm an honest man, that's what the photographer said, and I think I am anyhow. No, I know I am. I'm an honest man. I mean you're a nice woman, I can see that. And very attractive and kind and generous and I'm fucking no-one. Sorry, I didn't mean to curse at you.' The Irish was coming out. She was looked at me with an odd kind of interest. 'I'm in love with an American professor and she'd like it if I was an actor.' I stopped. I hadn't meant to say any of it.

'Sorry? What's your name?'

'Francis Riley.'

'And you're in love?'

'Yes. No. The truth is I wanted to be an actor before I met her so that's not entirely it. I mean I wanted to discover something. About me. Maybe you can see that, you're the professional, so's Louis and Jayesh. I did this film and I was suddenly roaring in the rain, it came out of nowhere, and I knew that there were things in me that I'd never realised. I mean I'd started being Irish for a start which I'm not, well I am by birth, but I don't speak it.'

'You sound it,' she said.

'Do I? Maybe I do. I mean now but not usually. You see what I mean? Things I didn't know I had are breaking out all over the place.' My hands were moving up and down, my head was at a strange and unknown angle. I looked round at the glass wall to my left. In the office beyond a middle-aged man in a scrunched linen suit was prowling round his desk shouting into a mobile phone. For a second I had no idea where I was.

'Oh fuck it. Shall I go now?'

'No, no. I'm intrigued.' Annabelle was smiling broadly. She seemed to be enjoying herself. 'Tell me, who's this American professor?

'Ah Jesus, for sure the most beautiful woman in the world.'

'How lovely.'

It might be, I live in hope. Can I go now?'

'I've never had anyone come in here and say all that before,' she said. 'You've made my day.'

'Anyway,' I said. 'that's who I am. And that's why I'm here.' I glanced down at my hands in my lap. They were clenched tight together making the backs of my fingers white. I felt stupid, shamed and at the same time somehow exhilarated like I was alone on the seashore and the waves were breaking and I could see the sky white with hope on the horizon. I breathed in hard. I wanted to run away. I never wanted to be anywhere else.

'Look,' she said, suddenly becoming businesslike. 'I can't represent you because to be honest there's nothing to represent, but everyday I have lists for commercials that come across my desk and if I think there's something you might be able to do I'll be in touch. It's not much,' she shrugged, 'but you never know it could be a start.'

Her eyes had become warm. I remembered Annie saying that good agents always think they're your mother. Oh no, not another one. I felt like I wanted to cry. 'Thank you, Annabelle, may I call you Annabelle? Thank you, thank you so much.'

'It's been a pleasure. And good luck with the American Professor.'

## 19

I walked onto a rainy Lisle Street feeling dissociated as Miriam would say. The pavement was spongy, there were roast meat, chop suey, Chinese smells in the air, footsteps came and went in the drizzle. People in anoraks, holding umbrellas, who didn't have an agent were passing me by. And I had one! Well maybe I had one. Anyway I could tell Abebi that I did. My step was lighter, I felt like doing a hop and a skip like Gene Kelly except there weren't any puddles except deep ones and my trainers leaked.

There were a couple of hours before I was meant to see Abebi and I was surrounded by restaurants. Why not? I went into the Long Moon and ordered chilli beef and a beer. Twenty minutes later I'd finished. They serve fast in Chinatown.

I walked through the red and gold lanterns of Gerrard Street beginning to feel ashamed of my outburst to Annabelle. I must have looked a right idiot. And all the Irish. What was that? I give up on that one. Had I somehow betrayed Abebi by using her to get myself an agent? Wasn't that somehow corrupt? Or weak? Was I weak? Yes I was. But it had worked, it had worked!

I went into a pub and ordered a pint. The bar was half empty and the walls smelt of beer down the ages. I sat at a table under a dark wooden wall covered in old posters of actors in Edwardian costumes posing down on me in sepia. I couldn't seem to get away from it. I was one of them! I'm on a stage with footlights blinding me, my arms are aloft, I'm declaiming howl, howl, howl! I'm sitting in an LA restaurant opposite de Niro whose brow is furrowed, his lips in a snarl, he's trying to scare me from under his eyebrows. I'm brash with a coloured tie. I tell de Niro to go fuck himself. I'm on the red carpet with Abebi. I'm facing thirty kids who don't want to know. They're sneering and hooting, you and de Niro, tell us another one, Mr Riley! I didn't care. I felt happy. I'd never see the kids again. I liked the kids. I loved those fucking kids. Ok, so I was just an English teacher but I was also a great English teacher. Two or three of those kids had learned a lot from me. And so what if they didn't give a toss for Jane Austen. Did I when he was at school? No I didn't. I hated Jane Austen, mainly because of Mr Petty, who was a bad English teacher, who could have made the greatest day of anyone's life boring. And now I loved Jane Austen. Things change. Everything changes.

Annabelle was one of those confident women who ran the world and scared me. But then she was nice. And the nicer she was the easier, no the freer, I became. I bet she lived in Kensington. She had one of those accents which could slice the air in half and also could be soft like a pillow too. She lived in a silver cage and she was going to put me up for a commercial! Alright then I'd sell Tampax and lawn-mowers. So what? Why had I been such a snob? I could love Sam Beckett and flog Durex couldn't I? And I'd be convincing about it too. Get your rubber johnnies here! And I'd love preening about in front of the cameras. Great art could come later. And the next time I saw John French I wasn't going to be a sad prat, I was going to be the hero he was trying to photograph! Sorry John, I love you too.

I bought another pint. Something had happened in that office. Sure I was a pathetic creep, but I was my own pathetic creep. I'd admitted, I'd opened up: I'd felt a piece of myself break away and come to the surface. Why should I be ashamed of that? Why not celebrate the crack in the shell? Why not laugh at my sad tears? And as for Abebi... she was going to see me for what I was, explosive, witty and wild. I'd tell her a few funny stories. I couldn't think of any off hand, but I would, on the spot. I'd have her roaring with laughter and she'd see me as free and full of an energy, an actor, a man that could be anything!

The pub was filling up, I was getting crowded into my seat. They were all young, in jeans and shirts hanging out all over the place. I was in my black baggy, but I didn't care. I'd rip it off in a phone box and emerge with a cloak and wings. So why had Tony given me all that bad advice about telling women they had great breasts? Was he trying to make a tit of me? Was he playing a game? And why had Abebi waited so long before she got back to me? Was she playing around too? Who was this Jordanian? Did he exist? I bought another pint. Tony was my greatest pal, I'd got an agent and I was about to see the love of my life. I looked at my watch. It was twenty past seven. Christ, I was going to be late. I sunk the pint and got out of there.

I hurried down Wardour Street, left on Lisle again and cut down to Leicester Square. Which cinema? I could see four. I should have asked her. I couldn't miss her now! I walked round the square. There was a fairground in the middle with fairy lights and a roundabout and people bobbing up and down on frozen horses. I wondered about taking a ride himself; how stupid can you get? I was already late. Maybe she wouldn't show. That would be typical. Typical of what? Her? I hardly knew her. But I knew for sure that she wouldn't come. She'd stand me up in Leicester Square, that was for definite. And there she was outside the Odeon bang on time looking like anybody's dream. I had no doubts now; about Tony, the agent and all the rest of it; this life, it was the best, everything I wanted. I put my hands on her shoulders and kissed her cheek.

'You been drinking?' she asked. 'I can smell it on your breath.'

'Just a quick half, I was early. Ah, how about...?' I looked around the square like it was London, my city.

'Over there,' she said. She pointed to a place with seating outside.

'Just what I was going to suggest.'

There were half a dozen tables sheltered under an awning. Three of them were free. 'Wouldn't you prefer to be inside?' I looked up at the sky as though I was an experienced forecaster of English weather. 'It can get worse.'

'I want to see London,' she said. 'Anyway it's warm rain.'

We sat down. I was full of it although I couldn't think of anything to say.

'You want to see a movie?' she said. 'Maybe take a ride? What's that?' she pointed at the roundabout. 'What do you call it? A whirligig or something?'

'It's a merry-go-round,' I said. 'As a matter of fact I was thinking of that just a minute ago.' She didn't reply. There was a faraway look on her face as if she was remembering something she didn't like.

'You been having a good time?' I was hoping she hadn't with the Jordanian. 'Has your friend..?'

'You mean, Omar?'

'Omar? That his name? Really? You know I imagined that was his name.'

'Did you? Why?'

'I don't know. Omar Sharif or something. He back in Amman?'

'He's gone to New York. He's doing some kind of deal.'

'You didn't go with him?'

'Obviously not.'

'Ah sure.'

A tall slender waiter with cropped hair came to the table. He was very polite and sounded Polish. She ordered water and after all the beer I thought I would be pissing all night, so I went for a gin and tonic. 'You sure you don't want something stronger?'

'Oh no. I don't drink much.' She looked out over the square again.

'Whatever you want. It's on me.'

'You're a great guy.' She was still facing away from me as she said it and I couldn't work out if she meant it. She turned back and smiled, but her dark eyes were downcast and I could see she wasn't too happy. I wondered if she was missing the Jordanian.

'Anything wrong? I mean, you don't have to tell me.'

'Oh, I'm great.'

'So am I.' I gave her my big smile. 'So, how was it with Omar?'

'You want to know? So. He wanted me to go with him to New York. He wants to marry me.'

'He wants to marry you?' My heart plunged, then rose as I realised she hadn't gone to New York. 'So what do you think about that?' I made it sound like it was just some interested enquiry from a distant relative.

'He's pretty rich.'

'Oh right, you'd marry him for the dough?

'You don't make a lot out of one book and flying round the world to universities, do you?' She sounded angry as she said it.

'Don't you? I mean I guess not.'

'A girl's gotta live.'

'Sure.' I felt good about all of this. She may have been doing so reluctantly but she was definitely saying no to Omar. Maybe Omar wasn't the big thing I'd thought he was.

'How was your day?' she said abruptly changing the subject.

'Oh not so bad. I've just seen my agent, just a routine meeting, you know. There's a few possibilities, a couple of things on the horizon...'

'What's that?' she asked, pointing to the envelope in my hand.

'Oh nothing?'

'They photographs?'

How did she know?

'Yeah, well, I guess so. No.'

'Let me see.'

No, you don't want to..'

She smiled properly for the first time. I gave her the pictures and she looked through them slowly one at a time.

'You're a really good-looking guy.'

'You what?'

She held a photo up to get more light. 'That's really handsome.'

'You think so? I don't think my agent...'

'I'm hungry,' she said. 'You want to eat?'

I thought it was probably better not to persist with the bullshit about the agent. Maybe I was already turning into an actor, hoping to build up the story. 'So am I.' I said. 'I haven't eaten all day.' The chilli beef had been on a small plate anyway. 'So let me get you dinner.'

'You'd buy me dinner?'

'Sure will.' I was relieved I had my credit card.

'I can't let you do that. I don't know you.' She gave me a low glance from beneath her eyelashes. I'd have bought her anything.

'Please. It'd be a pleasure. On me. I'd like to.'

She didn't answer and turned away again to the Fairground. The rain was getting heavier and the tourists were scampering around looking for shelter: the square was suddenly full of bobbing, brightly coloured umbrellas like some painting by Renoir. Her dark hair was damp and clung to the side of her face accentuating the sharpness of her cheekbones. I could feel she was distant and angry. The tall waiter bought the drinks. She sipped her water. Maybe she hadn't wanted to see me? Was all this some madness that I'd allowed to grow in my own mind, some stupid crush on a woman who had no interest in me and had never had? Why should she after my drunk and offensive behaviour in Alexander's club? But she had arranged to meet me hadn't she? And there she was sitting opposite me in a cafe in Leicester Square. So why do that if I was such a no-hoper? There must be some reason. I took a sip of the gin and made another effort. 'I really like being with you.'

She turned and looked me straight in the eye. 'Look, I've got to be straight with you, Frankly, I'm bust. I didn't go with Omar to New York because I didn't want to. Ok? You understand that, don't you? I mean you can't just go and get hitched because you want the money.'

'I admire that.'

'But then...' she touched her eye. 'But then, here I am.' She looked round. The rain was easing and the umbrellas were coming down: it was beginning to look like it could be a lovely night with the light bouncing off the wet paving; everything was soft and distant. 'I mean I love it,' she said. 'But I can't stay.'

'Why not?'

She shrugged. 'That hotel. God, this city is not cheap.'

'How much is it? I mean, the hotel.'

'Doesn't matter.'

'How much?'

'Two fifty a night.'

'Jesus.'

Her eyes suddenly filled with tears. 'And I can't pay it.'

'What do you mean?'

'I got a bill I can't pay, Frankly. Ok? That's all there is to it. Sorry, if I seem a little upset... it's none of your business anyhow.'

'I thought Omar... I mean you said he was rich.'

'I'm not going to ask him, am I? You can't turn down a guy's proposal and ask him to pay your hotel.'

'So you definitely turned him down?'

'Yeah I told him, no way.'

'What did he say?'

'What do you think? He's in love with me. He was begging me to go to New York with him. Told me he'd pay the fare, first class, book me in with him at his hotel. I can't, Frankly. I just can't! You know, you write books, and mine isn't what anyone's going to call a masterpiece, but you got to have some integrity, don't you?'

How could I not agree with that; I mean I'm a Sam Beckett fan. I wanted to touch her, hold her hand. I cleared my throat and said, 'I'll tell you something, I told you I saw my agent and all I could think of to say to her was, I just met this woman. I mean to say that to an agent? What kind of idiot is that?'

'What she say?'

'She laughed. I said I'd met this beautiful American professor.'

'Did you? You're so sweet.'

'That's what she said. Anyway I told her. I said that you'd made me want to do something with my life. That's it. That's the truth.'

She reached across the table and touched the back of my

hand. 'God, Frankly, I wish I'd never come to London at all. I wish I'd stayed back there in, what's the name of your little town?'

'So why don't you come back with me? Check out of the hotel and come back with me and... and we'll find somewhere for you to stay.' I was desperately thinking of where she could go and wondering whether I'd changed the sheets on my bed. I had. No I hadn't. I couldn't remember.

'I can't. I just need to be in the city. There are things I have to do. Anyway I can't leave my hotel until I've paid the bill. I guess I'm ok for another couple of days but then they're going to start asking for it.'

I could see her lithe lovely body stretching languorously across my bed. I'm on the sofa. She calls out, "Frankly..." I could check the sheets as soon as we got back; ask her to sit on the sofa and have a drink while I found new ones.

'You could do a moonlight flit,' I said.

'A what?'

'From the hotel.'

'You don't think I haven't thought about it? I've got a reputation, you know? It's not much but I'm working on it. I'd never be able to come back.'

'You definitely couldn't ask Omar?'

'I've just turned him down! He's going to think I've changed my mind. You want him to think that?'

'No.' Then without the thought passing through my brain. 'Look what is it? How much? I'll pay.' It was like being in the glass walls with Annabelle: I could see everything and go nowhere, but not this time. I could do what I wanted: maybe another piece was breaking off and things would be different.

'Oh no, you can't. That's so kind of you.' She squeezed my hand. 'But no, definitely no. I'm not. That's too much. But thank you. I'm sorry I've been mean to you. I knew when I met you that you were a good guy.' She leant over and kissed the side of my face.

'I'll do it.' The impulse was growing. I was going to go through those walls. 'What is it? A grand? And another couple of nights. That'll be fifteen hundred.'

'No.'

'Stay. It's on me.'

'I can't.'

'I insist and then I can see you for the next few days.'

'I got some meetings, Frankly. That's another reason I got to stay. There may be another book deal.'

'We can work round those.'

'I can't...' She began to cry. The gorgeous professor I was in love with had sweet tears running down her sweet face. I pulled my chair closer and put my arm round her. I nuzzled her hair. She kissed my neck. This is where I wanted to be: the waves were breaking on the shore; the only place in the world I wanted to be. She put her hands on my chest and pushed me away.

'No, I can't. I just can't Frankly.'

## 20

I took the train home. It was late and the carriage was empty. There was an old newspaper on the seat opposite me. I picked it up and glanced at the headline. It smelt of damp and I threw it back. I couldn't believe what I'd done. We'd gone to another Chinese Restaurant just round the corner from Lisle Street. It was bigger then the one I'd already been to that day and we sat at a large round table in a corner. Abebi didn't seem to care what we ate and sat silently as I ordered. I asked her if she'd like wine and she said 'Sure.' Her face was sullen and unhappy as she picked at the food, toying with it as she looked around the restaurant. I asked her again if she'd let me help her and she shook her head.

'Come on Abebi, I want to.'

'No.'

'Please, I have a lot of feelings for you.'

'Cut it out, Frankly.'

We ate and drank mostly in silence. I ordered another bottle of wine and watched as the hard beauty of her face relaxed into a softness and she slowly began to talk. 'See, Frankly, I had a tough time. Where I come from a favour is always followed by some kind of ask, nothing's for free, right? I mean I know I got to be a professor, let's be straight about that, I'm an associate professor in a small college, but I wrote a book and I look like this which helps. Men like...'

'Skinner?'

'And others. I told you and I want to be truthful, sometimes I took advantage of that. Ok?' Her eyes were black and defiant as she looked up at me; like she was daring me to comment. I didn't care what she'd done; it made no difference to me; she was there and I was desperate to hold her. I tried to take her hand across the white tablecloth but she pulled it back.

'I like you, Frankly, and I don't think you're too rich, so thanks for the dinner, but that's all.'

'Where do you come from?'

'They're called the projects, used to be, still are sometimes. I was on the South Side which were the worst, just with my mom after my Dad passed. I was six, she was white, she was Jewish and had a black kid. He didn't leave us much, he wasn't too regular as a player. I mean he didn't get paid too well, so no-one had any money, least of all we did. Anyway I don't want to sell you some sob story. I did ok, college, and Skinner told you the rest.' She raised her face and looked directly at me, the defiance was back. 'I slept with him.'

'You slept with Skinner?'

'Sure.'

I didn't know what to do with that. Skinner, the small

teeth; the fucking manbag he didn't have but could have done, flirting with Miriam, , and now this. It was no joke, no fucking joke at all, but somehow it made no difference. She was sitting in front of me eating lemon chicken and telling me the truth. 'Is that how you came over for the conference?'

'Yeah.'

My heart was beating fast. 'Did you? I mean did you, have you, slept with him in the UK?'

'No.' She sat back in her chair and wiped her mouth with her napkin. 'Why should I? I was here right? I'd got what I wanted.' There was a strange smirk on her face, as if she was going to cry but toughing it out. 'The Truth We Tell, right? That's what the book is. I mean I didn't want to make it too personal, but it's all there hidden in that academic shit.' She dropped her head. 'So now you know, Frankly. Guess I'm not all you thought I was.'

'I don't care,' I reached out my hand again and this time she took it.

The train rattled north through the suburbs. Dark silhouettes of buildings, rows of back gardens, empty stations flashed past the window. A young fellah in bright white trainers came on and sat in a seat a few rows in front of me and fell asleep. I grinned as I looked down at my own footwear: how had I thought Annabelle would be impressed by those? What did it matter? I'd told her my own bumbling truth and got what I wanted. And Abebi had told me hers. We'd walked from the restaurant to the hotel and I'd paid her bill plus another five nights. It had come to over two thousand quid. I didn't care, the plastic could wear it. I was as happy as I'd ever been. We'd walked to the lift and she'd turned to me and put her arms round my neck and pulled my face down to hers. It was the best kiss I'd ever had. Her tongue was soft and warm, her body pliant and close as I held her tight. She gently pushed me away. 'Not tonight, baby,' she said. 'Too much, too soon.' She'd faced me as the lift doors closed on her. And then, and this was the best thing,

I'd said, 'I love you, Abebi.'

# 21

'Two thousand, four hundred and forty-three?'

'And fifty-six pence.'

'Are you out of your mind?'

'Including tax. Don't tell Miriam.'

Tony's mouth hung open. It was three in the afternoon and we were back in the Calf. My pint stood untouched in front of me as Tony swallowed half of his in one long gulp. 'Why not tell Miriam?'

I wasn't entirely sure why I didn't want Miriam to know. And that wasn't the only thing I was unsure about. Arnold had called and told me that a slot had become available for a screening the next night at the film school for And So They Thought They Knew. The whole cast was invited including me. Would I like to bring a guest? Under normal circumstances, or according to habit anyway, I'd have asked Miriam, but the world had changed with that kiss by the lift doors. It was as if my heart had begun to flow and I'd breached some wall in myself, only to come up against another one, Miriam. And I wasn't strong enough yet to face what, for some reason I couldn't understand, felt like the last redoubt. It had always been the way with Miriam. She was either in the way or the gateway to something I wanted, or didn't want, and as usual I'd pushed it away to be sorted out another time.

On the other hand the day was too bright and joyous for me to be concerned with any of it. Everything seemed possible, there was nothing I couldn't do. Reality had carved its brilliant truth on the face of my dreams! What need I to imagine when the object of my reverie was there to actually touch, to walk with, spend my long hours with, to make love to? But it wasn't just bodies; there was another thing going on here. My desire was for her, the whole of her, this woman made flesh and heart and soul. I was in love with Abebi and more than that she'd made me be in love with myself again and nothing else mattered.

I texted her and invited her to the screening. She'd replied that she had a meeting with a publisher early that evening but would do her best to be there. And in the spirit of this new age of optimism I invited Tony too.

'You want me to come and see you act?'

'You can meet Abebi.'

'She'll be there will she?'

'Oh yeah.'

## 22

I could hardly watch and pushed my palms into the sides of my face ready to cover my eyes as soon as I appeared up there on the film school's screen which wasn't as big as some I'd seen but I still wasn't prepared for the size of myself projected above me. I seemed to be ten feet tall and towered over the audience of fifty or so of Arnold's friends and my own family. They were all staring avidly at this clumsy figure in an ancient anorak striding angrily out of the MacDonald's. I looked as if I was going to break out of the screen, trample the seats and storm through the auditorium. Fortunately I was stopped mid stride by Donna, played by Kate, who was sitting behind me in full midnight make-up.

My hands were closing over my face as I screamed the immortal, shameful line, 'Fuck off or I'll stick a spike up your cunt!' The look on Kate's face on screen matched my own horror. Even Tony, sitting next to me, seemed to recoil.

'Fucking hell,' he whispered. I looked down at my hands in my lap. The sheer fury up there was like something out of a primeval pit; my face had crumpled, my eyes bulged and my lips contorted into a deep and disturbing snarl. Even the sound of my voice was different; it had become deep, harsh and terrifying.

There was a palpable tension in those sitting around me and I felt them staring at the back of my head in a kind of wonder that such an evil presence could just be sitting there amongst them. It seemed out of kilter with the rest of the film which I could see was basically rubbish. But even stunned by myself and unable to meet the eye of Tony or anyone else, I felt a mischievous grin begin to grow beneath my hands. Now I knew. In the past few days I'd felt the weirdest, strongest emotions, none of which I'd known existed, at least not in me. It was as if something had suddenly erupted like some awful boil, and I'd taken a leap into an unknown version of myself. I was running through the heather and up the mountain again; the breakers were crashing down onto the beach.

If only Abebi had shown up.

But maybe she would and the fact that she hadn't seen the film itself could be to my advantage. She'd see the shock and horror of the crowd and know me for what I was; her heroic, slightly scary, benefactor.

After the screening everyone gathered in the small bar which doubled as a student cafe. I glanced around at the posters on the walls. Time was running out for her to make her appearance. I always thought she wouldn't come. I couldn't help it. No matter how I felt there was always doubt creeping up behind. On the other hand maybe the meeting with the publisher had gone well and they'd gone for a celebratory drink, or maybe she'd had difficulty finding the school, or maybe - and this sent a shiver of fear up my spine - maybe Skinner had got to her again. I refused to believe it, but you never know do you?

Kate, the Goth, came up to me at the bar. 'You scared the shit out of me. I didn't know what to do. I forgot my lines and went off in the wrong direction. I want to act with you again.'

I was amazed at my capacity for modesty. 'Oh you know, I doubt if I could ever do it again.'

'Arnold's doing another film. He wants you to be in it.'

'Oh. Well I guess I'll talk to him about it.'

'He's still writing it with some other writer. It's about a priest. He liked the Irish.'

'You mean he'll shoot it in Ireland?'

'Yeah, in Kilburn.'

Tony came up and banged me on the back, 'you're a hidden man, mate. What you having?'

Then Annie, 'Well little brother, I think you found yourself a career if there's anyone brave enough to cast you. Where's Miriam?'

Ah, she couldn't come, she's...' I stopped mid word. Abebi had appeared in the doorway to the street. My face was hardly able to contain itself as she pushed her way towards me. 'Sorry, sorry, couldn't get rid of the guy, then there's the damn trains.' She kissed me on the cheek. I knew she'd come. Always believe in the positive! That's what actors have to do.

'Annie, this is Abebi. My sister, Annie. And this is Tony.'

As I watched them nod hello's and shake hands I was hardly able to speak. Abebi had obviously done herself up for her meeting; her eyes were dark, her lips a deep red and her hair was pulled back behind her ears accentuating the classic lines of her face. She had on a pink silk blouse and a pair of black slacks which showed off her tall, slim and taut figure. She was smiling, open and relaxed. I could see Annie was impressed. Tony was something else. His mouth literally sagged open. For the first time since I'd known him he had run out of words. But not quite. He straightened his broad shoulders, showing off his bulk and said, 'Hi, staying in

London?'

Abebi's eyes sparkled, 'Sure, I'm at the Mayfair Garden.'

'Nice one,' said Tony. 'I'll get you a drink, as my friend here seems a little slow off the mark.'

'I don't think that's so true,' said Abebi.

'Yeah, I heard,' said Tony as he turned to the bar.

Abebi glanced quickly at me, 'Sorry I missed the film.'

'He was great. Great, great, great! And he's our kid!' Annie was proprietorial as she kissed me on the cheek again. Then to top it all, Paul came over with Alexander Hudson behind him. Sir Alexander fucking Hudson came to see my film! I was on cloud nine hundred and ninety-nine, my mouth was dry, my legs were shaking. Alexander put his hands either side of my face and said, 'A presence indeed!' Then he came closer and whispered in my ear, 'And now you must learn control, dear boy. It's called technique.' He smiled and patted my cheek.

My night was full, my year complete, my life perfect. There was nothing else I wanted now that I'd been complimented by Alexander Hudson in front of my sister, my brother-in-law, my best mate and most of all, my dearest darling Abebi. What else on this planet could be better? Fuck the heather and mountains, the breakers and the shore, this was paradise.

Drinks were bought, the presence of the great man seemed to electrify the entire room. Paul introduced Alexander to Arnold who in an excess of bonhomie put his arm round me and announced me as starring in his next film as an Irish priest. On seeing the surprise in my face Alexander smiled knowingly. Soon afterwards he left with Paul and Annie. Tony said he was heading for the the pub and invited me and Abebi to join him. I only wanted to be with Abebi and - probably for the first time ever - turned down a drink in the Calf. Tony kissed Abebi and said, 'Another time.' And was gone.

'Quite a guy,' said Abebi.

'The best.'

I held her hand as we left the school for the short walk to the train station. It was only a couple of stops up the line to my place but I was too nervous to ask her back. She pre-empted me anyway.

'Got to tell you,' she said, 'I had a great meeting. He wants my next book and there could be a big advance so I'll be able to pay you back.'

'Don't worry about that. That's not what I want.' I gently pulled her towards me.

'I want it too, Frankly, but tonight I can't. He wants a précis by tomorrow. I shouldn't even have come, but I wanted to see you.' She put her hand behind my head and pulled my mouth down to her hers. The kiss wasn't as deep and warm as before but it was enough.

'Couldn't you just...?'

'Not tonight. Sorry darling, I want to, but not tonight. Call me, text, whatever. That the train station down there?' She kissed me again and turned away down the road.

I went in the opposite direction. My step was light.

# 23

The manic face of my performance infiltrated my dreams and I hardly slept. Several times in the night I woke in a sweat terrified of myself. I lay trying to calm my beating heart by conjuring the other end of this strange spectrum; the lightness and joy of my feelings for Abebi: the sweet balm of our second kiss, only slightly tempered by its comparison with the first, flowed through me and distilled itself into a huge erection which I didn't want to exploit as it seemed somehow offensive and if anyone was going to relieve the pressure it had to be her. Those solitary longings and the lonely pumping of my wrist now belonged to the past. I was no longer a wanker. These noble thoughts slowly released me from my rage and I finally fell into sleep.

My first thought in the morning was to travel down to Lewisham and buy myself a burger for breakfast in the McDonalds, hoping that a return to the scene of the crime would bring me some understanding of what had flowed through me that day. But it would take me at least two hours to get there, it wasn't raining as it had been, there'd be no Arnold and his crew, and anyway I wanted to see Abebi again, immediately, which meant I had to call her.

Before I could do that I needed to get myself into the right frame of mind. First things first, a shower. Second, put some clothes on that would make me feel better than usual, which meant they needed to be clean although I wasn't going anywhere - not yet anyway - I hadn't ruled out seeing Abebi later in the day. And third? That was more complicated as it meant creating a plan for the day which I wasn't sure I was up to. After steps one and two, the bathroom and a bacon sandwich I found himself washing up. To do this straight after a meal was unheard of; I usually allowed at least two days before doing the dishes, allowing them to fester on the draining board and gain some kind of character as mementos of days past. But now things were different; life was brighter, sharper and would also be cleaner. I mopped the kitchen floor again, tidied the living room, straightened the sofa cushions, threw a pair of shoes into the bottom of my wardrobe, watered a plant, untangled the leads to my printer, considered marking the Year Twelve essays, decided that was going too far, then went out to continue my new fitness regime with a walk by the river.

In the spirit of precise planning I decided to get past the bridge, sit on the bench I'd frequently favoured for a quick cigarette and call Abebi from there. There was no reply and no voicemail either. Maybe she'd left her phone somewhere? No. It was just that she was so single-minded in her pursuit of the finances to repay me that she had her head firmly down into the précis of her undoubtedly brilliant idea for her publisher.

I sent her a text. Hi, it's me. wanted to touch base. when will I see you? Frankly. The problem with a writing a text or an email - I'd noticed this before - was that all the energy and resolve needed to send it was abruptly curtailed the moment you had and all that was left was a blank space waiting for an answer. Most messages weren't a problem, but all the yearning and confusion, not to mention pain, involved in contacting Abebi meant that the blank space felt like an eternity. Now I was staring at the screen, left dangling and anxious, and wishing I hadn't called her in the first place. It takes two to tango and there I was sitting by the river with my arms held out round an empty space.

I lit another cigarette and looked back down the path. There were two figures coming towards me. I soon realised that the girl was Molly Chang and she was with Sophie Rayner. All my thoughts of stardom, Alexander Hudson and Abebi were quickly replaced by the sour smells and clatter of school corridors, classrooms and my fear of Sophie.

'Hullo, Mr Riley,' said Molly as they came up to me.

'Hi Molly. Sophie.'

As far as I was concerned the conversation could have stopped there anxious as I was to return to the tension of waiting for Abebi. And anyway I couldn't think of anything else to say.

'Enjoying the break?' Sophie asked.

'Oh sure, it's a fine day.'

She gave me a friendly smile which I immediately took for a knowing look. Did she know I was aware of her and Tony?

'Er.. seeing Tony Braithwaite later,' God, it was so typical of me to reveal the context of my pre-occupation if not the content. Why can't I keep my mouth shut?

'Oh give him my love,' she said.

I thought that at least I'd wiped the smirk from her face.

'Still not going to Hong Kong,' said Molly sadly.

'Ah, maybe you will, maybe you will.'

'Bye Mr Riley.'

They continued on down the path. I wondered what they were doing together. Sophie clearly took her pastoral responsibilities more seriously than I did. I couldn't help thinking what a beautiful arse she had as they walked away. You didn't normally associate geography teachers with firm backsides. PE instructors for sure. The bums of the history department? There was enough material there for a dissertation, The Teacher's Arse; A View From Behind. And maybe she'd stop having a go at me about George Elliott. Next time she brought it up I'd make it clear that it wasn't my fault that she wasn't on the curriculum. And maybe we could have a drink later to talk about it like a proper man and woman and you never know. Now I had Abebi any woman was within reach.

My phone rang, my heart lit up as the screen did. It plunged as I saw it was a call from someone called Annabelle. I was tempted to turn the phone off when I realised it was Annabelle my fucking agent!

'Hi Francis. That Francis Riley?' She didn't bother to introduce herself, assuming I'd immediately recognise her Kensington tones and leap to attention. 'Look a little bird told me, and this may mean absolutely nothing, but Simon, he's another agent, casts Carter's Way, which I'm sure you'll know. They're shooting this week and there's a smidgeon of a part of a delivery man which they seem to have forgotten, or someone turned it down, who knows? One line. Day after tomorrow, Elstree studios. They don't have time to interview and they trust Simon and Simon trusts me, so there you are. It's carrying a parcel, anyone could do it, so I thought of you. Be there at seven.'

'Ah fuck. What?'

'Carter's Way, darling, been running for years. June

LeGrand and Barry Moss. Director's Allison Taylor, tipped for more, so get on with her and you never know. Get it right and I might consider representing you. Only joking. You were so sweet. I told everyone. They all want to meet the American professor. We're all guessing; Haile Berry? Close? Never mind. Let me know how you get on. Bye.'

I stared at the phone. Me? Television show? Delivering a parcel? You have to be joking. My head was spinning like some crazy top in an Italian realist film. The toy stopped dead and fell sideways to the ground as my phone jumped into life again and a text appeared. Sorry, sorry, can't do tonight. Got to get this thing right. Could be big money and I'm desperate to pay you back. Only got another day here. A xxx.

Three kisses! Well I was certainly going to ask for them in kind. Maybe I'd had the first two? Well anyway I'd make up for it with the third. I stared at the screen. What did she mean, Only got another day here? I thought I'd paid for at least another three. Things were so wild maybe I was getting confused. I texted back. Don't worry about the hotel. I'll pay for another few days. when will I cu?

The reply was immediate, Oh, you're such a lovely guy. Trouble is they want the money in advance. Can you put it direct into my bank account? I'll text details. A xxxx. Four kisses! It was getting better all the time. Then a PS. How about lunch tomorrow after I've seen the publisher? Some place I heard of called Gavroche. Ok? Can you book? Be a celebration my gorgeous Frankly. No more kisses. But I'd see her tomorrow!

The bank details came through and I logged into my account on my phone, shifted my savings into my current and sent her a grand with no more thought than I might have had buying Tony a pint in the Calf. Christ! An acting job and lunch with Abebi! Today must be my birthday. I got up and walked round the bench. Could the sky be any more blue?

I sat down again and glanced along the towpath. Sophie and Molly were sitting on a bench a hundred yards away.

Obviously my cunning, if not snide, mention of Tony had driven Sophie away to reflect on her previous aggressive behaviour towards me. One up for me. I gave himself a mental pat, then rescinded it. The sight of the pair of them brought back the school and the life I was going to abandon. Was I? After one call from someone who might or might not be my agent? I mean you can't know what's going to happen in the future, can you? Did I want to be an actor? Yes. To hell with the fame and money, it was my soul I cared about. Like Miriam said, to be free to be a gardener or work in a pub, to be whatever I liked. But it scared me to death. Anyway, the truth is, it didn't seem to have anything to do with me. I had no grip, events occurred, passed, something else happened, as if I was standing on some kind of moving stairway with no idea of where I was going. I was being swallowed by my own fate. Life at school was maybe ordinary but at least it was secure. Then there was Abebi. I wanted her that was for sure. Her kiss, her caress! Lunch at where was it? I checked my phone. Gavroche. What would we eat? Could I ever have a relationship with such a beauty? Would it last? Or would it all come crashing down? And what then, if I'd already left everything else behind? Au revoir Mr Pontini and Sophie Rayner come to that. Maybe half happiness right now was better than future disaster? These thoughts occupied me for barely a minute. How could I say no to being in a TV show? And to reject Abebi? That was impossible. But still I felt a slight but gnawing anxiety as my phone pinged a text confirming the transfer of the money into her account.

# 24

Carter's Way, according to the internet, was a tale of

suburban folk with nothing much to recommend it other than it had been on afternoon television forever. That was the extent of my research.

'I always knew you had the sun shining out of your arse. Don't ask me why; the rest of you is plug full of constipation,' said Annie, 'I tried to get in it for months and would have done if my fucking husband had managed to talk Louis Foster into taking me on.' She shot a dark look towards Paul who was outside mowing the lawn. Neither of them were working which is why I knew they'd both be in if I called round. There had been no way after hearing from both Annabelle and Abebi within the space of a couple of minutes, that I could bear to sit in my admittedly pristine flat all day. I couldn't think of anything else to clean.

I'd tried Tony but he said he had a cousin and his wife down from Sheffield for the weekend and he was taking them out for a curry. I'd considered Miriam but that was all too complicated. Annabelle and the soap was one thing, but Abebi and Le Gavroche, that was something else. I'd called the restaurant and begged for a table only to be told there weren't any. I pleaded, 'This is a special occasion!' I'd almost cried down the phone, 'She's going back to the States tomorrow, please!' The French maitre d' had relented, 'We always open for the special. It's why we're here.' And we were in. I'd looked at the menu on the internet and blanched whiter than several of the entrees. But in for a penny, in for everything I had. That was the way!

Annie was still going on, 'June LeGrand what a bitch she is. Worked with her once at Windsor. LeGrand by name... used to wear huge scarves and had enormous feet. I'm not kidding you, almost as big as her mouth. And as for Barry Moss, he's got a mean streak. Came here once. Nice enough if you like that sort of thing. They've both been playing the same part for years. Not what I'd call acting. Just being yourself, isn't it? Like getting lines for your own life He probably walks around the kitchen waiting for someone to tell him how to talk to his wife.'

Paul came in from the garden smelling of cut grass. I told him my news.

'He got it through the agency you didn't get me into,' said Annie, 'and that's in spite of me having Louis Foster round here for dinner at least three times.'

'I can't tell them who to represent, Annie.'

'You could have tried harder if you weren't so concerned with what they think of you. I could have been delivering this parcel to June LeGrand.'

'It's a delivery man, Annie,'

'You ever hear of gender free casting? I could have been a delivery person, what difference would it have made? Story of my life, Paul, always held back because I'm a woman and have a husband who doesn't care! Whole thing makes me want to puke!' She clattered a few pans around as she spoke. 'And him, my little brother, gets the part when he has no experience except for a cough and a spit in a film which we got him. For the love of God, what do I have to do to make some kind of way in this fucking profession? I mean I love it, but when you get faced with the reality that anyone can do it, including him...' she gave me a withering look. 'Well it makes you want to give up.'

'Just beginner's luck,' said Paul.

I'd thought they'd be all over me with congratulations. I could even hear a note of envy in Paul's voice.

'I say, "parcel for you, Mrs Carter," that's all.'

'Well you'll meet her then,' said Annie. 'She'll take it off you and spit in your eye.'

I stayed on for dinner. Their attitude to me was no longer affectionately condescending and I could see that they were more than a little irked, not so much by my delivery man, but because Annabelle seemed to have taken me on as a client. Or maybe me getting a job somehow made them feel rejected. I tried to flatter Paul by appealing to his superior experience.

'I mean how do you do it anyway?'

'Play a delivery man? Read the script, darling. Study it, look for the clues, the subtext, find out who you are. What's his name for a start.'

'Delivery man.'

'Not a lot to go on is it?'

'All I've got.'

'Where's he from?'

'A van. Or a bike. I don't know.'

'Well find out, Francis, you're the actor,' said Annie. 'It's your job.'

'How do I find out?'

'You've no gumption, have you?'

'Research,' said Paul, 'It's always the key to finding a character.'

'You mean get a bike and deliver a few parcels?'

'Look when I was the lawyer in Sparkbrook, which had an audience of three point four million by the way, somewhat more than Carters Way I'd say. Anyway I actually followed a real criminal lawyer for a week and learnt all the tricks. By the time I'd finished I actually could have been the real thing. People used to come up to me in the street...'

'We know all about that, Paul,' said Annie. 'You can't expect him to follow a delivery man around for a week, can you?'

'Don't have the time anyway. It's on Friday.'

'There you are,' said Annie, 'Just learn your line and be professional.'

Finally Paul poured me a shot of his favourite brandy to celebrate and that seemed to be the end of the conversation about my acting.

'But hey, I've got to tell you about Abebi. We're going to get lunch in Le Gavroche tomorrow!'

'Taking out a mortgage, are you?' said Annie.

# 25

See there's these two brothers called Roux, they're French, dead now, or maybe one, I don't know. They started it or their father did. That's him.' I pointed up to an oil painting of a chef with a beard hanging on the wall above our table. 'French. One of the top three cuisines in the world with the Chinese and Indian,' I added knowledgeably having read it on the internet.

'You seem to know a lot about it,' said Abebi looking round at the dark panelled walls and impeccably laid tables each with its own gold centrepiece. We'd been treated like royalty from the moment we'd entered Le Gavroche. and she was impressed. The maitre d' had come up to us as we'd sat on the tartan sofa in the reception. 'Ah the special occasion. Mr Riley I think.' He'd made it sound like I was a regular.

'It's nice of you to remember.' I grinned.

'And may I ask what the occasion is?' he asked.

I felt a gaiety and ease with everything in general. I extravagantly gestured to Abebi, who as usual was looking gorgeous. 'Here it is, Monsieur, Professor Abebi Musa from Baltimore and Los Angeles.'

'Ah such a beautiful woman,' said the Maitre d.' 'You are to be married perhaps?'

'God no!' said Abebi, then she reached over and took my hand,' Good friends,' she said. Very good friends. For now.' She gave me a brilliant smile.

The Maitre d', who seemed to have some experience and understanding of the situation, nodded and said, 'Well Monsieur Riley perhaps we can offer you one of our own cocktails. On the 'ouse.' He glanced to his right and a waiter appeared as if out of nowhere. 'Marcel, Le Gavroche sour for Madam et Monsieur.' The waiter disappeared as quickly as he'd arrived. The Maitre smiled again, 'Please enjoy your lunch.'

With a start like that I was prepared to ignore Abebi's fierce rejection of any marital prospects. I looked at her longingly, 'How's the cocktail?'

'Some kind of sherry?' she said.

'With lemon or something.'

'Don't usually drink,' she said, draining her glass.

Once at our table she perused the wine list.

'Your choice.' It wasn't a wise thing to say. 'Go ahead, it's a special day. There's your book and my TV show and here we are. Anything you like.'

'Well I'm not going to wipe you out,' she said, and chose a Bordeaux at ninety pounds. I paled briefly to the colour of the tablecloth but was too elated at just being with her to comment.

'You are such a priceless guy, Frankly,' she said raising her glass after the sommelier had poured. She ran the wine round the glass, sniffed it, and drank half of it in one gulp. 'Sorry what I said to the guy out there, you know. I didn't mean it like that. You're gonna be a great husband.'

'Ah but who to?' I asked with a mischievous smirk.

'Who can tell?' She gave me a knowing look and finished the rest of her glass.

I kept up with her, drink for drink, and we'd ordered another bottle, this time a Burgundy, before the main course had arrived.

'Maybe I should tell you about the publishing deal? she said and then described it at great length as the venison melted in my mouth. Her prospects excited her. The new book was going to be a sequel to The Truth We Tell sub-titled, Going Deeper. 'I want to get right down there, Frankly, right underneath it all.'

'Well you can start with me,' I said. 'I'd like to have a look round down there myself.'

'Well you never know I might write up a case study. I haven't got the structure yet, but I'll be in touch!' She raised her glass.

I could see the alcohol was having its effect; her eyes were sparkling and her cheeks going red. We finished the second bottle and without a glance at me she nodded over to the sommelier and ordered a third, this time another white to go with the dessert.

'So does all this mean you'll be around for a while?'

'I wish I could but I have to get back to Baltimore. There's people I have to see and there's a place I have up in the hills where I write. I need the peace to concentrate.'

I was with her as we walked under the trees, fished in the lake and made love every night when she finally concentrated on me.

'So does that mean, I mean, how long will you stay here?'

'Oh about a week I guess. I can't tell you how much I appreciate it, Frankly. I talked to them at the hotel and got a smaller room which gives me a few more days I guess. Thank you baby.' She touched my hand and gestured across the restaurant. 'And for all this. I'm just a plain old American girl and this is quite something.'

And it was. I looked round at the other diners. I had expected it all to be hushed and serious as they covered topics far out of my reach, but in fact their chatter was loud and joyous as if they were all congratulating themselves on being there. I couldn't imagine exactly socialising on a regular basis with them - they weren't like the drinkers in the Calf - but there they were sitting a few feet from me, the golden ornaments on each table glittered sparkling reflections on their faces as they happily laughed away their rich and privileged lives. Given a fair wind I could maybe be joining them every day for luncheon darling, gazing into the dark eyes - getting darker by the minute - of this gorgeous professor who was discussing her next book on the inner workings of the mind of man. What could be better? In fact I was only half listening to her, preferring just to inhale her presence and imagine our future, the house, the lake, the long soulful walks, the natural world, when my thoughts were suddenly interrupted by another entirely unexpected vision. A woman in a bright pink sari was standing over us and was leaning in to whisper in my ear. 'As a matter of fact I think it will be two point one million by the end of the year,' she said.

There was this Indian woman standing over us. I didn't know who she was. Yes I did. She was the one who'd received the hon. doctorship from Barr-Lyons. I stood up too quickly, rocked to one side and touched the table for support. 'Ah, Mrs...' I'd forgotten her name.

'Monica Mahdpuri,' she smiled. 'I remember you being interested in exactitude.' she said, 'so I thought I'd bring you up to date.'

'This is Professor Musa,' I said.

'And what a beauty,' Mrs Mahdpuri clasped her hands over her chest. 'Where are you from?'

'I'm American,' said Abebi. There was something hostile about her response. 'My dad was Nigerian if that's what you're asking.'

'Heritage, my dear. Don't be insulted, it's the most important thing we have. They see the colour of our skin and they get defensive.' She gestured to the restaurant full of the white rulers of the universe sitting contented and self-satisfied around them. 'I could show them a thing or two and I think you probably could too. Things they don't understand, you see? I'm sure you do.'

Abebi laughed, her anger gone. 'Good to meet you, Mrs Mahdpuri,' she said.

The Indian smiled down at me and nodded towards Abebi. 'Watch her,' she said. 'She will go far.' She indicated the entrance. 'So will I. As far as Tooting Bec anyway. My husband is waiting. We all disguise our origins don't we? But they are the source of our delight! Goodbye my dear.'

'Francis. Francis Riley.'

'Goodby Francis.' And she was gone.

I sat more heavily than I'd intended. 'She makes baby clothes and car parts. How can you make millions out of that?' This old world was getting stranger by the minute. Abebi was smiling at me. Was that love I could see in her eye?

'You seem to know a lot of people,' she said.

'Don't know how,' I said. 'Shall we go?'

I paid the bill on my credit card. It was nearly five hundred and I barely blinked and congratulated myself on having plastic money. What a great idea, a flexible friend!

I held her tight on the pavement outside thinking how much I loved Mayfair and especially all the hushed traffic; and then there were the footsteps of its denizens on the concrete; how solid and friendly they sounded. She kissed the side of my face then my mouth, my third kiss since I'd known her. It was less full and warm than the previous two, but my doubts faded as her body arched towards mine. I could feel the shape of her thighs and even more so, the response in mine.

'Let's go to your hotel,' I said.

'God I want to, Frankly, I can't tell you how much I want to.' She stroked my hair and kissed me again. The fourth time. When would I stop counting? There was a black cab coming conveniently around the corner and I shouted full and strong, 'Taxi!' Finally I was the mature man who could discuss property prices in Geneva. The cab came to a halt and I helped her inside. I somehow missed my footing and ended up kneeling on the floor of the passenger compartment.

The Cabbie turned, 'What's going on?'

I scrabbled up and sat next to Abebi. 'Sorry mate wet leaves in the gutter.'

I put my arm along the back of the seat and she slid over towards me. I gave the address of her hotel and pulled her face up to mine for a long languorous kiss. I'd definitely stopped counting now. She lay her head back on the seat and I let my tongue do the work as she nestled her face into my neck and I could feel the warmth of her breath under my ear.

She sucked the lobe as I held her as close and tight as I could. Slowly her muzzling quietened and I realised she was asleep. I didn't mind. It was always possible for me to make anything worse by talking. I was where I wanted to be, why ruin it? She lay quiet in my arms until we reached the hotel, when I gently shook her. She raised her head and opened her eyes seeming surprised that she was in a cab, let alone at her hotel.

'What?' she said.

'We're here,' I opened the door to get out, this time determined to stay upright and passed a tenner through the open window. 'Keep the change.'

'It's seventeen,' said the Cabbie.

'Ah, sorry.' I gave him another tenner and told him to keep the change from that one as well.

I reached along the back seat to help her out of the cab. She crouched toward me then stepped awkwardly down on to the pavement. I was holding her arm but not firmly enough to prevent her stumbling. Her right leg gave way and she staggered away from me. I yanked her back and brought her face to face, but my grip wasn't strong enough. She fell backwards ending up sitting on the bottom of the hotel steps with her back to the doors and with a look of surprise on her face.

'Oh God, I told you I never drink.'

I slammed the door of the taxi as it pulled away, then went and helped her up oblivious to the laughter of a couple passing by.

'You ok?'

'I don't know where I am.'

'You're at your hotel. I'll get you up to your room.'

'No, no.' She pushed me away and managed to stand up, concentrating hard on remaining vertical. 'I've got to go and lie down.'

'I'll get you up there.'

'I know how to do it, Frankly. She pointed at the entrance. 'I go through there and down that funny little corridor, I push the button for the elevator, I go in and push another button for the fourth floor.' She was concentrating hard. 'Then I wait till the elevator arrives and the door opens and I just walk out and I turn right, no left, get to my door and use this!' She produced her key card from her bag. 'Then I fall on my bed and go to sleep.'

'Abebi?'

She was already turning away. 'You're so great, Frankly.' The hotel doors swung closed behind her.

As I watched her disappear I was aware of a big red bus passing behind me and the buildings above slanting strangely in a day that was as bright as any I'd ever known.

## 26

I managed to get myself out of bed at five in the morning and make my way to the bus stop with one thought on my mind, Elstree Studios. What was I supposed to wear? What did a delivery man look like? I imagined some kind of contemporary superhero in a black helmet and green lycra, but didn't possess any of that and would feel stupid on the bus. Maybe it should be the old anorak again? Hang on, this was television for God's sake, not Arnold on Lewisham High Street. They'd give me a costume wouldn't they? I put on the anorak just in case and did my best to pull myself together as I walked down the street.

The first light was coming up silhouetting the rooftops and leaving the fronts of the houses still slumbering. More Dylan Thomas. Not useful. Then the sun came along, bright and cheery as I sat on the top deck of the bus. I ran through the route to Elstree that I'd planned the previous morning before seeing Abebi. The Gavroche seemed like a golden glittering vision of some long lost past. I remembered the

Maitre d' smiling at me, that Indian woman, what was her name? The wine slipping down, the kiss in the cab (fourth or fifth?), the hotel steps - what was that all about? I'd had the prize in my hands and let it slip as usual. I got down from the bus and clattered west on the train. I knew for a fact that her kisses were real. Hadn't she even put her hand on my leg? I saw the doors of the hotel swing shut behind her like the sudden end of a beautiful dream.

Well here was another one coming up fast. I was about to enter a television studio and had no idea what to expect. I got down from the train, took another bus, watching the electronic sign ahead of me. It pinged and a woman's voice said, 'Elstree Studios.' I stepped out through the doors as they folded back and suddenly every doubt I'd had ran redhot up my spine. I didn't know who I was, what I was or why I was there; I was falling back down the mountain; I wanted to go home and reached back towards the bus as it pulled away. I didn't know what to do. I looked up at the gates in front of me. The just seemed like ordinary gates. To hell with it. Why don't I just step through them? I was immediately stopped by a security guard.

A phone call later and a young woman in tight red pants and a clipboard was walking quickly towards me. 'Hi I'm Amelia, second assistant, and you're Francis Riley. This way.'

She led me towards the studio which I'd thought would resemble the magnificent facades of MGM or Paramount I'd seen in the movies; instead I was faced with a featureless grey block which looked more like a warehouse. I followed Amelia through a small set of double doors behind a row of green garbage bins and passed down a long beige corridor, then another, just walls, no people or anything even vaguely human. Finally we came to a smaller passage which at least had a few doors leading off it. Amelia opened one of them. 'This is your dressing room.' It wasn't much bigger than a cupboard. She pointed to a rack. 'And that's your costume. The director will come and see you soon. The green room's down there. Get a coffee if you want.' She turned round and left.

I sat on the one chair and looked into the mirror. I vaguely remembered Annabelle mentioning the director was called Allison Taylor who was destined for great things; and I knew that the green room was where the actors sat around before going on set. I looked at my costume which turned out to be an anorak like the one I was wearing, and a pair of jeans also like my own. I tried the jeans on and found they were too small so decided to stick with my own. I was as nervous as hell. A middle-aged man poked his head round the door. 'Costume alright?'

'They're a bit tight.'

'Look alright to me.'

'These are my own.'

'Fine.' The man went.

I'd decided to get myself a coffee when a tall energetic man with long hair, a moustache, and dressed entirely in blue denim came in followed by Amelia.

'Hi Tony.'

'I'm Francis.'

'I'm the director, Pete Lucas.'

'Oh I thought it was Allison...'

'Moved on to pastures new. Sorry you've got me.'

'Pete was the first for five years,' said Amelia proudly. 'He knows the show backwards.'

'He was the what?'

'Anyway,' said Pete. 'You got your script?'

I produced my folded page from the back pocket of my jeans. It looked crumpled and unprofessional: Annie would not have approved, she kept all her scripts in a smart black folder. I gave mine to Pete Lucas.

'Christ this is 4A. Why hasn't he got the latest?'

'Maybe in the recast...' said Amelia.

'What did you say your name was?'

'Francis.'

'You're not Tony?'

'He broke his leg,' said Amelia.

'Break a leg, hey?' I said. 'Lucky for some!'

'This is 4C,' said Amelia. She gave me a new page.

'Go through it with me,' said Pete. 'We're scheduled for nine.' He read from the script. She opens the door.

'What?'

'That's Mrs Carter, June LeGrand. She opens the door. You?' He nodded encouragingly to me. I was scanning the page and the several lines I'd never seen before. Pete said again, 'You?'

'Ah I've got a parcel for you.'

'Who are you?' said Pete as Mrs Carter.

It was slowly dawning on me that the delivery man's one line had been increased to three. 'You want me to say all these?'

'Yes, it's the new script.'

'Sorry,' said Amelia, 'we were expecting Tony. I guess we sent him the re-writes.'

'Right let's do it.' Pete looked at me expectantly. 'The door opens.'

'Ah, a parcel for you.' My voice was shaking. The unexpected trebling of the size of my part had thrown me badly.

'You're not going to do it like that, are you?'

'I've never done this before.'

'Jesus, who sent him?'

'Tony's agent,' said Amelia. 'Wasn't me, talk to casting.'

'Well we'll just have to make the best of it, won't we?' Pete gave me a sad look. I breathed in deeply, planted my feet squarely on the blue lino and took an imaginary parcel from beneath my arm. 'I've got a parcel for you...'

'...Mrs Carter.'

'What? She says, Mrs Carter?'

'No, you do, Your line's been extended,' said Amelia. 'Mrs Carter, June, thought she should know all the delivery boys.'

'Did she? Why?' I didn't know about TV prima donnas.

'You'll have to ask her,' said Pete drily. 'Read the script.'

I did and spoke more loudly this time. Somewhere in the back of my mind I felt pleased that June LeGrand wanted to know more about me. 'I've got a parcel for you, Mrs Carter.'

'Oh Alfie, how nice to see you again.'

'I'm Alfie am I? That's good I've got a name now.' It cheered me up no end. I'd known a boy at school called Alfie who was much taller than me and had big ears. We used to call him "Lummox" because he was always crashing into things. I immediately adopted Alfie's stumbling bass voice. A character! Annie would have been proud. I repeated my line.

'How nice to see you again, Alfie.'

'And you, Mrs Carter.' I wondered if I might try a wink but thought maybe I should hold back until I was in front of the camera.

Pete and Amelia, seemed satisfied with this new and improved delivery man and left me to it, so I decided to go to the green room which turned out to be like a cheap hotel reception with worn pink walls. I poured myself a coffee, took a couple of biscuits and sat in the corner on an old settee. There were two other actors sitting on the other side of the room. They were both reading their scripts and mouthing lines; one of them experimenting with extravagant gestures. I was still nervous but felt happy. There I was sitting in an actor's green room in a TV studio.

A make-up girl took me out and planted me in front of a mirror for five minutes while she dabbed my face with a dry sponge and combed my hair. 'You look good,' she said. And I wanted to agree with her; the soft lights around the mirror gave me a healthy glow and my hair shone. Francis the movie star.

Amelia came in to take me onto the set. The Carter home had been constructed in the centre of the cavernous studio. It was surrounded by cameras and hundreds of lights were hung above like great eyes waiting to open and shine on me. Amelia took me round to the side of the set to the Carter's front entrance. As I walked up the garden path a battery of lights came on and I thought for a moment I was outside some gigantic doll's house with a shiny brown door and golden knocker. Technicians were working quickly around me as I stepped over cables towards Pete Lucas who gave me my opening mark. After the fiasco on the Lewisham pavement I was well prepared for that. A camera was positioned behind me and a sound boom hovered above. I was amazed at the speed with which it was all happening. Pete went up to the front door and disappeared inside. I could hear voices from behind the door and realised that one of them belonged to the great Miss LeGrand. I stood on my mark and wondered if I was going to meet her before our scene together. Apparently not. Pete came out onto the path again and shut the door behind him.

'Right, ready to go.'

I noticed how unnaturally green the plastic foliage around the door looked under the lights. I thought it was probably best that I hadn't met June before the scene. Now I'd see her first as Mrs Carter and I would be forever her Alfie. Francis Riley? Forget it. Here, standing right here amid the luminous flora was none other than the great Lummox from Kilburn High.

'You go up to the front door and ring the bell,' said Pete. 'We'll take the scene in one. We may as well record the rehearsal. Shouldn't be too much of a problem. Don't worry we can do it a couple of times anyway.' He glanced at his watch.' But that's it.' He turned to the team around him. 'Alright. Camera, sound, action.'

I knew what that meant alright. I tucked my parcel firmly under my arm, marched up to the door and rang the bell. which chimed with a predictable suburban ding dong. And far quicker than I expected - too quick; everybody would think Mr Carter had been hiding behind the door - and there she was, June LeGrand, Mrs Carter in person. Her face was covered in orange pancake, her lips a deep red, her large eyes encased in dark blue mascara. All of it was topped by a messily contrived thatch of blond hair fetchingly tweaked to give this obviously older woman the appearance of gay carefree youth. But what shocked me most was her lack of inches. I'm not tall but compared to her I was a giant. Even standing above me in the doorway she was a good six inches shorter. Behind her and positioned close to her left shoulder was a huge camera pointing directly at me. I loved it; it excited me in the same way that John French's camera had. I suddenly felt alive.

'Parcel for you, Mrs Carter.' The deep, sombre tones of Alfie Canning had merged with my own lighter notes which once again had become Irish. Alfie was like Scarborough the detective, except this time instead of the rage there was an excess of charm and generosity. I didn't get it. I didn't care.

'Oh Alfie, how nice to see you again,' said Mrs Carter. Her face crinkled from within the ring of mascara and her mouth turned up at the corners in a wry smile.

'And you, Mrs Carter.' And then I couldn't help himself. I winked. I hadn't told myself to do it, it just happened like it was natural.

There was a pause. I saw a look of uncertainty pass over June LeGrand's face. I'd made a terrible mistake. My dreams crashed, Hollywood disintegrated, I was going to be humiliated in a way that only Francis Riley could. Her uncertainty became confusion and then suddenly she smiled in delight.

'Oh you're such a sweetie, Alfie.' This wasn't in the script and I was expecting an angry' Cut!' But there was only a silence which seemed to last for minutes but was probably less than a second, and Mrs Carter slowly and sexily winked back.

'Ah yer great, Mrs Carter.'

'And you tell those boys back at the depot that I want you

to deliver all my parcels from now on!' She inclined her head coquettishly.

That wasn't in the script either, none of it was in the script but I knew I had to go with it. 'I will, Mrs Carter, don't you worry about that! I'd deliver your parcels all day! Bye now.'

'Bye darling, see you again.' She gave me a great, flirty smile and stepped back as she closed the door.

'Cut!'

Pete Lucas stood up from behind the monitor as the door opened again and June LeGrand came back into the light. 'That was fuckin' marvellous!' Her semi-posh suburban accent had become a broad cockney. 'And I'm not doing it again, Pete.'

'It was a rehearsal,' said Pete.

'If the camera's ok. Are they?

Both the camera operators nodded as Pete looked down at his monitor. 'Yeah, sure,' he said.

'Then that's it. You can't beat perfection. What's your name, darling?'

'Er, Alfie. Francis. Francis Riley.'

'One take wonder, you are. Fuckin' brilliant darling. Thank you. Thank you!' She disappeared again behind the door as the camera behind me was rolled away and the boom above my head soared off into the darkness.

'Thanks Tony,' said Pete, as his monitor was pushed round to the other side of the set. 'Kitchen, scene twelve, shots 24 to 28 .' The lights went down and he was gone. They'd all gone. I was left looking down at the cables as they writhed across the studio floor to connect up to other cameras shooting other actors in other scenes. I wanted to be in them.

I sat in the green room not wanting to go home, but no-one talked to me so after a while I wandered off to the bus stop wearing the new old anorak I'd been given for the delivery man and leaving my old old anorak I'd worn for Detective Scarborough hanging on the rail in the dressing room.

## 27

It was still only four o'clock in the afternoon when I got back to my flat and I didn't know what to do. I stretched out on my sofa and considered gawping at pensioner's TV with my mouth hanging open and dribble on my chin and thought maybe I should give it a miss. Now I knew why actors couldn't relax after a performance; there was still too much adrenalin pumping through their veins and all they wanted to do was eat drink and be loud in restaurants until they were exhausted. There was nowhere I could go. Tony would still be with his cousins from the north and I knew Miriam wouldn't appreciate a call at that time of day. I considered a solitary pint in the Calf but the pub would be empty and I didn't want to stand at the bar not being able to tell anyone about my triumphant morning with June LeGrand.

What I really wanted was Abebi and another drunken lunch in Le Gavroche, with this time a glorious finale of riotous, beautiful sex on the bed in her hotel room. What a day it had been in the studio and all that, and it was still barely half way through. Yet again the Irish had just spilled out like the release of some ancient energy which didn't seem to have any thought or will, or come to that, a script. It was like the expression of some kind of sheer joy at just being there. Or at being someone else? I was just overjoyed at not being me? Maybe that was it. I didn't want to go there, it was all too complicated. I could hear Paul telling me that I lacked discipline; acting was an art and it wasn't enough to just release the turbulence in yourself; it required shape and form and most of all it required control. But the truth was, I didn't want to control it, I wanted the release, I loved the wildness of it! But then I had to face it, I had no real idea of what I was doing, no thoughts about what I was saying, or what would come next out of my mouth. If June LeGrand hadn't gone along with me it could have all ended in disaster. But she had, she'd grabbed the moment like I did. I would loved to have talked to her about it, to know what she thought of this crazy unknown suddenly winking at her. My gut creased in embarrassment at what I'd done, but at the same time I suspected that June LeGrand knew exactly what was happening and had enjoyed it as much as I had. You can say what you like about soap stars, but they couldn't have stayed there at the top without knowing what acting was all about. June knew, like Alexander, that it all started from some madness in yourself. Where else? But once you'd let it all out, then you had to control it without destroying it; according to Paul anyway.

I got up and walked round the room. There were too many thoughts rushing round my brain, more adrenalin I guess, bubbling around and driving me crazy for the want of doing something. I went into the kitchen and opened a bottle of red wine then sat back on the sofa and lit a cigarette. My phone rang. I looked at the screen. It was Abebi. My heart leapt.

'Abebi, I was just thinking about you. God I've had this day. I was at Elstree...'

She cut in, I could tell she was a little crazy herself. 'Oh Frankly I'm so excited! Everything is coming together. John Sheridan, the publishing guy, called. His company is huge and he's talking about an advance of fifty grand. Fifty! Can you imagine it? I'll be able to pay you back and keep myself for a while when I write it and no more conferences! I could maybe even get a sabbatical and write the book here. Maybe I could stay near you, that would be so good.'

'Oh that'd be great, Abebi. I could look for a place...'

'Look I'm so sorry about yesterday. I've never been drunk like that before. I didn't know what I was doing. And you were so good to me. God, I hit that bed and didn't come round for eight hours and boy what a headache. But I'm ok now especially since John Sheridan called. Everything's just wow shit! And you, Frankly, I'm so happy I met you. You're not like the others, I mean any other guy. It's all so good. How would you feel about me staying on to write the book?'

'You mean the UK? You mean here?'

'Yeah!'

'That would be so fantastic, Abebi.'

'I mean I like your little town, it's kinda quiet and peaceful like my place out in the hills and I could get on with things.'

'Listen, we should celebrate all this and I'll tell you about my scene with June LeGrand.'

'Who?'

'She's a soap star, great actress...'

'Yeah, let's do that. Maybe we could go away for a few days next week. Would you like that, Frankly?'

'Like it! I'd love it. Where d'you want to go?'

'Ok, just let me get through this weekend. John Sheridan wants a full treatment, like a synopsis, and maybe the first chapter. He says his editor won't go ahead without something being a little more fixed. God, I guess I should find an agent to negotiate all this for me. Or maybe I should do it myself. You know, I've been too weak in my life, Frankly, always relying on other people.'

'Tell me about it.'

'Well I guess it's time we both changed, right? We can both become more self-reliant, except with each other. I can rely on you, can't I, Frankly?'

'Oh you can, That would be grand. And a few days next week. We could find somewhere to stay in the country somewhere.'

'Yeah, let's do it. Just let me get through this weekend like I say. But Frankly, there's one thing. I need to ask you a favour.'

'Anything, darling.'

'God it's nice to hear you say that. Darling. Thank you, darling. Listen I got a call from the guy who owns my apartment in Baltimore. Like I know I'm behind in the rent and he's saying unless I pay up he's going to throw me out. Can you imagine that? I've been there four years and now he's threatening to evict me!'

'How much do you need?'

'Could you make another fifteen hundred? Then I'd be clear of him and be able to stay over longer. Maybe instead of a few days in the country we could make it a week. Oh God, Frankly, I'd love that! A whole week with you, the book proposal in and getting finalised and nothing to worry about. Could you do that? I'd just love you forever if you'd help me now.'

'Don't worry about it. Don't worry about a thing.' I'd said it before I'd thought it.

'You have my bank details?'

'Sure I'll do it. But this'll have to be the last, sweetheart, I'm coming to the end of....' I was thinking about Tony, You insane pal?

'Oh I know, honey, and you're so great about it. I promise I won't ask again and you'll get it all back with interest.'

'I wouldn't want any of that.' And Miriam's pitiful look.

'I know you wouldn't, but you'll get it anyway, Would you still have enough for a few days in the country?'

'I think I could just about manage that.' I didn't care. I wanted her too much. How much would I pay for a week with her? Everything.

'And do you think you could transfer it this afternoon, then I can get it off to Baltimore?'

'No problem.' And it wasn't. It was about the easiest thing I'd ever done.

'Then we're away, Frankly! Anywhere you like. Can you find us somewhere? From Monday? Sorry I'm asking you to do everything, but if I can concentrate I think I can get the first chapter done over the next couple of days. How about

Stratford on Avon? We could maybe take in some theatre.'

'I'd love it.'

'I'll leave it with you. Wherever you want to go, so do I.'

'Don't worry. I'll put the money into your account right now.' And I was tapping the keys of my phone as I spoke..

'Oh Frankly, I love you. Talk soon, baby.'

'Talk soon, sweetheart.' A fool for love? Maybe I was. And maybe I wasn't. I was in no state to tell.

I sat back on the sofa. 'Oh Frankly, I love you.'

She'd said it.

## 28

So I had a free weekend ahead of me. My fitness regime demanded another walk by the river and there was an anxiety in the pit of my gut which demanded a serious consideration of my finances. I'd somehow gone through over four thousand in just over a week and I was down to the last few hundred in my savings account which I hoped would be enough for our trip. But I was feeling nervous and could imagine what Tony would say. And I didn't dare tell Miriam. The problem being I was going to need her. The cottages to rent on the internet were outside my budget and all I could afford was to drive around to various Airbnbs. But I didn't have a car. And Miriam did. Would she lend it to me? Probably, but she wouldn't be so keen if she knew it was for me and Abebi. The ancient jealousy would resurface. I thought about it for a few minutes and decided to call her to test the water. As usual she was too busy to talk. Theo had asked her to help him clear up the conference. 'You wouldn't believe the paperwork,' she said. 'And then he's taking me out to dinner tonight as a thank you. Kind of him, don't you think?'

'The least he could do.' Even now I was irritated at the thought of her being with Skinner, but buried it as usual; not that it fooled Mitzy.

'I know you don't like him, Francis.'

'Well he hates me, what do you expect?'

'He hardly knows you.'

'And has he made any effort to do something about that?'

I wanted to tell her about the studio but thought I'd save it till we met. We arranged to do so the next day for a coffee on the High Street. Thinking about it I realised the fact that she was seeing Skinner could work in my favour, balancing any resentment she might have about Abebi. And if I played it right, without too many details, I might be able to finesse the loan of her car. Things were looking up.

That left the rest of the day. I thought of popping in to see Annie and Paul and telling them about my day with June LeGrand but on second thoughts didn't think it was such a great idea. I wasn't in the right state of mind to concentrate on school work so I ended up on a bench by the river again; a different one this time, as I didn't want my life to be too predictable. I stretched my legs out in front of me, lit a cigarette and watched as people passed me by on the towpath. I felt good. The day after tomorrow I'd be sitting in Mitzy's Mini with Abebi in the passenger seat like I was Jack Kerouac on the road with my girl. It would have been better if we'd been driving along the Big Sur but you can't have everything, and Hertfordshire was pretty interesting at this time of the year. Maybe after we'd made love, under an oak tree perhaps with acorns tapping down as romantic accompaniment, Annabelle would call with more work. What a life.

A young family with three kids dressed in circus colours walked by. A ball rolled to my feet and I kicked it back to a little boy who stared at me with wide blue eyes before picking it up. I smiled back as the kid ran off to take his mother's hand. Our little boy is kicking his ball and grinning up at me and Abebi as we crunch across the sand in our free and easy flipflops on Venice Beach. We walk towards the sea as the breakers break and the foam splashes over my storybook future. My latest book had been optioned for a movie, there's the possibility I'll direct ... The sun beat on my head. Four teenage boys on bikes whizzed by. A month ago if you'd told me that I'd wipe out my savings on a woman I hardly knew I'd have had a good laugh. Was Tony right when he said I was insane? Was I going to regret all this? A riverboat passed festooned with red, blue and white flags. Go with the flow, son, go with the flow, let it all happen. A girl on her own went by wearing very short shorts and looking thoughtful and reminding me of the girl in Jonny's with legs up to her armpits. Women. No problem. Legs that could go anywhere. Two gay men held their heads smartly high as if they didn't care what anyone thought. Why should I care what anyone thought? The old Francis was breaking apart, but not in a bad way; the curtain was lifting, there were new worlds there on the stage beyond. All I had to do was step through. Some old Doors song, Break on Through to the Other Side sung in my head. But the other side was scary. Carter's Way was frightening. Abebi terrified me. She was way ahead of me. Why couldn't I take the initiative and lead for once in my life like Mr Pontini said? I had a mind, I could learn, I had a body, I could run, I could even take on June LeGrand. What was stopping me? I wanted to see my dad and ask him what it was like to take a leap. How good would it be to drive Abebi to Cork and introduce her to my family? I didn't have the money for a start, and anyway I wasn't sure enough of her. Is that right? I'm not certain of her? Oh fuck, this uncertainty, this fucking mind, fuck the mind. Why couldn't I live in the spirit and just be joyous on this sunny day?

I got up from the bench and wandered back along the towpath, looking carefully into faces as they passed me by. Beneath the smiles, the chat, the silence, they were all solitary with lights flashing in their heads. Just themselves, like me.

# 29

I spent the Sunday in much the same mood, staring at the walls, watching TV, lying out on my sofa, letting thoughts float with no end to the flow and no organisation or meaning to it either. They were flotsam, they were jetsam? What's the difference? I knew but couldn't be bothered to say. Around six o'clock I pulled on my trainers and went out to meet Miriam. Whatever stratagems I'd invented to both borrow the car and avoid telling her about Abebi were forgotten, along with any notions of breaking through doors onto the other side and my rosy future. I was just kind of vacant, don't know why; sometimes you just are, like your mind is asking questions you can't hear.

Miriam was waiting for me at a table outside the Flying Duck, or the Dying Fuck as Tony and just about everybody else who took a coffee there called it. The cafe was opposite Guiseppe's the Italian we'd all been to after Abebi's paper. I sat opposite Mitzy and ordered an Americano and a glass of red wine being as it was virtually evening already. Where had the day gone? Miriam eyed me as I drank half the glass in one.

'Don't start, Mitzy.'

'I'm not. You can drank as much as you like.'

'How was it with Skinner?'

'He was charming. He wanted to thank me, that's all.'

'Didn't make a pass at you?'

'He flirted. What did you expect?'

'And you batted your big eyes.'

'And then we went home.' She took a sip of her coffee. There was something about her face that worried me. She'd never been very good at hiding her feelings and I could see there was something there that wasn't so good. I thought she was going to have a subtle go at me about Abebi.

'What's up?'

'Nothing.'

'You sure?' I leant forward on the table. It wasn't particularly private; the pavement that ran alongside us was busy; Sunday traffic was cruising past; day trippers looking for somewhere to park before going down to the river. Miriam looked across the road to Guiseppe's which was beginning to fill up for the early evening trade.

'Why are they all drinking that orange stuff?'

'They're Aperol Spritzers.,' she said. 'You had one when we were in Bruges.'

'Don't remember.'

'You never do. Professor Musa was in there last night.'

'Abebi? In Bruges?'

'Giuseppe's'

'Abebi was in Guiseppe's?'

'Yes. She was inside.'

'No she wasn't, Mitzy.'

'How do you know?'

'Because I know where she was.'

'You seem to know a lot about her movements.'

'As a matter of fact she was at her hotel writing the first chapter of her book. She's been doing it all weekend, she told me.'

'She told you?'

'Yes, Miriam, she told me.'

'Well she wasn't doing it last night, Frankie. She was in there.' Miriam pointed over to Guiseppe's She was at a table in that alcove by the door. I was outside with Theo and we saw her through the window.'

'I don't believe it.'

'Why wouldn't she be there?'

I didn't know how to answer that. Maybe she'd come to town trying to find me? She didn't have my address and she'd probably looked in the Calf and seeing I wasn't there had tried the only other place she knew, the Italian. 'She was on her own?'

Miriam looked down. There was an ominous look of kindness in her eye. 'No Francis, she was with Tony.'

'Tony?' Abebi had been in town with my best mate? This was all too much information too quick. 'She was with Tony?'

'Yes.'

'Did you talk to her?'

'Theo wanted too, but...'

'But what?'

Miriam paused and cleared her throat. 'They seemed very involved with each other.'

'Abebi and Tony?'

'I'm sorry. I had a feeling this was going to hurt you. Sorry Frankie. Theo was smirking as usual so I stopped him going in to talk to them.'

'Maybe you should have let him find out what they were doing.'

'They seemed very close.'

I sat back in my chair. What was I supposed to say? There was just a blank in my head. 'Tony and Abebi, well I didn't expect that. Maybe they...'

Miriam didn't say anything; she just looked out over the road and waited.

'I was going to ask you if I could borrow your car to take her away for a few days.'

'You're welcome to it.'

'Yeah, thanks, I'll let you know. You're sure she was in there with Tony?'

'Why don't you call her?'

'It's alright, Miriam, I'll work it out.' I finished my glass of wine. I couldn't handle it. Why would Abebi be here? She'd told me she had to work on her book. And why was she with Tony? 'Do you mind if I go now?'

'I am sorry, Frankie. I could tell that you were very keen on her. Everybody could.'

I could see tears in her eyes. 'Don't start, please Miriam.'

'No, I won't.' She looked out at the traffic again.

'Fuck it,' I said. 'I liked her.'

'She's really beautiful.'

'Yeah. Want another drink?'

'If you are.'

We sat for another hour and drank two more glasses each. She asked what I was going to do with the rest of his holiday. How should I know? She was at a loose end too but there was nothing I could do about that. Abebi and Tony, together? The woman I was in love with and my best friend? No she wasn't, couldn't be, that was all rubbish. But I knew that Miriam would tell me the truth, she always did. Tony and Abebi, the names seemed to ring together, It was like something out of Mills&Boon.

Mitzy gave me an affectionate and supportive kiss as we left the cafe. As far as I knew the only time Tony had met Abebi was after the screening at Arnold's film school. He'd asked her if she was staying in London. She'd told him the name of her hotel. Was that all it took?

I sat on my sofa looking at my feet. I'd given her fifteen hundred quid. The thought made me so angry that I picked up my phone and called her. I got number unobtainable. I tried twice more and then rang the hotel. Professor Musa had checked out. They'd ordered her a cab for Heathrow. 'You must be joking!' 'No, sir, I'm not joking.'

The horrible thought; was the money I'd put into her account for her airfare? Had I actually paid for her to leave me? Wait a minute, she'd said that Skinner and the conference had given her the plane tickets. I sat back on the sofa. I still couldn't find any anger, there was just this great weight. I'd told her the fifteen hundred was all I had. She'd robbed me of my last penny and taken off. Sometimes things just won't sink in.

# 30

I walked for days round the back streets of the town and for miles along the river. Summer seemed to be over and it was all the flat, dull, same old days of England. There was a faint wet drizzle in the air. I felt like I was walking through warm water and my own spirit was against me telling me to stop and don't move; sometimes it was difficult to breathe and I wanted to raise my arms and point my hands ahead of me trying to part the air and swim just to keep moving.

I wasn't even thinking about Abebi. I'd called the hotel again to see if there'd been a mistake and they got pissed off with me. She'd checked out and her room was now occupied by another guest, alright? Don't call again. I'd tried phoning her even after I'd worked out she must by now be back in the States. Probably with the Jordanian in New York, though I doubted it; Omar was probably just another lie. I'd even called the publisher she'd talked about and they'd never heard of her, or a John Sheridan. The title of her book should have told me; The Truth We Tell. I was in such a state, cast off, angry, I didn't care about humiliation any more, I needed to know. I phoned Miriam and got Skinner's number. Even if he hated me, he'd tell me. He'd probably enjoy it.

We met in a tea bar at the university. There was no point in fucking about so I let told him what had happened. I'd expected him to gloat but he didn't; in fact he was sympathetic.

'There's quite few of them around. They get some kind of temporary tenure at a small university. They're bright enough and publishing now is more about the author than the book. Abebi was beautiful and easy to sell so someone took a chance on her, even if the book is crap. So she hangs around conferences flirting with susceptible men and I include myself in that. Who's going to turn down Abebi? That's what most of these conferences are about anyway; academics fucking around while their wives are at home, or the other way round. I met her, sorry to tell you this, Francis, had a brief fling with her, and she persuaded me to pay for her to come over here. The rest you know. She gave a perfectly acceptable presentation, she's very capable of that, didn't have any further use for me and decided by the sounds of things to empty your pockets to extend her stay in London. Sorry, mate, it's the price we pay for letting our dicks lead us astray. When I saw you walk out of Guiseppe's with her I thought here we go again. I did tell Miriam to warn you but she seemed to think that you needed to learn your own lessons.'

'Don't blame her. Did you all think I was an idiot?'

'Not at all. She's a very attractive woman. Most of the guys were probably jealous.'

'Well thanks for telling me.' I looked up at the high ceiling of the tea bar. I was close to tears. Coming from Skinner it all seemed worse, like I was the biggest clown in town. I asked him, 'Did you always think I was a hopeless prick?'

'Not at all. I rather liked you. Still do.' He held out his hand. 'Next time you'll know. The world's full of them. Or maybe I should say that the world's full of them and us. I wish you well.' We shook hands. 'Give my love to Miriam. I'll be seeing her in a few weeks anyway.'

More streets beneath my sad, slow feet. I discovered parts of the town I hadn't known before; boarded up shops, a kid's playground with empty swings swaying in no breeze at all, an undertaker in a back street, a cul de sac full of Sikhs. And dead birds everywhere. Why so many dead birds? Dead birds in my head? I stopped. My feet refused to take me further. I was by a four foot high brick wall outside a terraced house on a small street somewhere at the back of the town. I felt hopeless, empty. I looked down at the top of the wall and put my hand on it to hold myself up. She'd abandoned me, I was a lonely boy, a mini man with my gut wrenched and burned. How could she have done this to me? I wanted to kneel by the wall and bang my head on the pavement. I burned. The wall held me as I bent down. I couldn't stop this. I was cracking, bending lower and lower, my head was level with the top of the wall. I pushed down with my hand to hold myself up but I could feel myself sinking. Down, down. Stop it, Francis boy, just cut it out. I wanted to retch, vomit up the pain and hurt. My body was bending even lower. Use it, dear, I heard Alexander say, use it Francis, it's part of it all, you burn, she's gone, so what? So what? So what...? So the kid rolled the ball, so what? It burns, so what? I'm still here bent down staring at the paving stones at the base of the wall. It all came and it all went, and it all came again and it went again. Good man, sucker, saint, fuck you Abebi, and I love you Francis, I love you Francis. I throw the ball back and rise a little. I'm holding on. I turn and I'm sitting on the wall. I slowly raise my head. I'm still here. My feet are on the pavement, my two hands are either side of me gripping the rough bricks. I am here. Francis I am. And whatever that is; whatever that will be; I am and I will be. St Francis the stoic. I push myself up from the wall. I stand straight again and began to understand that this wasn't even to do with her. In a strange electric flash I remembered the good times; her beauty, my lightness, Le Gavroche and her face going red with the booze. Was she pretending it? Why couldn't I have seen it coming? Well if I could it was my problem that I didn't. And it was her's that she did what she did. It was one thing her putting the boot in, why do it to myself? Slowly I began to breath again, standing by the wall again, staring at the pavement by my feet.

I'd done what I felt. Nothing wrong. Nothing; just me; Francis. And I'd got what I deserved maybe. She knew more than I did, that's all. Or perhaps she was just some idea in my own head, some fantasy. A fool for love? Sure. So now I knew. But so what? At least I'd loved. I'd been a sucker and I'd learn, but maybe not learn too much; not learn how not to love. I didn't want to do that. Some things maybe are worth a few quid. And anyway I'd get back my savings in a year or two and then I'll be the same dim, trusting bloke I'd always been, and what's wrong with that? It would be a kind of relief, it was natural anyhow; natural Francis. Me. And I'd forget about acting too. I couldn't even deliver a line straight. I'd go back to my school, my kids, football at the weekends and nights in the Calf.

And talking about the pub and the school, what about Tony? My best pal had steamed in and taken my girl. But I couldn't face confronting him. I'd just be nervous and inadequate; stand there shaking with the burn rising. It was bad enough I'd been humiliated but to sit opposite the man himself, who might be ashamed, or sneakily proud of himself; whatever he was, there was no doubt who'd been the winner and who'd been the loser. Tony had hardly called her up by accident, had he? I mean it had been him called her, must have been, how could she have got in touch with him? Maybe it was the one time they'd met at the screening. She could have enticed him with a sly come on. He wouldn't need too much enticement. She must have been very keen to come to the town she knew I lived in. My town, my place. How much longer was I going to stand by this fucking wall. How much longer was I going to avoid my favourite pub? Seeing Tony in our usual corner, with his usual pint, talking the usual bullshit. I didn't know how much Tony knew anyway. How would he know what Miriam had seen, or what she'd told me? But he must have noticed I hadn't been around.

I began to move away from the wall, I'd gone a few yards then it got worse and I stopped again as the burn burned again. Abebi hadn't left the country at all, the cab to Heathrow was a ruse. She was at this very moment staying with Tony who was right now pawing her with his great rugby hands, great rubbery lips, great thick fingers, fucking her with his great thick prick. Fuck it. This was no good, no good at all. I made myself walk again, slow at first - what else are you going to torture yourself with? You going to leave town, leave the country, be a teacher in Oz, go back to Ireland, or what? Come on, Francis, you need to know. Know what? Know it all. I'm walking more quickly now. Just the facts, the plain facts; just what actually happened. Face it like a man. Is that what you are? You think you are, so face it; then go home and cry. Right?

It was about four in the afternoon and the Calf was almost empty. I hadn't expected Tony to be there but thought I'd have my first pint anyway. I walked straight to the bar without looking back to our old table. Somehow the bar girl's demeanour, her friendly smile like nothing had happened told me Tony was there behind me waiting for me to turn. I picked up my drink, walked straight to the table, sat in my usual chair and faced him.

'How's it going?' I said.

'Alright.' he took a sip of his beer. The tension was strong. 'Haven't seen you.'

'Not surprising is it?'

'Isn't it?'

'Don't fuck about, Tone.'

'You know it all, do yer?'

'I know enough. My best mate went off with the woman I was... seeing.'

'So what?' It looked like he was going to brazen it out.

'What do you mean, so what?'

He shrugged and looked away. 'All's fair, mate...'

'Don't give me that shite.' If he was going to be that fucking cool, I'd... I didn't know what I'd do, but fuck that. 'You know what you did.'

'She was that kind of woman, Frankie. Everyone could see it. I did you a favour.'

'Did you fuck her?'

He looked at me, then away. He rubbed his jaw with his palm.

'I'm asking you, did you...?'

'No.'

'Why not?'

'Because of you.'

'Me?'

'You're my mate, Frankie.'

'So why'd you call her at the hotel?'

'How d'you know I did that?'

'You did, didn't you?'

'Alright, I did.'

'So why?'

'If I told you I did it for you it would be a lie, but it's part of it. I wanted to see what you were getting yourself into. Don't believe me. It's true. I also wanted to fuck her. That's true too.'

'Did she mention me?'

'No. Never said a word about you. Sorry pal. I could have taken her home but took her to the station instead.'

'Did you kiss her?'

'On cheek.'

'But she wanted to go with you?'

'You'll have to ask her.' He looked at me squarely.

'You seen her since?'

'No.'

'She tell you she was going back to the States?'

'No. She just went onto the train. That were it. How much did you give her?'

'What?'

'Money, how much did you give her?'

'Don't matter.'

'How much?'

'About four grand.'

'Shame I didn't get there earlier, in't it?'

'Fuck off, Tony,'

'I've been coming in every day, waiting for you. Want another?'

'No.' I got up and left the pub.

## 31

Opposite my sofa in my living room, hanging above the TV, was a print of a beautiful boy. I'd bought it a long time ago when my old man had wanted to to do a complicated novena on his rosary a few months after my mother had died. For once I'd had the money and time so I'd taken him to Rome and at around eleven o'clock every morning I'd left him in St Peters to say his prayers while I wandered off round the eternal city. On the third day I'd discovered the Sistine Chapel, which was empty, don't ask me why; so for a while I'd stood on my own with my mouth open, staring up at this dazzling wall and ceiling of saints and prophets and God. I was overwhelmed by this great tapestry of faith like a web round us all in its reds and blues, its browns and brilliant white, and maybe I was over-awed by it, or trying to escape it, but anyway there it all was. I bought a print of a cherubic young angel in a pale blue robe and had it framed and hung it on my wall. It took me a year or two to realise the angel was a boy. He looked off to one side as if he was too shy to look Michelangelo in the eye, or maybe the painter was too embarrassed to look into his.

Perhaps it was because my own feelings were so torn up by Tony, Abebi and the rest of it, or my energy so turbulent, or my mind so rushing, that I was seeing things I'd never seen before. The boy's eyes were lovely, his glance askance innocent, like he was nervously waiting for a love he'd lost. There was so much honesty in it that it made me want to cry, standing there on my own carpet, crying for love, or in love with love anyway, in my own fucked up way. Why was it so beautiful? This boy? Why was Abebi so beautiful? How would Michelangelo paint her? The outline of her cheekbone, the pale brown of her lips, the black in her eye, the twist of her hair, her long body in a long curve, her breasts soft to the touch. I didn't think so. Sure all that was in her and in the boy but none of it was what made either of them beautiful. It was something else, something unnameable, like some light inside them that was shining out, some light that blinded you and showed you who the boy was, that showed me who she was. Sometimes it had been more than I could manage just to look at her and not feel as if I didn't exist compared to this life force in front of me. And that was really what was making me want to cry as I looked at the Michelangelo. I'd seen something so precious in Abebi. I didn't know what it was and knew I'd never forget it.

Head down, arms hanging, slumped deep, how long did I stand there. I don't know. My phone rang. It was Paul who said that Richard Guest had collapsed in his flat and been taken to the Royal Hospital . I imagined the worst and knew I had to see Fat Dick before he copped it. I had a last look at the Michelangelo and took off out of the flat and ran down the road fast to the train station.

## 32

My hopes for a long and boozy lunch of pheasant and port in Fat Dick's club were quickly crushed by the walk down the antiseptic, corridors of the hospital. Gurneys and trolleys were lined up along walls dotted by bad art which wasn't Michelangelo. At least Richard had his own room even if it was just a bare white cube with monitors all over the place flashing green jerky lines. I quietly stood at the end of his bed. He was snoring, his plump cheeks quivered slightly as he breathed out through his mouth and nose; his skin was almost white where it stretched over his temples, and his great laughing jowls sagged from his ears to his chin and merged with his neck in furrows of fat. For a moment I thought I should leave. After the events of the past couple of days the last thing I needed was a brush with death.

He suddenly opened his eyes; startled and frightened as he gazed up at the strange figure at the end of his bed; then his face broke into a great, beaming smile.

'Ah, dear boy.' His voice was husky and low. 'How kind of you to come. What a vision to wake up to.' He raised his head and shoulders. 'Help me with these pillows.'

I pulled him forward and tucked the bedding behind him. 'Paul told me you passed out on your kitchen floor.'

'Did I? How very inconvenient. Don't remember a thing. Must remember not to be a nuisance. Sit down. Pull that chair over. Come close.'

I got as near to the bed as I could, 'Sorry I haven't brought you anything. Paul said, I er...'

'Paul said, I didn't have long?' he grinned. 'And you didn't spare the horses? Don't worry about gifts. Who needs a grape or an orange? As for reading, I gave it up several weeks ago. I have all I need in here.' He tapped his head then lay his hand down for me to take. I could feel the bones of his fingers through the dry papery skin.

'How are you now?' I asked.

'Nearly there, old love. I know I can be straight with you, you're not the sentimental type. Exactly what I need. Sorry, can't offer you roast duck and you wouldn't appreciate the local fare even if it's a very pretty boy who serves it. How are you?' He rolled his great head to one side and peered at me. 'You're not well are you? Can see it in your face. What's happened? Tell me. I don't care what it is. If I can't bear the woes of the world now I never will. The truth please.'

I told old Richard my story. By the time I'd finished it with a description of Tony in the pub, tears were streaming down my face. 'Sorry, Richard, this isn't what I came for.'

'It's probably exactly what you came for.'

'I don't know whether I loved her or not.'

He gently clasped my fingers and half whispered in what was left of of his deep baritone.

'"Oh what can ail thee, Knight at Arms/Alone and palely loitering/ The sedge has withered from the lake/And no birds sing." - the poets, darling they knew.' He smiled and continued holding my tearful gaze. '"I met a lady in the woods/ Full beautiful, a faery's child/ Her hair was long, her foot was light/And her eyes were wild/I made a garland for her head/And bracelets too and fragrant zone/And looked at me as she did love/And made sweet moan."'

'Thanks Dick, that cheers me up no end.' I grinned and wiped my face with the back of my hand. 'Old troopers never die, hey?'

'It's better to have loved and lost and all that, darling. I know, I know, love is hard. But I shall tell you the real thing takes years to mature. Yours was a romance. That's it, a romance, love's spear, the most wounding and delicious...Jonny Keats knew. What's so wonderful about a tree, a forest, a wheatfield? Hmm? They're all hard and uncomfortable, stones get in your shoe. But see them as the poets did and they tell you of everything that's bubbling away underneath. That's romance, you see?' He raised his hand and curled his fingers in the air as if to grasp the life it contained. 'It delights you at the thought that just for one moment you may revel in pure life, that you may witness it, you see? Perhaps you don't.'

'Like the light?'

'Exactly that, dear boy. The light that's streaming through it all. Nature, dear boy. This woman showed you how to see it. The light, very good. "She found me roots of relish sweet/And honey wild and manna dew/ And sure in language strange she said/I love thee true."

He breathed heavily and his eyes were this intense deep grey, so grey it was black.

'Sometimes for a little while with a lover or a friend and you can see it together. How marvellous that is. As if you're both saying...' His hand clasped the air again, '...see that. Know that. That's where we are. You laugh, you soar away. And then it's gone. But she'd been you see. She'd visited you. And you'd seen. "I saw pale kings and princes too/Pale warriors, death pale were they all/They cried - La Belle Dame sans Merci/She hath thee in thrall."'

He was tired, I could see he was tired, his skin was drooping, his eyes were glazed.

'You found her too, Francis, La Belle Dame sans Merci, and now she's gone.' He closed his eyes. 'Goodnight, dear Francis.'

'Richard?'

'I shall sleep now.' And within seconds he was snoring again.

## 33

'Simon said the casting director of Carter's Way couldn't stop talking about you. He said he'd never heard such a positive report about one of his clients. I said, excuse me, Simon, you mean one of my clients.'

'I'm your client now? I mean, you're my agent?'

'Well obviously.' Annabelle raised her eyebrows.

'That's official?'

'As official as it's ever going to get, Francis. Ok by you?'

'Oh yes. Thank you.'

It was the best news I'd had for days. Paul had told me

that Fat Dick had died and that had dulled me. The days had passed and that's all I've got to say about them. More walks, town and river, a couple of afternoons finally with schoolwork, evenings with TV. My acting career was stalled like some battered jalopy parked in no-man's land. I couldn't even get excited when Arnold had called and told me that the film he was making was now a play for the stage.

'It's inspired by an old French film by Robert Bresson called Diary of a Country Priest.' he'd told me. I've got this great young writer called Billie Jewell, worked on the Court's young writer programme. I'm setting it in a village just outside Dublin. I liked your Irish. Interested in playing the priest? The play's nothing to do with the film anymore, just short and sweet. Forty-five minutes. Great part.'

I'd told Annie and Paul who obviously knew more about it than I did.

'How much you getting?' asked Annie.

'Ah? Nothing.'

'Always the same. Used and abused. What did you say?'

'I said, yes.'

'No you didn't. You said you'd talk to your agent. What's the point of having one?'

'Arnold hasn't got any money,' Paul interrupted.

'Yes he has. Alexander Hudson's given him some, and so have you.'

'I didn't say I was giving him anything,' said Paul.

'But you are, aren't you? So if our money's going to Arnold I don't see why some of it shouldn't trickle down to my brother.'

'Annie, do you know how much it costs to hire a theatre?'

'The Threshold is hardly a theatre.'

'Yes, it is.'

'It's tiny.'

'Still costs. And there's the set, the publicity and all the rest.'

'Arnold asked me if I'd help out,' I said.

'He's asking you to pay him? He must be joking!'

'You're just pissed of that he hasn't asked you to be in it,' said Paul.

'Or you. When did you last have a job?'

'I did that Barclays Ad...'

I left them to it but took Annie's advice and called Annabelle. We met for a coffee down the street from her office. She was full of my success in Carter's Way. 'Anyway I called the casting director myself and said any further enquiries should come direct to me. And Francis...' she tucked her hair behind her ears, something she did when she was about to be serious, and leant forward across the table. '...she told me, strictly entre nous that June LeGrand had asked the lead writer to find something else for you.'

'Deliver another parcel?'

'Who knows where that could lead? She could invite you into her house!'

'What for?'

'Get to know her. You never know, you could end up being a romantic interlude. You could even replace Barry Moss!' She thought this was very funny and roared with laughter.

'Me? An affair with June LeGrand? She's about seventy.'

'You're thirty-nine, Francis, too old to be an ingenue. Anyway think of all those women you've seen in clinches with seventy year old actors pretending they're your age. Louis thinks I should look out for something better for you.'

'I've got something,' I said. I told her about the Diary of A Country Priest.

'A French film set in Ireland?' she said, looking interested.

'No an English play in a theatre just round the corner from me.'

'Oh. How much are they paying you?'

'Nothing.'

'Have you agreed to this?'

'Ah yes. No.'

'Tell them to call me.'

'There's another problem.'

'What's that?'

'It doesn't start rehearsing for another week and I have to be back at school.'

She did her best to imitate a wise old sage and repeated something she'd obviously heard from another wise old sage. 'Francis, there's no point in just wanting to be an actor. You have to need to be one.'

I wandered away into the streets of Soho with no idea of what I needed to be. I had no right to expect to be happy, and anyway the only way I could be happy was with Abebi and she'd gone. I crossed into Leicester Square and had a coffee in the place I'd been with her. I even sat at the same table in the hope that I'd find some clue as to what had happened to me. I didn't. I watched the crowd in front of me as they popped in and out of coffee houses and pubs carrying their new costumes in big store bags. It was an act, the whole world's an act, acting away, acting away, all of us. That's what Alexander had said. No-one was what they really were because they didn't know what it was and even if they thought they did they'd pretty soon find out it didn't exist anyway. They were all like me, trying to find some new jacket to put on as I walked out of the house. What a life. Well if that's what it was you may as well just do it. Just get on with it. Alright, Arnold I'll do it. I'll be an Irish priest, and like Paul said, I'll do the research. I still had a few days of my holiday left. I'd go to Ireland. There were plenty of Irish priests there and anyway I wanted to talk to my dad.

## 34

With the last of my money I bought a plane ticket, hired

a car at the airport and arrived at my old man's cottage near Cork late in the afternoon. He's a solid-looking bulky man in his early seventies with a red face and a mop of tousled grey hair. He's trusty until he's not, and leads a quiet life; most of the time just walking, fishing and drinking a pint or two in local pubs in the little town where he lives on a small inlet of the river.

'Gilly's miffed you didn't stay with her in the city,' he said as he greeted me with a big hug and a kiss. 'The boys'd like it too. I got some cake from the shop. Why don't we take it out back?'

As the kettle boiled I went out into the small patio garden and stood over the river flowing peacefully past pretty well under my feet. It was a different water from the English; slower for a start, you could think it was static, but like all things Irish, it came up on you unexpected.

I'd left Annabelle and Leicester Square and gone straight to my flat and packed a bag. I was running, I knew that, but wasn't stupid enough to think I could leave all that behind - I may as well as stuffed it in my rucksack; there was a lot of weight still hanging round my gut and heart. It was my father I wanted to see, which is why I was staying with him and not Gilly. There was something I wanted to talk to him about, although I wasn't sure what it was, but it was definitely there, like some nag in my soul if you think you've got one.

The old man bought the tea out to the garden and laid out the pot and the cups on an old wooden table under the garden tree that dipped its boughs into the water. 'The river and the rowan,' he said. 'They love each other indeed.' He nodded down to the leaves trailing and being tickled by the flow close to the bank. 'Would you look at that, what else do you need?' He poured the tea, sat, and looked up into my face with laughter in his eye. 'So where you been? What is it, three years? And you're not exactly regular with the post, are you?'

'No, sorry.'

'How's Annie?'

'Oh she's grand. The usual you know.' I opened and closed my fingers like my sister gabbing.

'Never did shut up, that one,' he laughed. 'And you? You didn't get married or something, did you?'

'No, Da.'

'Well I suppose you'd have told me if you did. You tell Gilly most of it anyway.'

'Why wouldn't I have told you?'

'Because you wouldn't. That's fine. I'm alright anyway. Pint in one hand, fork in the other.' He laughed again. 'I'm happy enough. You?'

'Why'd you ask?'

'Well I'd like to know.'

'I'll tell you later.'

'You came at the right time. Arthur Bean's got his birthday party tomorrow night at Mooney's. Some hoolie that'll be. Got five brothers and three sisters and all the nephews and nieces and the rest of it. Won't be like it was though, we're all too old for it. Still it'll be worth a look. Want to come?'

'If you're going, Dad, what am I to do, stay at home and watch the telly?'

'That's grand, and tonight we'll have fish and chips in the pub, how's that?'

The next day we walked along the river. The old man had bought his spare rod for me and we sat in the quiet under the shade of a grove of alder, the sunlight dappling our faces and hands. In the pub the night before I'd told him something about what had happened but not too much. The details should I wish to reveal them could wait for Gilly my youngest sister probably closest to me than the others, though piss-taking as hell, but with a love to it. After I'd mentioned it the old man hadn't said much apart from, 'there's plenty of fish in the sea, son.' And that was about it. Thanks Pa, but what did I expect, none of us had ever been particularly open with our feelings, except Gilly maybe, which was why most of the time she'd pretend to be acerbic. Anyhow I'd broached it with the old man which meant I was beginning to inch towards it myself, inch towards him I mean, with that something that nagged me.

I watched my float as we sat there; it was peaceful for a while anyway.

'You've got a bite, son!' the old man shouted.

I could see my float bobbing in the water.

'Reel him in. Not so fast. You've got to play him. Give him some line. Let him go.'

I followed his instructions and let my reel unwind fast as the fish pulled the float and the line away from the bank and headed up river.

'Let him go, then slowly pull him back. Could be a big one.'

'You want to take over?'

'No, son, he's yours. Slowly reel back. Don't jerk it now. You're going to have to tire him out. That's it, let him go again.'

The fish pulled away, this time towards the opposite bank.

'Don't let him get tangled in the reeds over there. You'll lose him and the line. Slowly pull him back. That's it, pull him back, then let him go again.'

I did as I was told. The energy of the fish amazed me, it's sheer power in the water, even with the metal hook in his mouth which must have pained him. I pulled it back as gently as I could, reeling in as fast as the line would allow without tightening it too much. It became slowly more taut as the fish came close to the bank. There was suddenly a flash of silver and brown as it leapt out of the water and then disappeared.

'It's a big trout,' said the old man. 'Don't let it get away. Let him him go again!'

'I'm doing my fucking best, Da! Which is it, let him go or reel him in?'

The trout pulled away fast, this time allowing the water to take him down stream. I allowed the reel to spin. This went on for a while as the trout took off then came back like he was playing with me. My arms were tiring, the rod was old and heavy. 'Christ, I never knew it was such hard work.'

'Life and death for him, son.'

What was worse than the pain in my arms was that I knew I didn't want to catch the fish. I wanted somehow to release the hook and let him go free; but the barbs were caught strong in the fish's mouth and anyway he was deep in mid river most of the time and I could only go with it. I began to slowly reel him in again, ignoring my father's shouts.

'Not too tight! Keep it nice and easy!'

'Shut-up, Da, I'm bringing him in.'

'You may need to let him go again.'

'I'm bringing him in! Would you shut up!'

Slowly the fish came towards me. I could see it now in the shallows as it writhed just beneath the surface. It was maybe eighteen inches long. My father grabbed his landing net and stood with his waders in the water as the trout thrashed and splashed. The old man was about to scoop him when I jerked the rod and the fish flew up and landed heavily, wriggling wildly on the bank, gasping for air. I threw the rod down and tried to pick it up.

'Help me get the hook out of his mouth!'

'Get him into the net, son!'

'Help me get the fucking hook out!' I glared at my father who threw his net down and picked up the trout. I held the head while he twisted the hook out of its mouth.

'Give it to me,' I said.

'What?'

'Give me the fucking thing.'

I took the fish and threw it back in the water. 'And that's the last fucking time I want to go fishing.'

The old man stared at me. 'What's the matter with you all of a sudden?'

'Nothing.' I sat down on one of the collapsible canvas chairs we'd brought with us. For some reason I felt close to tears. I noticed a series of small bubbles in the middle of the river and hoped it was the trout swimming away even if it did have a bleeding mouth. I picked up my rod again and slowly began to reel in the line. 'Sorry, Da.'

'Makes no difference to me, son.'

He baited his line again and cast off. We sat quiet for maybe another fifteen minutes. I could hear the birdsong in the trees as the question became real in my mind; it was the fish that had done it. My voice sounded loud in the silence of the trees, almost like it wasn't my own.

'When I was about two or three years old Ma brought me down here to stay with Auntie Pat. I can remember sitting on her floor under her table. Why'd she bring me here?'

The old man was taken by surprise. 'She was probably wanting to see her sister. We came down a lot from Dublin.'

'Yeah but you didn't come with her that time. Why not?'

'I don't know, son, it was a long time ago.'

'She was really unhappy. I can remember her crying.'

'How old were you?'

'Doesn't matter how old I was, I can remember it. And afterwards, back home, she was really unhappy for a long time.'

'Oh Christ, Francis, why'd you need to go over all that?'

'I'd like to know.'

'Know what?'

'Why she left you.'

'Why should I know? She was visiting her sister.'

'This was different. Why'd she leave you, Da?'

'She didn't leave me.' He was concentrating hard on his float on the other side of the river.

'She did. Why?'

'It's none of your business.'

'Yes it is. She was my mother.'

'And she was my fucking wife!'

'Come on Da, will you tell me? I want to know!'

'Why? Is this because of the upset you've been going through? I can tell, you know, you're not happy. Well don't take it out on me.' He set his face which was more red than usual; his eyes smaller. He stared down into the water.

'Tell me, will you? For fuck's sake, will yer tell me! What happened? Why'd she leave you?'

He slowly began to reel in his line. His face was hard and red, his mouth clammed, lips tight. He was staring down at the water. No words.

I shoved my rod into its cover and began to gather the weights and hooks and floats and stow them in the bag. We both sat on our chairs for about ten minutes not looking at each other, saying nothing.

'Why don't we go and get a pint for lunch,' he said.

His head was bowed like under a weight as we walked back along the river path towards the village. I sat in the pub garden as he went inside and got in a couple of pints. He sat down under the umbrella and took a long draw on his Guinness. I knew it was going to happen and it didn't take long. He was looking away from me. He said, 'She didn't leave me. I'd left her.'

'What?'

'You want to know?' He turned and faced me. 'Do you really want to know?'

''Yeah, I do.'

He put the pint back on the table and wiped the white from his lips. 'Alright then. You sure?'

'Yeah, I'm sure.'

'I'd been seeing someone else.'

'Yeah? In Dublin?'

He stared at me for a moment, his eyes were sad now. I knew he didn't want to tell me, but he would. I waited.

'Yeah, in Dublin. I was working for Mahoney. You know Mahoney? You remember? There was a woman there in the accounts department called Yvonne Brassit. I liked her, you know? You really want to know all this?' He kept asking. He knew I wanted to know.

'You're going to tell me, so why don't you?'

'There was some project in Galway the firm was doing it, I can't remember now what it was, some electrical job, needed an estimate or something. Mahoney asked me to go over and said take Yvonne to sort out the paperwork. I didn't arrange it, Francis, I didn't set it up, Mahoney did. You understand, it wasn't me that made this arrangement. It wasn't much, a couple of days. We stayed in a hotel and... and you know?'

'I know what?'

'Something happened between me and Yvonne which shouldn't have done.' He was rubbing the wood of the table with his palm. 'I mean I was married and so was she. We were both pretty hesitant about it, you know, just a thing that happened, probably after one too many drinks in the bar. Anyway we came back to Dublin and I think we both thought we'd just forget it, one of those things.' He coughed and took another drink. 'But we didn't forget it, we carried on seeing each other.'

'Behind Mum's back?'

'Yes.' His mouth was set in that line again. 'Behind her back. I loved your mother and wanted it to stop, but I couldn't.' Like through gritted teeth, like it was busting his heart to tell me.

I lit a cigarette.

'And you should pack that in for a start.'

'That's my business.'

He was looking at me, it was hostile. I was thinking he wanted to kill me for a second there.

'So you carried on seeing each other? Why?'

'What are you, the fucking Garda?'

'I want to know.' I turned and looked into my father's face. 'I want to know, so please tell me.'

He rubbed the back of his neck with both hands. His grey

eyes were darker. I thought maybe he was going to cry. He said, 'I thought I was in love with her, this Yvonne. It got really bad. I had all these crazy fantasies about going over to Birmingham or somewhere, getting a new job, raising another family. I mean she'd leave her family and I'd leave mine and we'd start another one. That's what I thought. And it was strong in me, like it was some kind of madness.'

He stared over at another table as a family, two kids, sat down. The kids were laughing and japing around. He watched them for a second.

'So I told your mother. I said I was leaving her. You know, the most stupid fucking thing, I hadn't even told Yvonne what I was going to do. I hadn't told her about going over to Birmingham and all that. How crazy can you get? Anyway...' He leant back, stretching his spine, 'So your Ma was broken up about it. So she walked out and took you down here to Pat's. So I was left there with Annie who was about six or something.'

'She know about all this?'

'Annie? No. Don't think so. She's never mentioned it. Kids, you know, they just get on with it, went to school and...I don't know. So anyway I told Yvonne what had happened and what I intended for us to do and she looked at me like I was insane. She had no intention of doing any such thing. She finished it there and then. We were in a pub, not like this, dark night, can't remember which one. She walked out. I never saw her again. Never again.' He brushed his eye with the back of his hand. 'So I'd lost both of them. I stayed on my own in the house for a while. I think Annie even came down here to Cork for a week, can't remember. And slowly I began to realise what I'd done.' He was talking easier now, like it was some relief. 'It was like I'd been in another world there for a while. I know it sounds crazy but I don't think during that time that I really knew who I was. It was like I lost myself. I had a pal at the time, a drinking buddy, Tommy Reardon. I told him all about it and he fucking gave it to me. He fucking let me have it.' Suddenly he laughed. 'Christ, what are friends for? Told me a few home truths, I can tell you. Woke me up. So anyway I came down here and begged your mother to forgive me. Took some time; a lot of tears and outpouring and all the rest of it; but she did. She came back to Dublin. End of story.'

'It wasn't for her.'

No, maybe it wasn't.' He was relieved now, but kind of shame-faced all the same. It was done. 'Nor me either. We were alright. Gilly was born. But you're right, you never really get over these things, do you?'

'No, I suppose you don't.'

'I know how you're feeling, son.'

'Does Gilly know?'

'No. And I'd appreciate it if your didn't tell her either. Let sleeping dogs lie.'

'And that's exactly what they do, Da. They lie.'

'Oh very good. What good would it do?'

'Thanks for telling me anyway.'

'Can't say it was a pleasure.' He tried a grin. 'You want another pint?' He half stood. You want to tell me anything? I mean, about you?'

'No, it's ok, Da. When I've got it worked out I'll let you know.' I didn't know what to say to him. 'You know Mum was unhappy most of her life?'

'That wasn't just down to me, Francis. She had that streak in her, you know? No excuses, but sometimes I had to put up with a lot.' The skin on his face was grey and sad as he stood straight, the sun over the pub behind him. 'And you're a daft bastard. If you'd let me take that trout we could have had it for tea, and set ourselves up for Arthur's.'

# 35

Arthur Bean had booked the biggest pub in town for his party. The place was packed before me and my father arrived. Arthur and his brothers were rolling about having a good laugh. We suspected they'd been there since midday. Now the sisters and all the rest had joined him, which seemed to include half the town, all boozy and shouting and talking a mile a minute and laughing like hyenas. There was a ceilidh band set up in one corner of the rec. room with a couple of fiddles, a guitar player and an old drum kit being thumped and snared by the oldest percussionist I'd ever seen. He was in an old sleeveless vest that showed his taut and skinny white muscles. The band played hits from the past and now, and what they didn't know they made up and nobody cared.

'We're waiting for the singer,' Arthur, who like his name was a bean shaped man, shouted over the racket. 'He crashed his car in Cork, but he'll get here, always does. How you doing Francis, long time no see. What you drinking?' And he was away, submerged by the noise and crowd.

My sister Gilly came up and hugged me. 'Did Pa, not tell you I was coming to the do?'

The old man had disappeared into a corner with his cronies and there was no way of asking. 'He probably did.'

'And you forgot. Typical! Where've you been? Why didn't you write? What's up with you? And here's Finn and Paraic and Steve your nephews if you can remember their names and that far back to know you've got a family, though I doubt you'll recognise them.'

I grinned at the three hulking awkward teenagers that I hadn't seen for three years, grinned and shook their hands. Paraic was drunk already and staggered away to find the bar to lean on. Gilly took me off to a couple of chairs at the side of the room.

'Annie told me. At least she calls, Frankie. You were going

to be an actor. Oh no, please God, no! One in the family is enough. And look what happened to her, she went and married that stuck-up snob, who doesn't like me to visit. Oh the God's truth he doesn't. Not enough room for three clunking Irish boys to run around his pretty garden and stomp on his flowerbeds. Happy enough to show us endless repeats of his TV shows though, isn't he? How are you anyway? We're all fine. I've got a new job teaching difficult kids. Difficult! Let me tell you...'

I looked around as she talked. I wished Annie was there and I wished my mother was there; I wanted all of them to be together in this fine old night. I could see my old man laughing away over the other side of the room, my nephews were lunging about in a circle taking the piss out of their own dancing and Gilly was talking nonstop down my ear. The singer arrived with a bandage round his head and everyone clapped as he walked over to the microphone and launched straight into song with a laugh and no explanation of the smear of blood on his face. Gilly got up to get new drinks and was immediately replaced by a tall, big-boned woman with long blond hair, a tight sweater and a wide grin; she had the fresh air of her life coming out of her every pore

'I'm Mary Doolan,' she said. 'I know who you are, you're Francis Riley. Pleased to meet you. Want another drink? Go on.'

'My sister's getting one. How'd you know my name?'

'You're Jamie Riley's son. Everybody knows everything round here.' She gave me a bright look out of sparkling blue eyes. 'And I'm not taking no for an answer.'

'You what?'

'You heard.' She put her hand on my thigh and kissed me on the side of my face. 'Because you're fucking gorgeous and I'm half pissed, alright? We have that clear now?'

I laughed as Gilly put a drink into my hand, gave me a big wink and pushed her way back into the crowd. The band struck up a number and Mary pulled me from my chair.

'Come on you, dance with me.'

After a hesitant and awkward start, clattered all round by sharp legs and arms and fuelled by the Guinness, I felt my own limbs find their way and my joints loosen. I'd been tense for weeks. I laughed as Mary whirled and gyrated around me in her own unique Doolan dance; everyone's dancing was unique which was what was great about it. I put my head back and whooped as some old joy came up and coursed through me; it was clearly still quite possible for me not to give a fuck and I decided that this is where I should have been all my life; at least for that night anyway. Mary tried to teach me her own moves, none of which I could do, and after a while I gave up and started going my own way, knees pumping, elbows sharp and arms flying. For a minute or two a circle formed around me like I was the town clown, clapping in time to the band as I high-stepped, jerked, made an ass of myself and didn't care. Mary thought I was hilarious. I sang along with all the old favourites, acted out my Whiskey in the Jar and remembered the words to most of the others. When the slow numbers started she was close and perfumed and more obvious that any woman I'd ever known, thrusting her hips at me and gripping my backside. The lights were lowered and she held on tighter.

'Oh no,' she said, 'Not fucking Danny Boy.'

'You got to listen to him, he's got a bandage round his head.'

We both thought this was very funny and fell into a clinch. I had my arms round her shoulders and my groin fitted so tightly into hers we could hardly move. The lights dimmed even lower and we kissed. I was going for it, but she stopped me and turned it into a soft, slow, melting embrace which turned me on even more. Halfway through I noticed out of the corner of my eye, my old man looking at me from across the other side of the floor. His smile was kind, as if to say, 'plenty of fish...'

Mary whispered in my ear, 'I think it's time we took a little walk.'

'Where do you live?'

'About fifty yards up the road.'

Her bedroom floor was littered with children's toys. 'I had my nieces over,' she said as we stood by the bed and kissed again. She stood back from me and in one extraordinary movement she lifted her sweater, pulled the cup of her bra down and revealed a shapely firm breast. At the same time, with her other hand she clasped me round the back of my head and pulled my mouth down to her nipple. 'Oh God,' she said, 'I've wanted you to suck my tits all night.'

She undid my belt and pushed my trousers down as I pulled off her sweater. She held my cock in her hand as I pushed her skirt down to the floor. 'Get your fucking shoes off and out of those pants!" She laughed and then stood back from me and by the glow of the street lamps through the window she was naked like some Greek statue with her strong shoulders, heavy breasts, slim waist and powerful thighs . 'You're fucking Aphrodite,' I said. 'Aaagh!'

'What's wrong?'

'I just stood on a My Little Pony.'

She laughed and grabbed me and we kissed again as we fell onto the bed. I lay up against her stomach with her knees round my ears. I fucked and fucked like I'd never fucked before. I could feel a massive orgasm coming as she pulled me further and further into her.

'Oh come, come, fucking come, but not in me.'

I managed to jerk himself out of her as I heard her howl her own joy and then grab my cock as I came wild and splashing. 'Oh Abebi,' I thought, 'here's one you didn't get.' Mary wanked me off to get the last ounce out of me and I lay curled in the warmth and flesh of her as she stroked my backside. 'I could feel you needed that,' she said.

My face was in her shoulder and I could smell her hair. She held me as I kissed her neck. 'Too fucking much,' I said.

'Never, never too much,' she laughed.

# 36

By the time I arrived back at the cottage the next morning my father was dressed for Sunday mass. He grinned at me as I came into the kitchen. 'Good time?'

Still half drunk I sunk onto the hard-backed chair at the table and stared at the sauce bottle and mustard jar lined up in the middle of it. 'Don't ask.'

'Want to come to mass?'

'Is that what a good catholic does after the night before?'

'We all find our way, son. How long since you've been to mass?'

'Can't remember. They still have the incense?'

'Will today, it's a high mass. Why don't you come for old time's sake?'

The church was only half full. It was like an old Ireland that I remembered from my teenage years in Kilburn which was like a slice of Dublin prayed over to London. In those years I'd followed the old man unwillingly to mass, but my church going hadn't lasted too long. After I'd lost my virginity I became so obstinate - how can you confess a fuck in the park? - that the old man had thrown in the towel and let me have my Sunday mornings back. This had begun I suppose the gaping of the gap between me and him, the parting of the ways; not too painful or regretful, or even hardly noticed but a drift away certainly; him to the places he knew and me into the inside of my own head and whatever I invented there. All splits and schisms come down to religion so they say. My Ma anyway had only gone intermittently to mass for years - I couldn't remember her ever taking communion - and she'd merely shrugged when confronted by my refusal. 'Let the boy be,' she'd said. And so I was. And so I am. No longer a Roman.

We sat in the back of St Marks which was a big, nineteenth century church; its exterior was covered in sharp black stone, like it was the flint heart of the town. The last time I could remember going to mass was for a midnight service when kids ran round the pews and drunks swayed in the shadows up the back. Here was the same hum of whispered response and the same smell of incense permeating the same walls with their alcoves for statues of Mary the Virgin, of St Mark himself with a full beard and a four foot rosary, and a giant and bloody crucifix just in case you'd forgotten to feel guilty.

I disliked the priest on sight because he reminded me of the others I'd known who were all arrogant bastards as they'd twisted and turned in front to the altar, their chasubles swishing, their heads up high when they raised the host. 'Look at me holding up God and we couldn't give a damn for ignorant boys only interested in football and sex.' The congregation seemed cowed. They were just ordinary people who believed, but didn't know for sure; who followed the priest who believed he did know for sure; which is why they followed him. What could I say? You can't argue with belief, can you? Which is what's wrong with it. I was just an ordinary person like them but one who didn't believe. That's them. That's me. Did it mean my soul was empty? Or maybe I didn't have one? Did that mean I had no nub, Alexander?

I knelt, or sat or stood, following my father if I concentrated, and missed a couple of kneelings when I didn't, or if my knees hurt and I literally sat it out. After a while though I allowed myself to breathe in the wax candles and be calmed by the responses and chants and all the smells and holy breath and shifting limbs and memories. I knew all this was somewhere deep in myself and knew that somewhere I was part of this community of souls, even if I didn't have one. Maybe the community did and I didn't. How could that be? I couldn't deny that this church with its alcoves and plaques and plinths and saints and martyrs was something I knew all about deep as hell, high as heaven. Here lies Francis, named after one of the most famous saints of all. Come little birds tweet on my shoulder. Even if my life was over I had to start somewhere. You were always starting somewhere. Or going back somewhere. And here I was sitting next to my father on an old wooden pew at the back of St Marks on a Sunday morning going nowhere.

The priest, whose name was Father Mulligan, began his sermon, which was something about a saint who came from a wealthy family and who was dissatisfied with his life of ease and so had struck out into the wide world to discover the truth of himself.

'And he was in a deep, dark wood, where there was no sustenance of any kind, including food and water and there were bears roaming. He came across an old wise man in a grotto.'

Where else?

'And the wise old man said, "Seek yourself, the kingdom is within."'

Which kingdom are you talking about, pal? I could hear Tony, or maybe it was the question I was asking but didn't dare and let Tony do it. I looked sideways at my Father, who was smiling as if he agreed heartily with Mulligan but I knew he was probably thinking about something else.

After the mass the priest stood on the church steps greeting his parishioners as they left. He seemed old and more frail than he'd been at the altar; maybe he only really existed in his vestments. I watched as the congregation went up to him like he was the centre of their universe and they wanted to check their orbits and share a minute or two of their lives in the sun and remind themselves they were catholics which was their beginning and their end of it. And it was my start anyway; I could take that for a fact, even when I was starting again. For a moment, some flash in my mind; I could see where I'd come from, what I'd been and the long trail of who I was, disappearing into the mist right back to now.

The old man had gone to get the car to drive us over for lunch with Gilly and her family. When most of the congregation had gone I went over to Father Mulligan by the church door.

'Hullo Father I'm...'

'Oh I know who you are I can see your father in you.'

'Can I ask?' I said. 'You said, "seek yourself, the kingdom is within."'

'That's right, son.'

'Did you mean the Kingdom of God?'

'It's whatever kingdom you seek.'

'You see, I'm not sure I believe...'

He laughed and took my arm. 'See that tree. Poems are made by fools like you and me, but only God could make that tree.' He patted my shoulder. 'I need my dinner now, if you don't mind.'

Dad was relaxed and content as we took the car, an old Peugeot, into the city. James Riley the good hearted gregarian had come back on the Sunday morning delighted with himself, his son, his daughter and his grand-boys. They, taking their cue from their mother, took the piss out of me for my self-effacing ways, and after Gilly slyly commented on it, for my going off with Mary Doolan the night before. I was tempted to tell them about spearing my foot on My Little Pony. They'd have loved it, so would Gilly, but she'd have to pretend she didn't. The table groaned under the roast beef and every vegetable known to Ireland. Even Dennis, the morose husband peeked out of his shell for a minute or two. The family larked like good families do; the dark spit of the past was a long way below.

The next day as I left the cottage the old man said, 'Thanks, son.'

No, thank you. You know? I'm sorry. I just needed to know.'

'And maybe I needed to tell'

We laughed, both a little embarrassed.

'You know what I'm going to do?' said the old man, 'I'm going back to that river and catch that fucking trout.'

'Good luck with that.'

We hugged and kissed then I got into my car. I didn't tell him that I was going to see Mary to say goodbye. We went for a pint and a pie in the Black Horse. As she sat in front of me with the TV screen above silently showing a game, I felt some stirrings of lust at the sight of her breasts stretching the fabric of another tight sweater; this one pink with a broad blue band round it just under the swelling. She was as direct as she'd been the other night; her smile was generous and her eyes sympathetic to us both. There was no doubt about it, there was something about this woman that moved me. I knew like she did that our one night together was probably our last. I felt the slight stirring of a love, but not like the one for Abebi; that was more like a dull pain. Anyway no regrets about Mary.

## 37

I unlocked the door to my flat and the shapes and smells of the past almost overwhelmed me with a sense of sadness and the dread of coming back to the beginning; where I'd been, where I still was. I picked up the pile of mail scattered on my doormat, dumped my bag and slumped on the sofa. I looked about, the same furniture, the broken blind, a grimy beer glass on the table by the window, and directly ahead of me the print of the cherubic boy on the wall. Now it seemed faded, just a picture after all. I guess I felt different now; Ireland had cheered me although I didn't know why; it was like a different place, another place, another world a long way away; Mary Doolan, Gilly, Arthur's hoolie, even Father Mulligan, but mainly my Dad, who I missed already. There was something I'd seen in his sad face; his loneliness, like life was over and what do you do now, son? 'If you want me to dwell on the past I'm not going to.' But I knew that he did and he'd carry that Yvonne Brassit forever; a madness like he said, like my madness for Abebi. I picked up my phone looking, I knew, for a text or message from her; some kind of last lunge at hope which I knew was hopeless. There was no message. I tossed the phone back onto the sofa on top of my post and saw an envelope with the Barr-Lyon university logo printed at the top and to one side. My name was hand-written, there was no address and no stamp. Inside there was a note from Theo Skinner. 'Received this from Professor Musa. She asked me to pass it on.' I took out a smaller, white, sealed envelope and opened it.'

Dear Frankly,

I know you probably don't want to hear from me and I don't blame you. What I did was unforgivable. I'm not going to say I'm sorry. I did it that's all and probably hurt you a lot. I guess I could say that I had to. Well I didn't have to, did I? Like everything else in my life I just kind of go ahead and do things even if I know that most of them are wrong.

God, where do I start? Maybe my book. We kind of met over it, didn't we? 'The Truth We Tell.' I can imagine your reaction to that title now and bet you're thinking, well I don't know about truth but that woman certainly knows about lying. Well let me tell you, she does, and she still carries right on doing it. I'll be straight with you - and you can tell Theo if you want to - most of my CV is just hokum. I just make it up as I go along, telling people what they want to hear and even getting a kick out of watching them swallow it all. And if anybody ever questions it I just make up something else. All liars know that there's always another lie which is why they're never caught. The last lie is always to yourself, but you never really know what that is, and if you ever find out, you can never admit it.

I know the reason that everyone believes me is because they want me. (I'm talking about men, women are something else.) I can see it in their eyes, in the way they move their hands wanting to touch me, in the stupid grins on their faces. I pretend to be having some kind of academic conversation about how I would enlighten everybody at their conference and I know all they want to do is fuck me. Oh boy, I've been there so many times that the way I lead them on has become almost automatic. I lie all the time. Pretty well every time I open my mouth a little lie drops out. And I thought, well if I add them all up maybe I can see the truth behind it all - that's the book - but I still haven't worked that one out - I mean what's the truth behind it all?

I could see you were honest and really liked me but that didn't stop me, did it? I named you Frankly because that was in some way a recognition of what I knew you were. Maybe I was sending a message to myself but I ignored it as usual. See, I didn't quite know what to do. I knew what you needed and I knew I was making you promises I wasn't going to keep and I couldn't give you what you were asking for. And even as I was stealing your money, I knew it was wrong, but couldn't do anything about it. Then your friend called and I thought maybe this was a way out. I could see what he wanted straight away so I played the same old games and he went away disappointed too, but I reckoned if you got to know about it you'd know what kind of person I was and forget me. So I hope that's what you'll do.

Ok, I'm writing this to tell you that you're a decent and good guy, and I'm sorry I came into your life and messed you around. There, I said it, I'm sorry, which I guess is a pretty big thing for me, at least I'm admitting what I did.

I'm not in Baltimore anymore, they fired me. Maybe these lies do get you in the end.

I actually really did like you, Frankly. You weren't the same as the rest of them.

In another life,

Abebi.

I read the letter twice then put it down on top of the rest of my post. I was numb for a while, even more numb than I was before, then I realised I wasn't thinking of Abebi at all; what she'd told me I knew already. I'd always known, hadn't I? Just couldn't admit it. And now that old mysterious ball of anxiety that had lain down there in my deep gut for most of my life, that had burst wide and open in the joy and wonder of Abebi, was now broken and in pieces. But as it all fell I felt a strange new energy as if all the pain was coursing up through me and demanding some kind of release, like I was kind of reassembling. If the old me was lying around like the junk used to be around my bed, now I needed to pick it all up again and make some other version of myself. I had no idea what that was. It wasn't that I was angry or even unhappy. I seemed to be staring at another me that was waiting in a kind of blank and unthoughtful way to appear, like some other thing that was pushing up through the depression and demanding to be seen. I knew I had to do something. I didn't know what it was, but just sitting there meant I'd sink back through the sofa and never emerge again. Something? What? I needed to act that was for sure. I mean, sink or swim. I mean, why not?

I called Tony. We arranged to meet for a drink. I didn't want to go to the Calf, but he did, so we compromised and met in the small back room of the pub rather than at our usual table by the front window. The room was ancient wood painted brown, small and dark, the kind of place where conspirators met and planned to fuck up the world. There were only two tables and on one of them was a full pint waiting to be drunk. I sat opposite it and a minute later Tony came in from the gents.

'Hullo mate, haven't seen you for a while.'

'Been in Ireland.'

'Good time?' He sat opposite me and picked up the beer.

'Corking.'

'Right.' He took a long sip. I thought he looked smaller, thinner in the face, his sheen of fitness had dulled.

'I got a letter from Abebi.'

'Yeah?'

'You said you turned her down.'

'Aye.' He was looking a bit shifty.

'She said, in her letter, that she left you disappointed.'

'She would, wouldn't she?'

'So which is it?'

'Which is what?'

'Don't fuck about, Tone. Would you have gone off with her if she'd have let you?'

'I already told you.'

'Tell me the truth.'

'That's a dangerous game, son.'

'It's not a game.'

His voice was sharp. 'I thought I could have her but didn't want to because of you.'

'I think you're lying.'

'Up to you, pal.' He tipped his pint down and looked at his empty glass. 'Want another?'

I wanted to walk out. I wanted him and Abebi out of my thoughts and life. There wasn't any point in this was there? I'd known Tony for years, there'd been a lot of good times, a load of laughs, but he was lying and I'd never trust him again.

'I'm asking, you want another pint?' he said.

I looked down at my drink untouched on the table in front of me. I didn't know what to say. Finally I looked up. 'Tony, just tell me the fucking truth, will you? And then I'll tell you if I want another pint.'

A moment passed. He held his empty glass in both hands, gently rocking it on the table. 'Alright. So maybe I'll never see you again but this is what happened. The moment I saw her I wanted to fuck her and I had the feeling she were up for it so I called her at her hotel. I couldn't believe how quick she agreed to meet. And she wanted to come here too. I'd have preferred London somewhere. Anyway she came, and I did want her, I really did, and it's my opinion that she would have done. She obviously doesn't agree. But....' He looked down his at his glass. 'Can I get another drink?'

'No.'

'Alright I did want her. I would of done it. But I didn't want to. And that was because of you. That's true. If she'd have led me on a bit more, maybe I would have done. But maybe I wouldn't too. And I'll tell you this I think she was thinking same thing. We didn't mention you, not once, but you were there, Frankie, like some fucking ghost at the table. And that's why it didn't happen because of you.' He stood up. 'And now I'm going to the bar. I'll get you one too and if you don't want it I'll drink it meself.' He went out.

I thought maybe I'd just been told two half-truths, one from her, one from him. Did that make a whole one? How could I know? I didn't think that either of them knew either. It was all too murky down there, no-one ever really knew what was going on. As Alexander said, 'You just have to make a decision.'

Tony came back with the beer.

'Alright, Tone, I forgive yer.'

'Good.' Tony sat back on his chair, looking down. He didn't smile or look happy about anything. He just looked down. I suddenly felt very sorry for him. The great know-it-all Tony was gone. He was just another fellah like the rest of us. He looked up and there was the beginning of a tear in his eyes. He said, 'You done something no-one else has ever done.'

'What's that?'

'Made me feel ashamed of meself. I wouldn't want to lose you, mate.'

'Well, fuck it, I'm going to be an actor.'

'Thought you were already.'

'No this time it's the real thing. On the stage.'

## 38

'It's not exactly based on the film,' said Arnold, 'Or the novel. It's a chamber piece.'

'It's an original play,' said Billie Jewell. She was a short skinny writer from Manchester who wore tight jeans, basketball boots and had spiked blond hair. Her face was set in a perpetual serious frown. 'It's a distillation of the idea,' she went on. 'The focus isn't on the priest, it's on Chantal, the landowner's daughter, breaking out from the confines of village life.'

I could see I was going to have trouble with Billie; there was something about the thrust of her thin shoulders which said one thing, fuck you.

'So what happened to the landowner?' I asked.

'We don't need yet another patriarchal figure,' Billie tried not to sneer.

'So who's Chantal fighting against if it isn't her father?'

'You, the priest. The great weight of religious tradition that's infected her sprit and everyone around her.'

'I represent all that?' This acting game seemed to be turning serious and I was already worried that it might be beyond me.

'Just do the lines,' said Billie. 'They're all you need.'

We were in the second day of rehearsal in an old church hall that Arnold had found. The play was called the The Lost Secret, which was a line from Bresson's film and was about how Chantal grew up from being a wealthy landowner's daughter and became a modern woman.

'It's the absolute truth that without women the world will never achieve its proper balance and it's time we realised it.'

Billie glared at us, especially at me. I wanted to shout out, 'I'm innocent!', but I knew she wouldn't hear.

I thought Bresson's film had been about the priest's idea that it was only in having the deepest faith in the good, the good of God, that humanity could save itself. There was probably some truth in both our ideas but I could see that she wasn't having any of that. It was clear enough to her, the priest was the villain who was going to have to be shown the way. Remembering Father Mulligan on those old church steps surrounded by his parishioners I could see it was all a bit more complicated than maybe she thought. If nothing else the priest was a man living in his own house of confusion and well may he have thought that God shone through the window but down there in the basement was the usual writhing of a lot of old snakes that Billie didn't know about. And I did. Or at least I was beginning to thanks to Abebi.

The play was now a series of scenes played out in a small room of the landowner's mansion in a small Irish town a hundred years ago. It was the day of the funeral of the landowner's wife and as he and the wealthy villagers met in the main drawing room, Chantal created her own havoc with: a) a slovenly maid who in her view required a revolutionary shot in the arm; b) her previous governess who she suspected of having an affair with her father and; c) the local priest, who was me, who she saw as a symbol of all that oppressed her and every other woman. Which was a bit much if you ask me.

The fact that the priest was now only in three scenes at first disappointed me because as usual I was imagining myself as a star again. The film was called The Diary of a Country Priest wasn't it? And who was the country priest? Anyway. But in the end I'd felt relieved when I realised I didn't have so many lines to learn. I was finding it difficult. At first I was in one place and the lines were in another, but as I became more familiar with them they came closer. Now I was still in the one place and the lines were sort of on my forehead but not in myself. And that was a problem I couldn't get over. How do you get them under your skin? How do you actually become it, or him; how do you become another person? I also discovered that acting required inter-reacting with other characters and moving about the stage and not bumping into the furniture as Arnold had wittily pointed out. It seemed a lot to learn, but the plain sad truth of it was that I didn't know how to act. The Irishness of it all was a relief to me and I felt ok to represent a generalised view of people I understood. But how to get these thoughts down from the general to the particular, in other words how to actually be this other character, was a mystery I couldn't even quite define let alone master.

The school term was in full swing and I had only a few evenings and weekends in which to rehearse. Chantal was played by Kate, the black-haired Goth who'd confronted me outside the McDonalds. I was amazed to see how she'd transformed herself from angry London street kid to a haughty, semi aristocrat from the West Coast of Ireland. I thought her accent was better than mine and she was certainly a far better actor. I wasn't helped by the fact that I could see that I wasn't going to get much help from Arnold who obviously didn't know what acting was, or from Billie, who didn't care.

The set was marked out on the floor of the hall and a few old pieces of furniture were dotted around to represent what would actually be there on the three nights we performed the play in the Threshold Theatre. I became more and more terrified as I realised the extent of my inadequacy and my lack of basic understanding of what an actor did. It was one thing to agree to do a bit of it but quite another to actually go on stage in front of my sister, her husband, Miriam and fifty or sixty others I didn't know sitting in judgement on my performance and I was sure having a good laugh at it.

Arnold decided to stand it up as he put it and block the play. As far as I could see this meant more or less asking the actors to move around the acting space for no apparent reason according to his whim.

'You come in from there,' Arnold said to me, 'and go up to centre stage by the fireplace.'

'From where?'

'The door to the room, it's marked on the floor.'

'Ah, I see.'

'And you go up to the fireplace.'

'Why?'

'It's just a preliminary blocking,' said Arnold.

'Is it because I'm cold? Is it snowing outside? I seem to remember it was snowing several times in the film.'

'This isn't the film, this is my play,' said Billie who was sitting importantly on a chair just behind Arnold with her fingers propping up her chin looking like she was praying.

'Anyway,' said Arnold,' you haven't come from outside. You've been in the drawing room talking to Chantal's father and the other guests.'

'Oh I see. And then I went outside and got cold so I come back in and go up to the fireplace. Did I know there was a fire in here?'

'Maybe you did. There's the fireplace.'

'Where?'

'It's marked on the floor, like the door.' Arnold was getting impatient.

'So I am cold. I mean I could shiver a bit.'

'Francis, it doesn't matter at the moment why you go up to the fireplace. You go there because that's where I want you to go.'

'Oh, right. Why do you want me to go there?'

Arnold leant back and crossed his legs in a pose that I could see had come from his father. 'Look Francis, I know you're not very experienced in the theatre, so let me explain something. If you imagine for a moment that you are watching a play and then someone turns the sound down..'

'What?'

'And you couldn't hear anything.'

'Why wouldn't I be able to hear anything?'

'Just imagine it for a moment, please.'

'Oh, maybe I suddenly went deaf?'

'Alright, you suddenly went deaf and you couldn't hear anything. But you were watching the play. And if the blocking was good, so you could see the movement of the actors, then you'd still be able to tell what was going on.'

'Would I?'

'Yes, Francis, because their positioning on the stage would tell you.'

'Oh right.'

'So come in and go up to the fireplace.'

'So what does that tell the audience? Ah! I get it! I'm cold.'

'For God's sake.'

'It's alright, Arnold I understand. Just the one little thing, one last little thing. Why am I cold if I haven't been outside?'

'Fucking hell!' Billie threw her script on the floor. 'Can we please do my script please.'

'Oh I will. I mean I will, but I just need...'

'Can I help?' said Kate, who throughout all this had been standing on the other side of the room waiting for the scene to begin. 'Look Francis, you've been in the other room talking to my father, but maybe you felt a bit awkward...'

I could imagine that, it was the story of my life. 'Because I don't get on with him too well, because I'm kind of impassioned and a kind of solitary religious person entrapped by my own belief?' I was hoping to ingratiate myself with Billie with my profound understanding of her play.

'Oh for fuck's sake,' she said.

'So,' said Kate. 'You leave my father and go out into the hallway, out there.' She pointed to the wall of the church hall. 'And it's cold and you're shivering, so you see the door and you come in here, see the fireplace and go for it.'

'Brilliant, thank you Kate.'

'You're welcome.' She grinned.

'So can we start, please?' said Arnold. 'You come in through the door.

I went over to the door, 'Oh just one last tiny little thing. Will there actually be a fire in the fireplace?'

'I don't know yet, Francis, I have to talk to the electrician.'

'Oh an electric fire. Did they actually have one of those back then?'

'It would be some kind of imitation fire. Did you think we were going to have three bright red glowing bars?' said Arnold grinning.

'And a shilling in the meter?' Arnold and Billie both roared with laughter.

'Im just doing my best to fucking understand what I'm doing, Arnold!'

'Alright, alright,' said Arnold backing off and perhaps worried he was going to experience some of my rage that he'd last seen on Lewisham High Street.

'We'll just walk it through,' said Kate. 'Don't worry we'll talk about it later.'

I knew then that if anyone was going to help me it would be Kate. At first this made me happy but as the rehearsals went on I began to realise that although I could imagine what I was feeling and what I was meant to do, actually doing it without being self-conscious was another matter entirely. Everything seemed false and clumsy and I even discovered alarmingly at one point that I'd forgotten how to walk. I knew I was awful and so did everyone else. How do you do it? How do you take that leap into being someone else?

I looked over at Kate who was sitting at the side of the hall with her nose in the script and peeling an orange. Every now and again her face would change and she made shapes in the air as she mouthed her lines. I remembered the actor in the Carter's Way Green Room doing the same thing. These were real actors who knew what they were doing. And I wasn't.

# 39

'Dear Richard, great Richard,' said Alexander.

He was sitting with me on a bench outside the crematorium where Fat Dick was probably even now just smoke and ashes. We were waiting for the car which was to take Alexander to the gathering in memory of Richard and he'd kindly invited me to ride along.

I was glum, not only at the death of my friend but couldn't help continually returning to what seemed the intractable problem of transforming myself into someone else; and being surrounded by actors at the funeral, all of whom knew perfectly well how to pull off this magic trick made matters worse. The previous evening's rehearsal had been embarrassing, I'd reddened and wanted to be out of there. I could see that Arnold had lost all faith in me, Billie had walked out twice, and even Kate was giving me pitying looks. I'd managed to get the day off school to pay my respects to Fat Dick but the memory of this desperate failure was so all-consuming that I could hardly concentrate on the death of my old friend. What a heartless mess I am. Alexander didn't help.

'Richard was a great actor,' he said. 'Superb, better than all of us I'd say. Technically untouchable, could do anything, but that's not what was great about him. He had breadth, the greatest understanding, such a deep and rich knowledge of his fellows. He could tap into it whatever the circumstance and of course for whatever he was asked to play. Over the years he has helped me many times. And so brave too, never frightened of what he was, and never judged others either.'

I was sitting, nodding, as I sat leaning forward on the bench scuffing the fallen leaves at my feet and thinking Christ I don't need more tales of great performers, I can't even take my first step. Not that Alexander noticed.

His voice became softer, 'I remember one time when we

were both young and playing small parts in some god-awful repertory company. You weren't allowed to be gay then, but Dick was what he was, flamboyant, kind and clearly homosexual. He didn't give a damn what anybody thought. There was a young boy in the cast who was also obviously gay, but perhaps didn't know it, or at least couldn't admit it, and was very unhappy. The company was run by a fool, as they often were, often are now. His name was David Harber and he was a tyrant and a bully. How he became a director I'll never know. He picked on this boy mercilessly and rehearsal after rehearsal was agony for him as everything he did was derided and he was humiliated. It came to head one day when he just stood in the middle of the rehearsal floor in front of the entire company, his arms by his side, his head hung low and with tears streaming down his face; an absolute picture of misery. Harber, nasty piece of work that he was, shouted, "Oh for God's sake, do we have to witness this sentimental claptrap? Either do your job or get out of here!" The boy couldn't speak. He slowly turned and began walking towards the door. There was absolute silence. The boy was desolate. What could we say? Then Richard stood up. He was bulky even then, but let me tell you his presence counted for far more than any body weight. He said, "No, it's not him that should be making his exit, sir. It's you."

Now you must remember that Richard wasn't a well known actor then. We were all callow, just starting out. I'd been second footman, a doctor, five lines, six lines until I gave my MacDuff to Richard's Banquo, a marvellous performance by the way. Me I mean. Suffice to say that we were both junior members of the company and there he was standing up to this well known director. He then turned to the boy who was still standing by the door and said, "please would you do me the honour of sitting by me. You are brave, so terribly brave to stand up on the stage and reveal yourself; and it's a privilege for us all to act in your company." Then he turned back to the director and said, "and you are a bully, and like all bullies, you are a coward."'

I could see tears coming to Alexander's eyes as he told his story, whether they were of approval, or rage, or grief, I don't know.

'The boy walked slowly over to Richard and sat by him. We were all expecting an explosion from this ridiculous director but all he said was, "well, we'd better get on with it, hadn't we?" He'd been beaten down and utterly crushed by a much better man than him. And do you know why? Because Richard meant every word he'd said. You could see it in his face, hear it in his voice. In right is might, dear boy, and Richard didn't doubt for one second how right he was. I've never had so much respect for anybody. Greatest performance he ever gave.'

'You think Richard was just acting?'

'Not just acting, Francis. Being the best he could be. Ah, here's our car.'

He sat preoccupied as the limousine cruised out of the cemetery and onto the main road towards the nature reserve that Richard's friends had booked to hold a reception for him. Suddenly he said, 'Even the most fervent faith, the most powerful belief is an act that comes from within, from what you are. I don't know whether that's the most terrifying thing I know, or the most optimistic.'

Drinks were laid out in the large bright airy room overlooking the marshes. The river glistened silver in the distance under a sky full of the clouds of Richard's passing. Affixed to the walls were a series of large, blown-up photographs of him in his most memorable roles; smiling, or glowering down on his friends as they drank his health and recited their stories of him. I had a short conversation with Annie and Paul and was about to leave when I was abruptly confronted by a woman in a spectacular black dress, a half veil and a riot of blond hair piled high on her head.

'The delivery man!' June LeGrand held her arms outstretched. 'How wonderful to see you again! I remembered our scene together for the rest of the day!'

I was almost overpowered by the strength of her perfume as she kissed my cheeks, leaving traces of lipstick on the side of my mouth. I could feel the grease on my tongue as I licked it off. 'I told the lead writer that I wanted you back,' she said.

'How many parcels can you get?' My modesty had become so becoming I'd become an idiot.

'Well cast him as something else, I told them. But it was all the usual excuses. You were wonderful, darling, absolutely wonderful! You gave Mrs Carter a new lease of life!' She laughed and turned away. 'Jonty! Hullo darling!' And she was gone.

'You seem to get around.' It was Alexander who'd been standing nearby.

Maybe it was the boost to my confidence given me by the flattery of June that made me blurt out what had been on my mind all day. 'Alexander, do you mind if I call you Alexander? How do you act? I mean how do you not be yourself?'

My look must have been so pathetic that Alexander's cheery greeting was immediately replaced by a look of serious concern. 'Ah,' he said, 'I had a feeling there might something worrying you.'

'It's worrying me terribly. I can't even concentrate on Richard.'

'Come. Come with me.'

He led me out of the room to a long balcony that ran down the side of the building overlooking the river. We sat at a black whicker table facing the water. A flock of Canada geese glided down, skimmed the marshes and took off again. He listened gravely as I told him about my failure to play Father O'Brian.

'I know about everything about him, how he walks, how he talks. I can imagine the lonely life he leads with the bread and the wine; they're his only food, in the film anyway. I know about his immovable faith. I mean I know about God, I've been there myself. And I know about Ireland. I know everything and at the end of it all there I am, still me, like stuttering and totally embarrassed. How do you do it? How do you get to be him?'

Alexander reached out and touched my hand. 'I'll tell you how,' he said. 'Take all that knowledge and forget it. Don't worry it will still be there, but now it's no use to you. You have a vivid imagination?'

I nodded. At least I thought so.

'So we start at the beginning. It's called a play, you're playing a part, so play. Play like a child, throw your hands in the air, speak in strange voices, walk with your feet splayed, or tucked in, or raise your knees ridiculously high with a stupid grin on your face. Play. Just play. I am Father O'Brian, look at me.' I did. 'I am happy, I am not happy, I am concerned, I don't care.' He pulled a series of clownish faces, his mouth turned down, his eyebrows went up, even his ears were part of his amazing conjuration of every mood. 'Now they're just silly, aren't they?' He pulled his chin into his chest and thrust his belly out, then spoke in a gravelly Irish accent. 'Dominus Vobiscum Tuo.' He laughed, 'Now you do it.'

'Do what?'

'What I just did.'

I did, copying him. 'But that's not Father O'Brian.'

'Then do it again like him. Play, Francis, play. Doesn't matter whether you believe it or not, just play. Be serious, be jovial, who cares, it's up to you. The choices you make are there for you in the script. It says be earnest...Dominus Vobiscum Tuo...play with it; and he was earnest. Be angry...Dominus Vobiscum Tuo...play with it; and he was angry. You're under threat. Laugh, cry, you can see him do it...Dominus Vobiscum Tuo...play. Do it, just play. And play and play.'

I began to repeat the phrase over and over again letting whatever mood I felt dictate the tone. 'Dominus Vobiscum Tuo, Dominus Vobiscum...'

'Let it be in your whole body, your voice and your hands.'

'Dominus Vobiscum Tuo. Dominus Vobiscum Tuo...'

'And in your imagination. And in your laughter and your tears...

'Dominus Vobiscum Tuo. Dominus Vobiscum Tuo...'

'And in your soul....

'Dominus Vobiscum Tuo. Dominus Vobiscum Tuo...'

He laughed and so did I. I began to relax and enjoy myself, then I stopped, 'But am I now myself doing this?'

'Of course you are.'

'You said there was no such thing.'

'Self? Absolutely there is no such single thing. There's hundreds of them, dear, hundreds of you. The number of you's is infinite, dear boy. Dominus Vobiscum Tuo. Dominus Vobiscum Tuo,' it was as if he was conducting me; his hand went down and his hand went up and so did my head and voice.

'So who's deciding which one of all that I'm supposed to be?'

'You are,'

'So who that fuck is that, Alexander?' And oh boy I meant it as I said it. I was almost in tears.

He slapped the table as he roared with laughter. 'Do you know, Francis, I think you are going to be the most wonderful actor.' He stood up, ' Remember Dick Guest and his defence of that boy? That was his decision. Took guts, didn't it? Only he could have done that. And only you can do, Dominus Vobiscum Tuo. Dominus Vobiscum Tuo...' He turned away, laughing and repeating the phrase as he went through the glass doors back into the reception.

I thought about following him but didn't want to meet June LeGrand again. 'Dominus Vobiscum Tuo. Dominus Vobiscum Tuo...' I looked over the railing to the marshland and knew I had to get out of there. I decided to walk along the river home. As I went along the gravel path through the marshes I repeated it; Dominus Vobiscum Tuo over and over in time to my footsteps; Dominus Vobiscum Tuo, clickety-click, Dominus Vobiscum Tuo, clickety-click, My stride quickened and my breath became shorter. The image of Father Mulligan greeting his parishioners by the church door came to me and I stuck my belly out like Alexander had done. Dominus Vobiscum Tuo, Dominus Vobiscum Tuo. My accent became rich and from the West of Ireland. I began to laugh as I nodded the phrase to a plump of moorhens as they splashed up from a clump of reeds. I saw my old Aunt Ella, a mean stringy woman with broken hands and a walnut face and rasped it as she would have done, Dominus Vobiscum Tuo you little brat, get out of here! I came to the river, walking even faster. Dominus Vobiscum Tuo in my old man's baritone. I shouted it louder, Dominus Vobiscum! A young couple passing with a baby in a pushchair gave me a strange look. Dominus Vobiscum Tuo! I blessed them. They grinned back. The woman even crossed herself with a playful smirk. I remembered my mad cousin Lennie, a joke-a-minute drunk, Dominus Vobiscum Tuo in Lennie's crazy cackle. Dominus Vobiscum Tuo, have you heard the one about...? I thought of Fat Dick and looked into the deep murk of the river passing by slow as a funeral. I felt sad and gave it the camp bass as Dick would have delivered it to the martinet director back in those days. Dominus Vobiscum Tuo to you my dear, now get out of my sight! I liked this voice and repeated it, La Belle Dame Sans Merci, watch out she doesn't drown you. Then Abebi with her husky, sexy, LA accent. Dominus Vobiscum Tuo, hi Frankly, I'm not really a liar. And Tony answered in broad Sheffield, Dominus Vobiscum Tuo, Nor me, pal, I just wanted to fuck her, want another?

I thought maybe I was crazy. No I'm just possible. All this is me and I'm possible; weird, but that's what I thought. I tapped my side in rhythm as I recited a line from the play, "I know one thing, Chantal, and that's my faith." Dominus Vobiscum Tuo. I repeated these lines again and again adding Dominus Vobiscum Tuo every time I lost the line or its meaning to me. I was a kid again, dancing in the rain, up to my elbows in mud on the pitch, scoring, missing a tackle, getting thumped on the back of my head by some bastard in the fourth year, eating beans on toast with a lashing of ketchup, shouting at my Da. I didn't care! I played. I got angry as I understood that Father O'Brien was expressing the deepest things. "I know one thing, Chantal, and that's my faith." I shouted it at the river which paid no attention. Walkers stopped and stared at this madman losing his mind by the Thames. The rage that had come to me outside the MacDonalds, the rage of some other time and place, the rage of me; it was here again, but this time in a way I could understand. I roared, "That's my faith!" My body was rigid and I could feel the sound cutting the back of my throat. The words were nothing to me, but they were everything to Father O'Brian.

## 40

The rehearsals were better. The lines weren't those huge problems I'd thought they were. I began to see them as friends, like the tips of mountains of all kinds of stuff that I could play with. And when I did that things came out that I didn't expect about O'Brien, but also out of myself. Sometimes it was fun, sometimes it was stupid but I didn't care and anyway Kate laughed even if Arnold didn't. For a while I was enjoying myself; it was like rehearsal was some big playground where you could do what you liked; in other words play as Alexander had told me. Billy came in, went out, looked pissed off especially when I forgot, or changed, or just ignored her script, but as time went on I became more accurate because somehow what I had to say was infiltrating me or maybe even exploiting me in a way I didn't really understand; in other words there was something opening up in me. Mostly I was still confused but I was finding a way and sometimes I'd break through this invisible barrier between myself and O'Brian for a second or two and be in another world. Then I'd wake up and see to my surprise that I was standing by some old chairs in the church hall and I'd forgotten who I was and had actually become the country priest. Kate smiled at me at those times. I knew she believed in me which was a relief, but still it was only happening in little moments and I didn't know how to make it a whole thing; how to join it all up together into what I knew about the priest and what was in myself. I felt I almost wanted to explode, could see the fuse, but couldn't find the match. There was still something missing, something beyond me and I couldn't fathom what it was.

I was intrigued by this problem which I began to see as within myself, not in O'Brian, or Billie come to that, although the words I was saying were her's. It was as if there was something I'd never admitted, or never known about, some root, Alexander's nub, that I was circling round, taking a nibble at every now and again, but never fully seeing or understanding. Whatever it was the whole process fascinated me.

I thought that concentrating on all this would have a bad effect on my school work, but it didn't and I actually found that I was enjoying my classes more. I was happier, more open and had more energy. I didn't see the kids anymore as a kind of wall, they were more like a fertile garden. My lack of preparation over the summer had become an advantage as I was forced to improvise and actually talk to them from some part of myself which surprised me. I wasn't droning on about all the usual stuff, I was actually listening, as if actually they had something to say, and then they'd talk about it. I discovered that if I encouraged them they were very capable of mimicry and pastiche, they could act the scenes out and then take the piss out of them. In other words they could play, like I could play. And sometimes it was funny and sometimes even actually riotous, and every now and again we learnt something. Even one time when some scene or tone or other reminded me of Abebi, tears came to my eyes and all the girls went aah as if they'd moved me so much they'd made me cry. Well the truth was that sometimes anything at all could make me laugh or make me cry. Maybe I was going mad.

After one class, Angela Griffiths came up to me at my desk as said, 'You've changed, Mr Riley. What happened?'

'Oh nothing much. As a matter of fact I had a bit of a difficult summer.'

'You got sad?'

'No. Well, yes. And happy too.'

'Which?'

'Both.'

'You can't be both.'

'Well to be honest, Angela, I think you can.'

'That's interesting,' she said.

'It is, isn't it?'

As she left the classroom I thought how you could be one thing and then another and back again which is why I could have tears in my eyes about Abebi and at the same time hate her. I had some big sympathy for her growing from somewhere; she didn't know what she was doing, did she? And if she didn't know, it meant that she like me, was shooting from one feeling to another, or in her case one lie to another. There were even moments when I could imagine putting my arms around her. I liked those moments best, until I was disgusted with myself for being a wet sucker and threw her down onto some imaginary floor. Then I picked her up again.

And there was Tony. Things between us were getting back to a kind of normal. We still met for a drink when I had time, and talked about football and all that stuff, but there was a difference. He actually listened to me when I spoke, and I knew that it was because I'd accepted what he'd done with Abebi, whatever the truth of it. I wasn't quite sure how all of that worked, but I knew things had changed. I even managed to talk to Sophie Rayner in the staffroom without feeling like a small boy with my tongue hanging out and waiting for a slap around my ears, and I'd actually laughed with her which was a first. I sat at home staring at the Michelangelo and there were moments when I wanted to rip the boy's face out of the frame, but other times when I just sighed because I could see the beauty again. Maybe it was all to do with Mary Doolan, or my Dad, or Kate, or myself. Spring and storm were breaking out all over. I couldn't work it out but knew I needed to because the first night was coming up fast.

Arnold had asked me to come in for a dress rehearsal on the afternoon of the premiere, as he called it, which meant taking more time off school. As I'd already taken a day out to go to Fat Dick's funeral this wasn't going to be easy and I went with some trepidation to see Mr Pontini to plead my case.

'I've only got the one class that afternoon. I'm really sorry, but..'

Mr Pontini was looking at me through his over-sized red perfectly round spectacles. 'What should I do, Francis, tell your pupils to go and play on the street? Or perhaps they should teach themselves? From what I hear of your recent classes - and hear is the word, we can all hear them from one side of the school to the other - they're doing that already.'

'Well I think they've been going quite well.'

'Do you?' Pontini looked at me as if I was something he might have found in the bottom of a desk drawer. 'So you want to be an actor?'

'Oh I don't know about that.'

Pontini arched his brows above the rims of his glasses. 'Well if you don't, who does?'

'I'm still making up my mind.'

'And if you decide to do so, you'll give up teaching?'

'That might be a bit premature. I was in a soap, just a bit part, you know it? Carter's Way?'

'No.'

'Well it goes on in the afternoon. Maybe I should forget it. It's probably just a stupid fantasy, I don't know, I'm... well to tell you the truth, Mr Pontini, I'm getting quite interested in it.'

'Are you?'

'Ah, yes.'

'Why?'

'Because, well, it's very interesting.'

Pontini continued to look at me. 'I like you, Francis, I always have, but you never seem to be too clear about where you're going with your life.'

'That's my problem alright.'

'But you're certain enough to want next Thursday afternoon off?'

'I'd really appreciate it, Mr Pontini, I really would. I am clear, I think, I am certainly clear in my own mind, but I can't blame you for thinking I'm also a bit confused, because I am. You see, if I do this play it'll help me make up my mind. I mean if I'm useless I'll know won't I?'

'And if you're a great success?'

'I doubt that. I doubt that alright?'

'But you want to do it?

'Please. I do.'

There was a pause. Pontini pursed his lips, 'alright, Francis. I'll take your class myself and find out if they've been learning anything.'

'Thank you, Mr Pontini, thank you so much.'

'I wish you well, Francis.'

As I left the school at lunchtime a couple of days later to get to the dress rehearsal Tony came up to me by the gates.

'Good luck tonight, son.'

'You coming?'

'Didn't get an invite.'

'You may as well, everybody else is.'

As I went on down the road for a minute I wasn't sure where I was going and for a moment I didn't know if I'd ever be back. I mean, I did know that I'd be back but somewhere else in my head I wasn't so sure. I'd fixed a short date with Miriam because as always in such times I needed to talk to her. She didn't always say what I wanted to hear but it least it meant I was focussing on the problem, or at least what I thought the problem might be. The fact was that I was as nervous as hell and doubted I'd even be able to walk on the stage let alone deliver a line and I needed to tell someone.

When I arrived she was already sitting outside the Flying Duck at the same old table where she'd told me about Abebi meeting Tony. As I sat down opposite her I glanced over at Guiseppe's and imagined them sitting opposite each other and holding hands.

Miriam was drinking coffee. 'I thought I'd get you a glass of wine,' she said, 'but wasn't sure if actors drank before a performance.'

'Better not, I'll take what you're having.' I gestured to the waiter and pointed to Miriam's cup. It was another fine day and the traffic was flowing along the road a few feet away. 'Fucking fumes,' I said, 'the death of me.'

'How are you feeling?'

'Shitting myself.'

'Don't you have to go in early to prepare yourself? Do all those vocal exercises, bee, bee, bee, aah, aah, aah and those tongue twisters?'

'How should I know? Maybe I should get some training.'

'Bit late for that.'

'Bit late for everything, you ask me.'

'God, I'm rushed off my feet,' she said, needing to get her own life recorded before she could move onto mine. 'Theo, without any warning, has dropped a new module into my lap, the confidence of the New American Dream. How am I supposed to know anything about that?'

'The American nightmare,' I said.

'Have you heard from her?'

'Got a letter. She's gone, Mitzy, and that's that.' It wasn't entirely but what else was I going to say.

'I feel partly responsible.'

'What because you saw them and told me?'

'I never liked her,' she said.

'You spent all your time creeping round her.'

'She was a contributor to the conference, Frankie.'

'Doesn't matter.' I was beginning to sulk, something I often did when I wanted reassurance from Miriam.

She could see the signs. 'Well it's not so bad, you've got the play, haven't you?'

'I don't know if I have. It kind of comes and goes. It's like I keep seeing myself coming back. How weird is that? I psyche myself up to be this Father O'Brian then find it's me standing there on the stage.'

'You're not over thinking it, are you?'

'Sure I am. What else? I've got a mind, Miriam. I can't close it down. It whirrs, it goes, it shoots up and down.'

'Not much point asking you to relax is there?'

'You could try.'

'Relax.'

'Fuck off.' I sipped my coffee and wiped the froth from my top lip. 'She sent her letter to me via Skinner, you know? He must have walked round to my flat and hand delivered it. I saw him at the university too.'

'He told me.'

'He was alright. He's an appalling bastard but he's alright too.'

'Aren't we all?'

'Are we?'

'I think you're very brave, Frankie. Being someone else is a very difficult thing to do. I couldn't do it. Or maybe it's a wonderful thing to do.' She was looking at me in a wondrous way as if I was shape-shifting before her eyes.

'And they're all going to be there. Annie and Paul, even Tony, he's coming now.'

'And me.'

'Oh I know you'll be there.'

'I always am, aren't I?'

'I guess so, Mitzy. I guess you are.'

'You'll do it, Frankie.'

'Will I?'

## 41

The dress rehearsal was a disaster. At first it went well. We were in the theatre for the first time, a rudimentary set had been built with flats representing the ante-chamber to the drawing room of the great house. There was a carpet on the floor and some good period pieces of furniture had been borrowed by the stage manager. No fire was in the fireplace, but all that seemed so long ago that I hardly noticed. When I'd walked in they were playing a tape recording of the low conversations being held at the funeral gathering offstage and the lighting designer was positioning his lamps.

Arnold had found me an old black cassock which fitted well and I swished it round my ankles trying to feel priestly as I paced the tiny dressing room we all shared behind the stage. Kate looked sexy and dangerous as Chantal and the maid looked like a maid out of a French farce in her black dress and white apron. I smarmed my hair back and down with a gel that I'd bought in the chemist on the High Street then walked back onto the stage and looked out at the auditorium. Various lights came on and then went down. Finally the full rig lit up and caught me staring out at the rows of empty seats. Francis spotlit for the world to see.

The stage manager shouted from backstage. 'Your half hour call, ladies and gentlemen, your half hour call.'

I sat for a long time opposite my mirror dressed as Father O'Brien, looking like Father O'Brien but not entirely sure who Father O'Brian was. 'We're all narcissists, aren't we?' said Alexander. I grinned at my face and liked what I saw, then out of nowhere that old Doors track again Break On Through To The Other Side. The fifteen minute call came. I thought I saw my image dissolve for a second and there was no-one in the mirror, but then I came back so that was alright. The five minute call. Chantal and the maid got up and left the room to open the play. I heard the tape of the crowd in the main room come on, and then Chantal's voice as she began the scene.

I got up and stood in the wings. The maid exited on the other side of the stage as Chantal sat down. This was my cue. I walked into the room beneath the bright lights which was make believe but the real thing. I confronted Chantal who was no longer Kate but the landowner's daughter. And I was Father O'Brian. My voice was full and strong. My first lines seemed to be coming from someone else and I knew I could bend them to my will and make of them whatever I wanted to. I didn't know how but somehow I was in control, or someone was in control. It wasn't me, but it was me. I could hear everything Chantal said and answer her back in kind as she responded to me. I was somewhere else. It was a wild and crazy feeling. It couldn't last. I wasn't me, or O'Brien, but some weird being who was both of them.

Suddenly Chantal's voice was faltering, she'd forgotten her speech. Then I knew I wasn't in control at all. I saw that her carefully coiffed hair was just a wig, her make up came from tubes and boxes I'd seen in the dressing room, the embroidered black dress was the one she'd borrowed from her aunt. She was Kate the girl who'd yelled at me outside the MacDonalds, Kate the actress who'd helped me. She was as confused and uncertain as I was, hunting for the Chantal who she'd lost.

She yelled, 'Line!'

The stage manager prompted her immediately from the wings and she began to pick up the scene and slowly return to Chantal. But it was too late. It was as if I'd seen through the mirror and was standing there naked. I didn't know what to do or what to say. My throat was dry, my knees buckling. For some reason I decided to sit down, which wasn't part of Arnold's blocking, and which only made matters worse. I didn't know where I should go next. Chantal was looking at me waiting for my line. I didn't know what to say.

I got up and left the stage.

Behind me I could Arnold shouting, 'What the fuck is he doing?'

Then Billie, 'I told you to get a real fucking actor!'

I pulled the cassock over my head and dumped it onto a chair in the dressing room. I could see the Maid and the Governess sitting in front of mirrors looking at me strangely, as if they were afraid to speak to me. I walked out of the room and into the small yard behind the theatre where I was confronted by a huge skip full of broken flats and theatre rubbish. Behind it was a wooden fence, and in the fence there was a door leading out into a back alley. I couldn't work out how to get to the door.

'Francis?' Kate had come out of the dressing room after me. 'What are you doing? Francis?'

'I got to get out of here.' I fumbled for a cigarette. 'I can't stay. How do you get to that door?'

'It was my fault,' she said, 'I dried. Because you were so brilliant, you threw me.'

'I can't do this. This fucking skip stinks. How do I get out of here?'

'What are you doing?' Arnold had come out of the dressing room with Billie behind him. 'Where's your costume? This is my career you're fucking up! And her's. You know how long it took her to write this?'

I was moving round the skip. I thought I could see how to get to the door. Then it was easy. There was a gap between the skip and the fence. 'I'm going now.'

'You can't fucking go!'

'I'm going.'

And I was through the door and into the alley and walking fast towards the light at the end. I stopped, lit the cigarette and looked around. I was in a small street with terraced houses either side. I thought it looked like the street where I lived but knew it wasn't. I turned down another street, and then another. The streets seemed to be getting smaller, hemming me in either side. Then another street where there were no houses, just sheer walls either side. I saw a gap in the wall and turned down into a narrow alley where the walls were so high that they cut out the sunlight. I could see a pub sign, The Mitre, swinging from the wall and thought, why not have a drink? Why not indeed? I could call Tony. But I couldn't find the door of the pub. The sign was above me alright, but there was no door. I seemed to be having big trouble with doors these days, first the one behind the skip and then this one that didn't seem to exist. I felt along the wall and came to a wooden edge that jutted out. It was a door! I pushed at it and went into the pub which was just a room with a couple of tables and a bar at one end. There was no-one there but I had a feeling that someone would come and I stood in front of the bar and waited.

Sure enough after a couple of minutes a woman came out from behind the bar. She reminded me of my mother. She had the same dark hair and dark kind eyes. She was a bit plump too, not too plump but kind of middle-aged plump, like my mother when she died. Just for one split second the curtain at the back of my mind opened and in that split second shaft of light I saw my mother in her last hours worn and wasted in her cancer. And I knew then she'd been a stranger but had loved me. And I suddenly realised with a shock that rooted my feet to the floorboards that she'd had a secret life; a life I'd always known but never seen; a life that was silent but full of her own adventures.

The woman said, 'How can I help you?'

'I said, 'I'd like a pint please if you'd be so kind.'

'A pint of what?'

'Oh the usual.'

She began to pour a pint of Guinness.

'That's grand.' I said and noticed that my voice seemed lower. Not much lower but lower than it had been. I watched as she poured the pint too quickly allowing the top to froth and swirl. I thought, they don't know how to pour Guinness over here, and immediately wondered who "they" were and what I meant by "over here."

'Thanks very much,' I said as she gave me the drink.'

'You're welcome, dear.'

I took the pint and sat at a table by the wall. There was no doubt about it, my voice was definitely lower. I looked round the dingy room wondering why I'd never been there before. I knew most pubs, but not this one. Maybe it was just out of my usual area of boozing.

I sipped my pint. I didn't know if I was I; or if I was he; or if I was the big you looking down over all of it. I am all of them maybe; I, you and he. I thought I may as well do something useful and began to recite my lines from the play. They came quite effortlessly and easily. At first I thought I could hear them in O'Brian's voice but there was something different about it. It wasn't quite the priest's but it wasn't my own either, something, somewhere in between like the moment in the dress rehearsal. Whatever it was, it was ok. The woman was gone from behind the bar and I began to speak the lines out loud, my voice getting bigger and stronger and humorous and confident. I was playing around, having a laugh. The woman must have heard me and came back behind the bar.

I said, 'Ah landlady, another pint of your excellent Guinness if you wouldn't mind?'

'You from the Threshold?' she asked as she poured.

'Where?' I said.

'The little theatre round the corner,' she said. 'I could hear you speaking and thought you must be an actor.'

'No, I'm a priest,' I said.

She laughed. 'Oh so that's why you drink in the afternoons.' She came from behind the bar and walked towards me; a stout woman with the stout. 'Sorry about the pouring, my husband usually does them. He's away at the moment.' She put the pint on my table and left me to it.

I spoke out loud to the empty room, 'I know one thing, Chantal and that's my faith.' I said it now as if I was considering it, as if there might be a doubt. There was still some rage there like outside the MacDonalds but now it was more measured. Everything I said felt good and I let the lines flow out through me as the time passed and flowed out across the floor and out of the door. Then it was time for me to go. I got up and went back to the theatre.

## 42

They were all there in the dressing room. Arnold looked pale.

'You alright, Francis?' said Kate.

I sat in my chair and looked into the mirror again. Cassock, hair gel, still the same old O'Brian.

'We don't have time to finish the Dress now,' said Arnold as Billie walked furiously out of the room. Kate sat down close to me. 'You'll be fine,' she said. 'I promise you.' Her hair was blond and whispy, her lips carmine. She smiled at me as if she understood. I stood up and smoothed the cassock with my hands, and then sat down again.

'The house is open.' I heard the stage manager come into

the dressing room. 'Fifteen minutes.'

The time seemed to fly by or maybe it didn't exist at all. Chantal and the Maid got up and went out. I heard the tape recording of the funeral reception again. It seemed very loud. Chantal was saying something, then the Maid. I stood up and stood in the wings watching them under the glare. I could see rows of the audience through a split in the flats. The first person I saw was Miriam sitting in the fourth row behind Annie and Paul. Over to the left there was Tony sitting closer to the stage and at the back I could see the blond hair of Annabelle tied up in a top knot. I remembered sitting in her office telling her about Abebi. The thought of Abebi made my gut churn for a second then I forgot her. I was staring intently at the stage. The wings were dark and I thought I was in the underground club with Alexander. I was saying, 'You know Alex, sometimes you can love yourself too much.' The great actor's eyes crinkled in wisdom and kindness. 'Oh is that so?' he said. 'Yes,' I said, 'You have to forget yourself and see what's beyond.' And I felt the original pain beneath spreading and buckling and infesting me and somehow becoming part of it all and filling me with the energy of myself.

The Maid left the stage and Chantal sat in her chair. I walked into the room and everything was exactly as it should be; the carpet was under my feet and the chairs were in the right place. I was as clear as I'd ever been and felt good. I knew as I spoke that I was certain and strong in the great heat of attention from all the people watching me. I thought that was really good, people watching me, it made me feel bigger, kind of outside myself and very exciting as if I was finally myself, my whole self and nothing but myself, the centre of their attention, the centre of the universe. As a matter of fact it was the best I'd ever felt. It was the bliss of being nothing at all and knowing I could be everything I wanted; the bliss of knowing that everything changes all the time and I was part of it, rolling with those old waves that crashed down on the shore; and I was there in that moment, feeling all that could be and choosing what to feel. I was as free as that trout in the river, unhooked.

Chantal, this girl, was looking up at me. I thought she was very beautiful although her face was drawn and hard and suspicious. She tilted her chin in a haughty way and her voice sounded condescending. I smiled and let it go as if it meant nothing to me because I knew my opposition to her came from this place I was in that she could never be. That was my place and also O'Brian's faith which I knew was way beyond her, and she could never understand. My tone was tender although I knew that what I knew was way past tenderness. She could see what I was doing and she responded, playing with me and we fenced, each trying to take the upper hand. The scene came to an end as it should with a stand off between us. I made my exit as the Governess came on from the other side.

I didn't go back to the dressing room but stood in the wings watching as Chantal prowled the room and attacked the Governess with what I could see was the rage of a woman and the plaintiveness of an abandoned child. It was all very very clear, but the effect of the Guinness was wearing off and I wished I could toss back a fast Jamesons or at least take a drag on a cigarette. My stomach was beginning to churn again. I could see the back of the stage flats, a costume hung on a nail; the bleak reality of it all was like a smack in the gut. I was terrified again and was falling back behind the curtain that was between myself and the other place I had been in just a few moments ago. This other place which was where I should be. For eternal seconds I kept passing through this curtain backwards and forwards from here to there, from panic to elation, from dark to light, from myself to nowhere. I saw the Governess leave to be replaced by the maid again. Chantal was speaking harshly. In minutes, in more eternal seconds, I'd be there again, facing her.

As I walked on I fell back behind the curtain; my previous

energy seemed to have deserted me, the power had gone in the vapour of the Guinness. I was lucky that Chantal was the first to speak. Her delivery was assured and I loved her more than I'd ever loved anyone even if she had a look of hatred in her eye; her chin was set high and there was a sneer on her lip. My voice came back and I had broken through the curtain again and was some new self again, something I'd never known before and I knew would never be again, but it was complete and strong and belonged just to me. I'd never felt better. I was flying in a space I'd never known.

She said, 'You think you know, don't you? You think you know the big secret. But even if you did once, you've lost it.'

And in that final eternal second I did know. The lost secret was in me. O'Brian was the way, that was all. I was the kid playing football, the son of the father, the tears of the mother, the passion of Dolores, the love of Miriam, the acolyte at Tony's knee, the forgiving angel above, the ecstatic desire of Abebi, and the sad clown hardly able to walk through the air. I was an English teacher, Mr Pontini's pet, the angry maniac, the delivery man... and I was right now able to summon any and all of them and that included Father Patrick O'Brian who was all or some of them.

My body opened up, everything seemed right. I fixed Chantal with a look and smile and said, 'I know only one thing, Chantal, and that's my faith in myself.' I'd changed the words but it didn't matter. 'And that belief tells me that abandoning your father is wrong.'

She was shocked by my intensity, my realness, my whole truth. There was a silence in the auditorium. I was glorious. I stood there in my space in the bright circle of light, just me, all of me, being me and knew there was nothing that could touch me. Chantal hadn't expected this force and meaning, but she didn't yield. 'We will speak again.'

We'd both gone off script but neither of us cared. I only had one last scene to play; a short and sharp goodbye and pass my best wishes to her father. And it was done. As I came offstage I fell to my knees and looked down at my hands on the wood floor as the power drained out of me.

The applause was warm. I discovered I didn't know how to bow but managed to creak forward with a silly grin on my face. Tony was the first to stand, then Miriam and Annie both clapping wildly. Paul was more circumspect turning back to congratulate his son in the back row. I saw Billie smile for the first time. And at the back Annabelle stood with her hands over her head as she applauded. I wondered if I'd ever see her again in her transparent box and didn't care much. You see Annabelle, to be an actor is to be free, it's the career that fucks you up. Alexander you were right. I have it all in me ready to be plucked and plundered and revelled in. I may not know who I am, but now I could be everything.

After the show there were drinks in the bar.

Miriam said, 'So now you know why everyone wants to be an actor. And you can even get paid for it.'

'I didn't get a penny.'

'Oh Francis, stop being so miserable.'

'Fancy a pizza?'

'I think we can do better than that.'

# ACKNOWLEDGEMENTS

I'd like to thank all those who have read this book and for their comments; Alice Clark-Platts, Avril Clark, Cate Riding, Vincent Brimble, Jenny Farnon, and especially Gerrard McArthur for his editorial expertise, Justin Nardella for his brilliant cover and Christopher Hurrell for his taste and technical expertise.

# REVIEWS

Please leave any comments you may have regarding this book on the Amazon or appropriate website.

# PREVIOUS NOVELS BY MALCOLM McKAY.

## THE PATH

The Path is a journey of a lifetime to self-discovery.

It is the story of a group of international travellers who walk the Camino de Santiago, the ancient eight hundred kilometre pilgrimage from the Pyrenees to the remains of the apostle Saint James in the Cathedral of Santiago de Compostella in Northern Spain. (A journey made famous famous many years ago in Paulo Coelho's bestseller, The Pilgrimage)

The group are of all ages, all professions, all religious denominations (and none). They include a British army captain, a Danish business woman, a manic Austrian architect, A Welsh painter, a driven American priest and a comic mother and daughter due from Canada.

The thirty day walk is tough and demanding. They relate intellectually, spiritually and sexually as they search for their own deep and personal truths which are not always what the expect - or want - to find.

The climax is a terrible and shocking death which changes their views of themselves forever as they arrive in the holy city.

Published by Baseline and available on Amazon, ebook or print.

# THISTOWN (For young people)

Somewhere beyond the rain, the wind and the stars, and as far from the earth as it is possible to be there was a town so old that no one can remember how or when it began. It was a town where everyone stayed exactly the same, a town where no one grew older, a town surrounded by a million miles of yellow corn which was so strange that if you entered it you disappeared immediately.

And perhaps Thistown would have always stayed the same if they hadn't found the sleeping man.

He changed everything forever.

Amidst the turmoil a group of young people battle to save the town from tyranny and oppression but when they are forced to flee friendship and survival take on a new meaning.

'Down with Rasper!! The kids discover democracy!'

'Original, fresh, funny and inventive... highly recommended.' Juliet Stevenson.

Published by Baseline. Available on Amazon, ebook or print.

# THE LACK BROTHERS.

Charlie Lack, Soho aristocrat, is found dead at the Sunset Hotel. He leaves many debts and one asset, the Lack's restaurant, a prime piece of central London real estate.

He also leaves three sons: Arnie is fond of alcohol and women; Ronnie is unsure on both counts; and lastly Bernie, a vast twenty year old with a mental age of eight who seems to have celestial protection.

According to his scrap of a will Charlie has left the property to his wife, Violet, who walked out on him and his sons when Bernie was born. She hasn't been seen since. Unfortunately Luis Riss, local Maltese mobster, also has a compelling claim on the restaurant. To enforce it he unleashes the ultimate and extreme sanction of a contract with the McCarthy Twins to eliminate Violet.

Not only must the Lack brothers find their mother before the twins do, but they must also submit their own meagre existence to the judgement of altogether higher powers. As they begin their quest they are pursued by angels who have descended to make final judgement on Charlie Lack and to investigate the mysterious break up of the family twenty years before.

A breath-taking and unique novel with many diverse elements, The Lack Brothers is part comedy, part tragedy, part Arthurian quest, part love story and part thriller, all of which coalesce into a riotously riveting whole.

"A wonderful achievement. I loved it." Timothy Spall.

Published by Transworld, Black Swan.

# I AM THE GONG MAN

## (A Philosophy of Evil).

An intellectual thriller set over ten days on a Buddhism and meditation course in the Himalayan foothills of Northern India.

The Gong Man prowls the heat and shade of the Buddhist Campus ringing out the hours of the course timetable on his brass gong. He studies and meditates on Buddhist teaching. At the same time he describes to us his philosophy of the ultimate freedom to think, to act, and finally to both murder and create mayhem.

We discover that over the years he has travelled the globe in a search for his divine partner and when he finds her he kills her. By the time we meet him he has killed three times. Now on the second day of the course he meets his fourth potential victim in the form of a fellow student, Magdalena, a beautiful German journalist. He intends to kill her too.

All that stands in his way is Joshi, the Hindu mystic and meditation teacher who places profound philosophic and spiritual obstacles in his path, and the Rhesus Monkeys that live alongside the humans on the campus and who embody within their primitive existence, the only powers that could possibly be a match for him.

And then there's Magdalena. The victim herself appears to have been waiting for him and turns out to be much more than he bargained for.

"Let me tell you, evil is the natural state. It is freedom, it exists where there are no limits and no constraints. It is not immoral or amoral; these are just sad attempts to frame it. Evil is the act, the thing itself, the sound of laughter spinning through time. You get the picture?"

Published by Tangent Arts. Available on Amazon, ebook or print.

# FORTHCOMING TITLES.

THE PERFECT STATE. A billionaire philanthropist goes rogue. Ranald Vesey one of the wealthiest men in the world runs Fountainhead a philanthropic organisation that funds action against the effects of climate change and world poverty. Following Vesey's lead they aim to create the perfect state on an island off West Africa which has a population of five million. Fountainhead will provide everything, infrastructure, a sustainable economy and world-beating health and education. Their perfect state will be a beacon to the world showing the best humanity can achieve

Vesey will stop at nothing to achieve this, believing as he does in the power of the good. Unfortunately he faces a problem; the system of government. Is the island to be a democracy or an autocracy run by Vesey and his billionaire friends? The sitting president, an old friend of his begins to doubt his intentions, and so does a terrorist group with the power to disrupt the well-publicised assumptions of The Fountainhead. How does Vesey react to this threat to his ultimate ambition?

Charlotte Rivers is a sergeant in the Counter Terrorism Command. Two women are found dead in a London Hotel. Her investigations into The Fountainhead lead her to conclude that Vesey's obsession for the good is leading him into acts of violence and mass murder that reveal his perfect designs are driven by a ruthless desire for power and control.

THE SECRET COMPARTMENT OF LOVE. Ruth is happily married with two teenage children. She is a successful businesswoman with all she needs in her life. Then she meets divorced Irish artist Marc at a party and everything changes.

Where Ruth is controlled and contained, Marc is a searcher and emotional explorer. Their affair soon develops into a powerful relationship in which their most intense and unspoken desires can be expressed. Ruth, in particular, finds within herself a profound longing for something in her life which she has never before been able to articulate.

Ruth and Marc decide that their relationship will exist wholly within what they call The Secret Compartment of Love. It will be completely hidden from the world outside. Through a series of emails we see that the affair is becoming increasingly erotic and emotionally challenging. But in their secret place, can their passion for each other develop and grow? Or will their isolation from the rest of their lives, their children and friends mean that they will eventually turn on each other and their love will fail? A sudden death with her family leads Ruth to end the affair but Marc won't give her up. He pursues her to the last. Can The Secret Compartment of Love stay intact? Or will the outside world destroy what Ruth and Marc have created?

# APPENDIX

## ACTING AS AN ART INTRODUCTION

This is the introduction to a masterclass I gave to various international groups of actors and students over the years 2014 -2019. It is based around the core principles of the teaching at RADA in the 1970's and 80's, but is still relevant today.

## ACTING AS AN ART

How many of you have ambitions to be famous or at least working actors? Not knowing any of you, your talents or your backgrounds, I am sorry to tell you that it's unlikely that most of you will succeed. That may sound harsh and hopeless but it's the fact of the matter and we may as well face it before we start out. However, there is perhaps a chance of success but it may not be in the manner you hoped. I'll try and tell you what that is a little later, and why, despite the odds against you, it is perhaps worth persevering.

As a structure for what I have to say I'd like to describe to you the ten years I spent as a director at the Royal Academy of Dramatic Art in London. At the time it was a famous drama school.

Over that ten years I worked with between three and four hundred students. A few of them have achieved the fame, success and stature as actors that we are talking about. People like Kenneth Branagh, Mark Rylance, Ralph Fiennes, Fiona Shaw, Imelda Staunton and so on. A mere handful compared to the number who attended the school.

Below these there would be another ten percent - these

figures are very approximate - who would create a solid, respected life for themselves as actors, with a few ups and downs perhaps, but who worked continually, were in demand and earned a decent, if not great, living.

Then there would be another perhaps twenty percent who could properly call themselves actors, inasmuch as that was their trade, but who in fact didn't work continuously, had a handful of acting jobs a year, and often had to subsidise their work in other ways.

That leaves around seventy percent - and remember these are talented young men and women who went to one of the most famous drama schools in the world. What happened to them? Some of them scrape the occasional job on the edges of the profession and the rest have left it. They have failed in what they set out to do. I'll come back to that word failed, because it's perhaps not quite as harsh and hopeless as it sounds.

By the way I'm talking about people who completed their studies in the 1970's and 80's. I see many of them frequently and know their careers, or lack of them. And incidentally, with the rise in numbers of drama schools, university courses, and acting classes, in addition to the decline in drama productions in TV and theatre due to rising costs or lack of experimentation, there are fewer and fewer opportunities for actors. And this at a time when everybody seems to want to choose acting as a profession.

Not a good prospect is it? But maybe there's hope. Before I go into that let me tell you a little bit more about the RADA of thirty years ago.

First of all, it was very difficult to get into. There were generally between 1500 and 2000 applicants for around 25 places; 18 men and 7 women. It was biased towards men because at the time RADA gave a classical acting training and as you know, there are far more male parts in the classics than female. There was no such thing as cross-gender casting then.

So these 25 students entered the portals of RADA on their first day and were presented not only with an imposing bust of George Bernard Shaw, but with an extraordinary fact. In this great classical drama school there were no acting classes. And no acting teachers either. The Principal at the time, a great man called Hugh Cruttwell, didn't think you could teach anyone how to act. You could give them the tools and the space and privacy to create, but other than that there were no systems, tried and tested or otherwise.
There were, however, what were known as professional classes. These were Voice, Movement, Fencing and stage-fighting, improvisation, and make-up. I think there was also one hour a week devoted to text analysis. Plus tutorials. I'd like to spend a moment on a couple of these.

The first is voice training. At the time there was something known as the RADA voice. This could best be described as something akin to an old actor reciting Shakespeare in a big, booming, over enunciated, pompous and self-serving manner. It actually was entirely untrue that such a thing existed, let alone was taught. RADA at the time took more of the youngest and more working class students than any other drama school and had some very effective voice teachers who would have no interest in such a manner of delivery. They were concerned with and were very aware of the one absolute fact that may give you the best chance of success; that your voice is unique.

Nobody makes the same sounds as you do. There are of course technical aspects that can be learned and practised which will make your own (voice) sound more effective. But what is essential to remember is that your voice is an absolute expression of you. It is the sound of who you are. And the more you develop and expand your voice, the more you develop and expand who you are, then the greater your possibilities as an actor.

The other vital dimension of these professional classes was movement. At the time it was based around the Laban system. Again I'm no expert, and I'm not here to extol one system over another. But as with your voice, your body is unique and an absolute expression of you, where you are and what you are. And once again the more you can develop and expand your physical capacity, your flexibility, the more you will be able to express all the endless possibilities of yourselves.

Ultimately that's the work of an actor. In ideal terms to be able to cross the entire spectrum of humanity from light to dark, high to low, funny to tragic, quiet to loud, this character to that. No-one is entirely capable of all that, but that's the aim, that's the dream. And the two most essential tools for achieving that dream are your voice and your body. They need to be looked after and trained to be flexible, strong and absolutely within your control.

That's the power of the voice and body. But aside from this there is another quality, perhaps the most powerful of all; the imagination, which is the greatest and deepest, the most important and central quality of art.

Art. I'll stop there for a second to ask a question. Is acting an art? What is art? Don't buy the bullshit, 'State of the Art,' 'Artistic Director,' and all the rest of the self-serving tags attached to, in my view, the greatest human activity. What is art? What is the real thing? You will have your own answers, but I'll give you mine.

Firstly, all art is personal, it comes from you and can't come from anywhere else - where else could it come from? Although if we all examine our attempts at it we would probably be surprised to discover how much we think of as 'ours' is in fact an imitation of something we've seen or experienced elsewhere. That's not something to be too ashamed of, it's an inevitable part of the learning process, but as we attempt to grow as artists, the more we should be trying to reveal our own and personal vision. Ultimately, in my view, art is the individual and precise creation of the only form that can express the unique self.

So can acting be an art? I think it certainly can be, but only if the creation comes from what you are, or more exactly what you discover you are and that involves the exploration of self. I keep referring to the idea of the unique self and will do so again, because the self is all there is. You may know all sorts of things, you may discover new worlds, experience the most extraordinary feelings, but ultimately all that information can only reside and affect one thing, the self. That's where it all sits, where it all begins, and the more you understand that, the greater your possibility of art. It seems to me that this notion is fantastically exciting and inspiring because it means that right now as you hear this you already have all you need. It doesn't matter how small or great your experience is, if you express what you are and all its inherent possibilities with the greatest integrity and courage then you're on your way.

I return to thoughts about imagination. Where does it come from? We will all have different answers to that, but it is worth bearing in mind that an actor is asked to play a part in a play. To play. Like a child plays, unconsciously and with total commitment to a world he/she or they are immersed in. Children often play to create a space that they control and feels secure in. Within that there is the freedom to be whatever they want to be. That perhaps is the way that an audience experiences a play/film. They are watching something that, although it may be alarming or disturbing, is safe, in control, unthreatening and over there.

This space is created by an actor playing with all those visible and maybe invisible constituent parts of the self within the boundaries set by the words and story of the play. Of course to imagine within the constraints and ultimately artifice of the work, and to find the vocal and physical forms for the results of that imagined being, is the trick, and the difficult bit.

But it can be done. If you ask most people to imagine Richard the Third, they don't think of Shakespeare, they think of Laurence Olivier. His creation of that character, even sixty or seventy years later still surpasses the writer's creation. What Olivier did, and what many other actors have done before and since, is acting as an art; that is, creating a being that has been given form from within the possibilities of self. Only Olivier could have created that particular Richard. There is no such thing as Hamlet. He doesn't exist. There is only you. Your imagination is your possibility. You learnt and/or discovered that when you were a child.

So back to our student arriving on their first day at RADA and discovering that there are no acting classes. What do they do for the rest of the time? Well, in this particular period in the history of the school the answer is that they worked with directors. First on projects and then on plays. After a few months these would be performed to other students; after a year, to outsiders and the public. I'll come onto the ramifications of performance in a second, but for now the student had the prospect of working with initially a couple of directors a term and by the end, five or six a term. They were continually faced with different views of acting and the theatre. Some of these directors they liked and related to, others they didn't. But the essence of the matter is that outside of their professional classes, they were called upon to put into practise what they'd learnt.

This meant that the learning process existed within the work itself and not outside of it. All acting is ultimately measured within the frame of the play itself. This is part of the discipline of the art. Without this over-arching goal the acting can only be judged in a vacuum, and be created for its own sake without a final purpose.

It may be valuable to ask for a moment what exactly is a teacher? A person of learning and experience certainly, perhaps also someone of wisdom, but it's perhaps also worth considering both the context of the teaching and the relationship between teacher and student. Imagine three natural science teachers who are going to give a class on the life-forms to be found in a forest near the school. The first teacher takes the class to the edge of the forest, sits them down and instructs them to take notes while he/she describes what's inside it. The second teacher takes them into the forest and points out the various fauna and flora as they pass them by. The third teacher says to the class, you go into the forest and I'll follow. If you trip over something, I'll pick you up. Which of those teachers would you prefer?
These examples may be a little simplistic but it seems to me that RADA at the time practised the method of the third teacher. And that is why so many students tripped, stood up again and slowly discovered themselves and what they were capable of.

At the heart of this RADA of thirty years ago was the idea that acting was the art of transformation. That the job of an actor in the very simplest, crudest terms is to convince an audience that he/she is not an actor at all, but is actually the person/character that they see in front of them.

I don't go to the theatre or to see a film in order to see actors, or witness great writing, or to marvel at the effects of a director. I go to be immersed in a story, to experience another world, both emotionally and intellectually. Don't show me good acting, show me another person that I believe in. If you, the actor, have immersed yourself in the character you have taken on, if there is no outside, self-conscious or objective signifying within your work then you are more than halfway to convincing me.

At RADA the students performed frequently. It was how they developed their work. There is sometimes a debate in drama schools about whether a young actor should be pushed to perform before they're ready. There are probably many views about this, but mine is that performance is such an intrinsic element of both the psychology and art of acting that it can hardly exist without it. Maybe tough, but ultimately necessary.

OK, that was RADA then. Now there is a different RADA and many other drama schools, acting academies, and classes that will all have different systems and thoughts on acting. So where does that leave you? Go to one and you will learn this, another and you will learn that. Much of it will be valuable purely and simply in terms of the knowledge you gain, but mainly in terms of you being able to practise with other students.

I move on to the actual process of creating a character. There are many ways to rehearse; talking, games playing, exercises, improvisation, straightforward blocking and so on. But whatever is the process it is clear that the actor having worked on their voice/body in general terms, now needs to focus on the particular, the part, the play. The obvious beginning of that is research. Any character you play exists in a context, so start there; period, country, town, beliefs, attitudes and problems of the people/society they come from. Then narrow it down; class systems, power structures, aspirations for success, reasons for failure, values, fundamental and religious attitudes of the particular group the character leads their life within. Then deeper, and apply all these things to the personality of the character. Some basic questions; who they, what are their idiosyncrasies, what do they want, how do they expect to achieve it, both in general terms and in specific moments of the action. Look very hard into the text itself. How does a character express himself/herself, what words/images/rhythms do they use, what do other characters think of them, do they achieve what they want to achieve, what obstacles do they have to overcome? Ask questions and keep asking questions, until as the Buddha says, there are no further questions left to ask.

Having done this before and during rehearsal you will be armed with a series of facts, some useful, some not, and others more problematic. But the point about all these questions is that that the answers are all potential triggers for the imagination. Any idea that comes from this process could inspire a physical and/or vocal response, which could lead to the dream-state that is, in my view, the basis of all truly great acting. What I mean by that is the imaginative transference from yourself to another being. To imagine, to dream, and to manifest that dream in movement and voice.

The specific job of an actor is to evoke another being within the parameters of the group and the work. All the clues have been researched and are laid out before you, but ultimately where does this new being come from? Well, it comes from you. One real and unique person creates another real and unique person. You begin with yourself and then you expand and create from the material that is within you. Any character starts and ends with you and what you are. There is only you.

Always expand your possibilities through your work on the physical and vocal aspects of yourself and through your imagination. This is the heart of the matter. As I've said, you are unique and therefore what you create will be unique. Mozart was a great composer but he couldn't write Beethoven's Fifth, only Beethoven could do that, and only you can create what you create. I'm ramming this home because it's at the heart of the matter. You are the creator, and what you create can only come from you. You are the possibility - with ultimately no limitations. The power of the imagination working through the materials of the body and voice.

So that is essentially what happened at RADA. The students were given a set of professional skills and then thrown into the deep end, at the mercy of the whims and talents of their directors. Some thrived, some didn't. But in the end they were left with what they were as actors, and as unique human beings.

And so, they enter the profession, and what actor, whether they admit it or not, doesn't somewhere in their being aspire to become a movie star? To become the one in a million with the money, attention and the world spread before them. But the fact of the matter is, that as they have climbed the crystal ladder to stardom these stars have, more often than not, actually limited their possibilities as actors. Remember that to be an actor is to express the possibilities all across the great spectrum of humanity? A movie star is not allowed to do that. They are asked to do what they are good at, to play out the particular aspect of their personality that the public loves them for. And nothing else. Occasionally an actor believing his/her publicity will demand a part that takes them into another territory. Usually this is a disaster and they scurry back to the roles they are known for. The more sensible of them know exactly what they do, are wanted for and are paid for.

An example. John Wayne was once asked to read a script for a film. He did so, liked it and accepted the part on the condition that one scene was cut. The director asked why and John said because in that scene I have to be petty, and John Wayne is never petty... he knew, like all other enduring stars that his public image was everything. In other words he was no longer an actor, he was a brand. All the most well-known and successful actors know this. This is the downside of your uniqueness. Once refined, polished and accepted, it becomes a trap you can't escape. That's success for you.

The same thing happens to the next ten percent, those who make a good living as professional actors. The dreaded casting director will only consider him/her in parts that resemble the one they did successfully a couple of films ago. Their broad acting ambitions are narrowed. That's success for you.

But what about all the others who trained, who worked, who did everything they could possibly think of to become a success? What happened to them? Was it worth all those years of desperation and humiliation? On the face of it, no it wasn't. What they aspired to wasn't achieved. Hang your head and get out of here.

But see it another way. Look at acting as an exploration and expansion of the unique self, regard it as a source of knowledge, as a broadening, a deepening, an understanding of others, as a direct challenge to the imagination, as a means of becoming a fully creative person, and there you may have it. Acting isn't a route to becoming a movie star; it's to enhance your possibilities as a human being. That's art for you.

Malcolm McKay Paris, May 2019.

Printed in Great Britain
by Amazon

22681011R00145